WORDS
IN
COMMOTION

 AND OTHER STORIES

WORDS
IN
COMMOTION

AND OTHER STORIES

TOMMASO LANDOLFI

WITH AN INTRODUCTION
BY ITALO CALVINO

TRANSLATED AND EDITED
BY KATHRINE JASON

VIKING

VIKING
Viking Penguin Inc., 40 West 23rd Street,
New York, New York 10010, U.S.A.
Penguin Books Ltd, Harmondsworth,
Middlesex, England
Penguin Books Australia Ltd, Ringwood,
Victoria, Australia
Penguin Books Canada Limited, 2801 John Street,
Markham, Ontario, Canada L3R IB4
Penguin Books (N.Z.) Ltd, 182–190 Wairau Road,
Auckland 10, New Zealand

First published in 1986 by Viking Penguin Inc.
Published simultaneously in Canada

All but four of the stories in this book are from
Le più belle pagine di Tommaso Landolfi, published in
Italy by Rizzoli Editore, © 1982 Rizzoli Editore, Milano. "The Test" is from
A caso (Rizzoli), "Chicken Fate" from *Racconti impossibili*
(Vallecchi Editore), "Uxoricide" from *Le labrene* (Rizzoli)
and "The Ampulla" from *Del meno* (Rizzoli).

"Gogol's Wife" and "Dialogue of the Greater Systems" are
originally from *Gogol's Wife and Other Stories*, by
Tommaso Landolfi. Copyright © 1961, 1963 by
New Directions Publishing Corp. Translated by
arrangement with New Directions.

LIBRARY OF CONGRESS CATALOGING IN PUBLICATION DATA
Landolfi, Tommaso, 1908–1979.
Words in commotion and other stories.
I. Title.
PQ4827.A57A24   1986   853'.912   85-41063
ISBN 0-670-80518-1

Printed in the United States of America by
The Book Press, Brattleboro, Vermont
Set in Bodoni Book
Design by Levavi & Levavi

For my mother and father

I am tremendously grateful to Nino Gulli, whose illuminations of the Italian text and whose patience and generosity over the course of this project were invaluable to me; I also wish to thank my hardworking "close readers"—Lucille Lee Jason and Peter Rondinone, my husband; and Frank MacShane, whose friendship and guidance over the last ten years led me to Rome and circuitously to Tommaso Landolfi, and this book.

K.J.

CONTENTS

INTRODUCTION
PRECISION AND CHANCE

The idea behind this collection is to offer the reading public a new encounter with Landolfi. He had that great gift for capturing the reader's attention and inspiring his awe (he inherited a taste for the "shocking" story from the masters of "black romanticism"; but it was his own acumen, panache and incomparable wealth of verbal resources that made for his highly affective writing). Yet his reputation for being an impractical and peculiar character gave credence to the conviction—which still holds true today—that his writing is only for "a select few." This selection offers an opportunity to reconsider his work—inasmuch as "an introduction" to Landolfi can represent the various aspects of this extraordinarily idiosyncratic author.

In a work like Tommaso Landolfi's, the first rule of the game established between reader and writer is that sooner or later a surprise will come: and that surprise will never be pleasant or soothing, but will have the effect of a fingernail scraping glass, or of a hair-raising, irritating caress, or an association of ideas that one would wish to expel from his mind as quickly as possible. It is no surprise that Landolfi's closest literary forebears, Barbey d'Aurevilly and Villiers de L'Isle-Adam, title their story collections *The Diabolical Women* and *Cruel Stories*.

But Landolfi's game is even more complex. Starting with a

simple but nearly always wicked, obsessive or lurid idea, an elaborate story takes shape, related by a voice that usually appears to be an ironic counterpoint of another voice (just as a great actor has to alter his own diction ever so slightly to define a character); or it may pretend to be, say, a parody of another piece of writing (not by any particular writer but by an imaginary author whom everyone has the illusion of having once read) which, in fact, is ultimately immediate, spontaneous and faithful only to itself. In the verbal spectacle that unfolds, theatrical effects are precisely paced, but they can also turn into the most fickle fancies imaginable.

This is the kind of story Landolfi writes when he wants to employ his inventive versatility and his fixed ideas to construct some precise mechanism, or to set up a calculated strategy. But on other occasions, many other occasions, another mood prompts Landolfi to strip the act of writing of any pretense of constructing a complete, easily accessible and enduring story and instead he substitutes a careless gesture, a shrug or grimace, like someone who knows that the creative process is a waste, insubstantial and meaningless.

The extent to which Landolfi adopts this attitude is proved by this statement (in *Bière de pécheur*):[1] "Could I ever really write at random and without design, thus glimpsing the chaos, the disorder in my own depths?"

"At random": the same phrase becomes an existential program in the story "Mano rubato": "Living at Random" is then the title story (in *A caso* [1975]). But this insistence, which could be seen as some kind of aspiration toward automatic writing in literature and as an apology for the "gratuitous act" in life (thus validating the surrealist tag others inevitably labeled him with), takes on another dimension in the above-mentioned story. Here he shows the impossibility not only of a random murder but also of a

---

[1]The titles of books or stories that are available only in Italian editions will not be translated in this introduction unless translation is needed to provide clarification.

narrative developed outside of some logical framework.

Actually, chance was a god to which Landolfi showed feverish devotion even though he was constantly led to doubt its existence and power. If an absolute determinism dominates the world, chance is rendered impossible and we are condemned to our fates, without any hope of escape. This hypothesis of the nonexistence of chance is explored in the June 24, 1958, entry in his diary *Rien va:*

"It's difficult to believe that a chance happening (which is always and nevertheless an event) could be casual and it is certainly difficult to take chance seriously. Something that happens is not necessarily casual—we should be able to confirm this beyond a shadow of a doubt, although it is not so easy and it may be impossible to demonstrate such a fact. But somebody invented chance and everyone believes in and accepts it: even those who attempt to refute it as an ordering or disordering principle of the universe are thus implicitly admitting to its existence every minute of the day."

And the passage concludes thus: "The truth is that the spirit must lie in chains, regardless of who forged them."

That this problematical relationship with chance was so essential for him should come as no surprise, considering his great passion for gambling. After observing him on various occasions at the roulette table (he spent a good part of his last years at San Remo, and I knew that I had to go to the casino to see him), I had the impression that he was not a good player for the very reason that he played "at random" without any strategy or design (or at least it seemed so to me), instead of following one of those forced patterns or systems with which shrewd gamblers attempt to capture and trap the shapeless fluidity of chance.

It is likely that I was the one who understood nothing. What could I know of the imperatives and illuminations which move a gambler by vocation (or damnation?). I, whose only rule would be minimal risk were I to gamble. Perhaps in his passionate relationship with chance, which was both a courtship and challenge, he alternated between strategies too sophisticated to ever be revealed to anybody else and a "rapture" of dissipation in a maelstrom where all losses lead back to the loss of oneself, which is the only possible victory. Perhaps chance was the only way for him to test nonchance. And since nonchance par excellence is the most absolute thing, in other words, death itself, chance as well as nonchance are two names for death, the one fixed meaning in life.

In fact, when I saw him manipulating the chips on the green felt (and reflected on the words "at random," which kept going through my head like a motto), I came up with a comparison between Landolfi the player and Landolfi the writer. For, in both, there was the use of a rigorously determined form or formula which might stave off chaos and contain it, on one hand; and on the other hand, a gesture of supreme nonchalance which scorns any work or any value because the only basis for any action or discussion lies in the equation chance-chaos-nothingness-death; and the only possible stance toward that is ironic and desperate contemplation.

But another possible link between gambling and literature— what part need and what part the unknown play in both—has already been explored by Landolfi himself. In the story "La dea cieca e veggente," a poet drawing upon words at random ends up writing *The Infinite* and wonders (like that Borges character who considers himself author of Don Quixote) if this is really his own work or Leopardi's. Seeing that he has been lucky in stumbling upon highly improbable combinations, the poet decides to test his gifts in a game of roulette; the results are disastrous and he loses everything. The game of chance refuses the order which poetry can attain, being an impersonal system or preserving— thanks to its internal mechanisms or probable combinations— the secret oneness of the individual.

Governed as they are by necessity and chance, man's actions always disappoint his demand that they influence events to suit his will. For this reason, Landolfi's relationship to literature, as to existence itself, is always twofold: It is the gesture of someone who commits himself wholly to what he does, and at the same time throws it all away. This also explains the interior split between his dedication to formal precision and the indifferent detachment with which he abandoned his completed work to its own fate. After throwing himself into his work and enjoying it, he lost interest in the completed book to such an extent that he didn't even bother to correct the proofs. He once told friends about opening a recently published book and discovering an error that rendered an entire dialogue incomprehensible; this would have made me bang my head against the wall, but he laughed as though it were of no concern to him.[2]

In making a selection of Landolfi's works and sifting through the collections published over the course of forty years—some ten volumes containing pieces of varying character and value—one naturally tends to favor the real stories (that is, the more finished compositions, the attempts at virtuosity inspired by a desire for perfection) over those pages which arose from passing moods and whims, especially when his intention was to provoke or disillusion. But one soon realizes that a truly representative selection must take both moods into account, for if the pieces more lacking in form were discarded, one would rightly have to discard the excessively "well-done" and refined pieces as well. That is why I have not included some of Landolfi's most critically praised stories like "La muta" [The Mute Girl];[3] likewise, none of the three works in his volume *Tre racconti*, which I would categorize as narratives of more ample breadth (long stories or novellas, among which my favorite is *Racconto d'autunno*), can be included insofar as one must take them or leave them as books in themselves.

The "real Landolfi" whom I hope this volume will represent is one who prefers to leave something unresolved in the work, a

---

[2]In the misprint that Calvino refers to here "Francesismo!" was changed to "Franceschino!," thereby changing the word "Gallicism" into the name "Frankie."

[3]"The Mute Girl" appears in a translation by Raymond Rosenthal in *Cancerqueen and Other Stories* (The Dial Press, 1971).

margin of shadow and risk: the Landolfi who squanders the stakes that he puts on the table and then swiftly withdraws them with the horrified gesture of a gambler.

A gambler—nearly always in first person and sometimes in the third—is the most frequent character in his stories and meditations, the backdrops most often cities that house casinos; above all, the city which for me was associated with my family's roots and with all my memories of youth and childhood, and which for him was associated not only with the devouring passion of his whole life but also with the role of husband and father which he took on late in life. Very different memories link us to the same streets, to the same seasonal colors and landscapes. For example, the story of his first trip to San Remo as a young man (although I can't find this among his writings, some of the stories he told aloud are etched in my mind in the shape and style of the printed page) concerns his arrival in a train; leaving his suitcase hurriedly at the hotel, he ran to the casino where the hours of the afternoon, evening and night were spent breathlessly at roulette or chemin de fer until the croupiers shut down—I think it was five in the morning—and the last tireless players, still fantasizing a comeback, were forced to quit. Then he returned to his hotel, which was right across from the casino ("L'Europa e Pace," I think); sleepless, he gazed out into the dawn light and across to the windows of the room he'd just left. The windows had been opened to air out the smoke-filled rooms and he saw the cleaning women bustling about vacuuming and polishing the tables; he prodded them on mentally so that he could resume his position as soon as possible. And counting the hours that would separate him from the next game, he didn't take his eyes off the place.

In real life, I never knew the alternate mask that Landolfi's "I" narrator wears in the stories (more frequently in the earlier than in the later work, regardless of the fact that the ancestral home in Pico amid the olive groves of Ciociaria remained a stable point in his life until the very end): the character of the noble peasant who grows old as a bachelor and "son" in an environment that intensifies all his lunatic obsessions. But here we enter an area where grotesque transformation predominates over auto-biography and is expressed with a cruel and painful scowl if not with sadism and impotence. (This mask in all its particulars has already taken shape in that first story which established him, "Maria Giuseppa," dated 1929; and then the "Vera storia di Maria Giuseppa" [The Real Story of Maria Giuseppa] or confession twenty-five years later, which was an act of reparation and mercy upon the real Maria Giuseppa's "coeur simple.")

And there's yet another Landolfi, the hardworking and competent literary scholar and the gracious and precise literary translator, scribe of thousands of pages whose only signature is a characteristic grace (as opposed to the Landolfi in pursuit of the most meager rewards, which, according to him, dominated his every thought and intention). This is a character we rarely meet in the stories (though sometimes we come across him in the travel stories, suggesting that movement was the real necessity in his sedentary existence), but he lives on in his friends' memories, mostly friends from his decisive prewar period in Florence.

Landolfi's relationship to himself, if one traces it throughout his writing, reveals an egotism of the most complex and contradictory nature. One moves from the narrative theater where he rages against himself and the world, to a direct and open autobiographical vein where moderation and control reveal the suffering. And tracing this same continuum of psychological constancy, we begin with his memories of boarding school at Prato and end with one of the last sketches published in the *Corriere della Sera*, "Porcellina di terra," which has never before appeared in book form.

At this point I will not delve into the question of how much of his internal torment was real and how much of it was theatrical: the simple fact that he wanted to entertain his readers or himself by parading his suffering "I" redeems his stance, whether it is egocentric or all an impersonal game. Likewise, it would be pointless to establish whether the obsessions and phantoms of his sexual imagination are purely fictional or correspond to some pulse in his unconscious: in his exhibitionism he seems to leave himself open to psychological interpretation (and thus, using the story "A Woman's Breast" as a point of departure, [the critic Elio] Sanguinetti traces a constant sexual phobia, or more precisely a fear of the female sex, throughout his work; at the same time, the absence of interior censure weakens such an interpretation since it would suggest that the real unconscious lies elsewhere).

Any exploration of what Landolfi really *says* has yet to be made. Because while he claims to have "nothing to say," he always follows the thread of the discussion at hand. Eventually his philosophy will be unraveled from the knot of questions without answers, contradictions, proclamations and provocations surrounding him. If our intention here is simply to pass on the pleasure of reading Landolfi superficially, that is because it is the first necessary step. And it is also only superficially that we are pointing out his taste for fake "treatises," fake "conferences" and fake "moral works," though not without noting that at some point we might establish that they were "fake" only to a certain degree; that there is a thread linking Leopardi and Landolfi, a similarity between the two rural villages where they lived and the two paternal dwellings, between their youths spent laboring over paper, and their invectives against human destinies. (As for the dialogues, which Landolfi writes frequently, especially recently, I must say that I like them the least of all his writing. If I can trust my own superficial reading, they seem written in a much less successful vein. In any case, any exploration must begin from the diaries *Rien va* and *Des mois*, which I didn't feel I could include in the selection since, once again, they are complete in themselves.)

It is too easy to say that what Landolfi writes is always a mask of emptiness, of nothingness, of death. One cannot forget that this mask is nevertheless a whole concrete world, full of meanings. A world made up of words, naturally. But of words which are significant precisely for their richness, precision and coherence.

Take an emblematic text like "La passeggiata."[4] The sentences are constructed from incomprehensible nouns and verbs, much like Lewis Carroll's experimental "Jabberwocky," in which words from an invented lexicon have make-believe meanings. If it were the same thing, there would be no new amusement or gratification. However, if the reader only takes the trouble to consult a good old Italian-language dictionary (Landolfi used the Zingarelli), he would find all the words there. "La passeggiata" is a text with complete meaning; the author simply set up a rule to use as many obsolete words as possible. (He himself couldn't resist the temptation to reveal this secret in a later volume, thus poking fun at those who had not caught on.) So Landolfi the "mystifier" becomes the "demystifier" par excellence: he gives meanings back to words which have lost them (and instead of leaving the common reader in the wrong, he takes the trouble to patiently explain what he has done).

But Landolfi's inquiry into language had begun long before this. The title story in his first book (*Dialogo dei massimi sistemi*, 1937) [Dialogue of the Greater Systems] contains a discussion of the aesthetic value of poetry written in an invented language that only the author (and maybe not even he) can understand. I don't think it is mere hyperbolic irony that the story and volume were decorated with such an illustrious title:[5] It is as though Landolfi wanted to point out that beyond the text's paradoxical humor (and beyond the satire, which clearly arises from the then-predominant philosophy of Croce), the problem that concerns him is one of language as a collective convention and historical inheritance, and of the individual and mutable word. And this is the first document which reflects a concern—a concern no less serious

---

[4]Landolfi refers, if somewhat satirically, to his story "La passeggiata" and the stir it created among critics in "Personaphilologicaldramatic Conference with Implications," included here.

[5]"Dialogue of the Greater Systems," the "illustrious title" that Calvino refers to, is borrowed from Galileo's principal treatise *Dialogue of the Two Chief Systems of the World*.

or rigorous for its acrobatic tone—which will appear in all
of Landolfi's work right up to "Parole in agitazione" [Words
in Commotion], that crystalline little fable from his last book
(*Unpaniere di chiocciole*, 1968) abut the "signifier" and the
"signified."

I can't account for the sources of his knowledge; certainly, one
couldn't say that linguistics (much less DeSaussure's structural-
ism) were the order of the day in European literary culture when
he was educated. And I would doubt that he gave it serious thought
even later when linguistics became a "pilot discipline." And yet,
everything he writes about it seems to have such scientific "ex-
actitude" (in terminology and concept) that it could be used as
a text in the most up-to-date university seminars.

From Landolfi's stories and diaries, I think one can extrapolate
a linguistic theorization whose basic assumptions are innate mental structures (see his reflections on his child's first attempts at
speaking in *Des mois*), the arbitrariness of linguistic symbols,
and most importantly, the nonarbitrariness of language as a system, a historical creation and cultural stratification (Ibid., pp.
9–10, from which I have taken the following quotation):

"The delightful attempts of those who seek new languages and
are necessarily forced back into some ancient system of relationships which cannot be avoided! Ancient, and I would even say
innate. I challenge anyone to invent a truly new game (of substance not style), or else a new relationship with reality (or un-
reality): all the possible results seem to fall inevitably into one
set category or another, and there are a finite number of them,
ab aeterno."

The poet's individual and unpredictable work is only possible
because he has at his disposal a language which has rules with
established uses, a language which functions independently of
him. Landolfi's reasoning always revolves around this point (in
conversations as well). I remember the first time I talked to him
twenty-five years ago, he somehow ended up discussing language
and dialects, and he refuted my argument that we could have a

literary Italian with its roots outside of the Tuscan dialect.

In any case, it isn't the avant-garde's innovative thrust which prompts Landolfi's acrobatics. On the contrary, he is a conservative writer in that particular (and even metaphysical) sense that the gambler cannot but be conservative because the immutability of the rules guarantees that chance will not be abolished with every throw of the dice.

His most faithful critic and companion (up through the Florentine years), Carlo Bo, has written many times that Landolfi was the first writer since D'Annunzio who could do whatever he wanted with the pen. At first the comparison between the two names astonished me: even if both came out of the mold of the nineteenth-century dandy (like Huysmans' des Esseintes), D'Annunzio had gone in the direction of the erotic-euphoric, while Landolfi tended toward self-irony and depression. Indeed, their personalities, their literary presences, their relationships to the world were diametrically opposed. But reconsidering it, I realized the real common element between them was something else. It could be said of each of them (and of them only) that they wrote in the presence of the entire Italian language, past and present, and that they made use of it with a competent and knowing pen, as if they could draw abundantly and derive continuous pleasure from an inexhaustible patrimony.

Certainly, one must consider Landolfi's first-rate translations, and not from a language "everyone knows," but from Russian (which remains a language for specialists in Italian literary culture, and surely this is not the case in Italy alone: The only famous precedent I can remember is Mérimée, who translated Pushkin's stories). One must finally speak of his particular pleasure of bringing distant and complex accents to life in a voice tuned to the Italian key, and with the clarity and the shadows of his Gogol, the breathless speech of his Leskov, the precious falsetto tones of his Hofmannsthal (*Il cavaliere della rosa*, to mention one of his other languages).

But this relationship to one dimension of European literature,

without which Landolfi would not be Landolfi, must remind us
of his dominant passion for Italian literature. This fact is little
documented in his writings (even when he wrote literary criticism
on a regular basis for Pannunzio's *Il Mondo*, he was concerned
only with foreign writers). But he betrayed himself in conversation: he was enthused by discussions of Manzoni or Foscolo, or
by pointing out linguistic usage and vocabulary in the classics;
and even when he spoke of his contemporaries, though he appeared rather disinterested in the present, it was their language
that drew his attention. (If he ever saw any literary merit in me,
it was because in one of my stories I used the word "pesceduovo,"
which is the correct Italian word for omelet.)

This love of his for vocabulary, it must be noted, never became
an overly precious or songlike exaltation. Here I will quote [the
critic] Giacomo Debenedetti:

"It happens that in reading Landolfi one comes across words
that are actually too beautiful, too right to be real, but indeed
they can be found in real dictionaries where they are waiting for
someone to find them. In fact, he employs them without batting
an eyelash: the sentence isn't overjoyed by them, it doesn't consider itself any better for them, for they seem to arise from the
normal memory-bank from which we draw everyday words. A
baroque stylist or a decadent would have searched them out too,
but to bring them forth in the voice's highest register. Landolfi
levels them with the lovely timbre of his bass baritone."

The question of words which are not immediately comprehensible but which have meaning is being reexamined today in an
essay by Giorgio Agamben on "glossolalia" (in this sense "speaking in glossary," that is, "with words foreign to present usage")
whose point of departure is Pascoli. (The essay is an introduction
to an edition of *Il fanciullino* by Giovanni Pascoli, Feltrinelli,
1982.) Could Agamben's theory of "dead words" as "the death
of language in the voice" be applied to Landolfi as well? It seems
to me that all language, including "dead words," is a part of life
for Landolfi, but precisely because death is only steps away and

on every side. In the end this may be saying the same thing, but in Landolfi there is a dramatic power that springs from the consciousness of the living man. Isn't the moral of the diaries (*Rien va* and to an even greater extent *Des mois*) really the fact that all his negative meditation unfolds before the imposing presence of life, represented by Minor and Minimus,[6] that is in his acceptance—despite everything—of a vital continuum?

The physicality of existence is constantly present both in his imagination and in his reasoning. A death urge—fear and attraction—imposes itself upon his thoughts at all times, but is ultimately represented by bodily emotions. The disembodied abstraction of the philosopher's mind is not for him. His problem is with the body's fixed, physical and palpable presence, his own as much as others', which provokes in him tumultuous reactions such as horror and homicidal cruelty. However, these are merely the extreme points of a gamut which includes all emotional possibilities.

This might explain why real reflection—and the need to keep a diary—begins for him when he feels he must come to terms with a new "biological" fact—paternity in his mature years, which suits neither his ways of being nor the predictable roles in his repertory. And even here he allows the whole gamut of possible attitudes to spring forth without denying any: from the most open tenderness to the rapture of sadistic infanticide (though the latter is actually less frequent). And it is the experience of the relationships between human beings—one's fellow man felt as a physical closeness—which will determine the course his ideas take, and not the other way around.

(This also explains the meaning of the before and after in his "erotic" fantasies: the accounts of attraction and repulsion, spells and aversions are remarkable precisely because they are erratic and open-ended.)

---

[6]Minor and Minimus are the nicknames Landolfi used to refer to his daughter and son respectively in his diaries *Rien va* and *Des mois*.

And death then? Can one create a palpable image and experience of it? In the romantic and symbolist writers, the main theme of fantastic stories was ghosts, the living dead, that uncertain boundary between the world-beyond-the-tomb and our own world. Landolfi reaches far and wide in that repertory and apparitions from the beyond are not lacking in his two major novels, *La pietra lunare* and *Racconto d'autunno*. However, I would say that the world of the dead never comes into the foreground in the shorter stories from which I made my selection; for him, the obsession which overrides even that of death is the pathology of living. The dominant theme of necrophilia in Poe, with whom he is often compared, is not to be found in Landolfi. We find only the complementary theme of the anxiety of a mistaken death and premature burial, as in the story "Le labrene" [The Labrenas], but it is a subtle pastiche and ironic homage to the master.

Death and nothingness, which are often named but seldom represented, belong therefore to the restricted number of abstract concepts in Landolfi's always concrete world, a concept that represents a necessary boundary, a breath, a rest from this world so dense with existence, so loaded, so intense... Landolfi's real nightmare is that nothingness does not exist. His two books of poetry (*Viola di morte* and even more *Il Tradimento*) often return to this theme which is expressed in a passage in *Rien va:*

"Existence is a condemnation without name and without redemption; there's nothing to be done against it. And perhaps it is only hope—our need to catch our breath, as if from the sharp pain of a wound—that allows us to imagine a state outside of existence; a nothingness. My God, perhaps everything exists, has existed and will exist in eternity. There is nothing we can do against life but live it, just as there is nothing to do in a closed, suffocating, smoke-filled room but go on smoking."

I owe my own meetings with Landolfi, which unfortunately were rare, and whatever I learned of him indirectly which allows me to speak of him as a man, to Filiberto Lodi. Lodi was a dear friend of his and mine (as well as of Soldati and Bassani, who introduced his fellow citizen from Ferrara to us all). When Landolfi fell ill and Lodi died suddenly, many threads broke for me as well. It is to the memory of Filiberto, who always accompanies me with his calm and calming footstep, his concern for his fellowman, and his lightness, that I dedicate this work.

—Italo Calvino

FANTASTIC
STORIES

THE LABRENAS

1

Labrenas—a boyhood friend from Venezuela called them, and I sometimes call them that too. Actually, they are no more than a common gecko, more precisely the one zoologists call (if I'm not mistaken) *Platidattilo muraiolo:* a sort of miniature crocodile that frequents and meanders along old walls, and sometimes invades inhabited rooms where, as is its habit, it eyes and then sneaks up on various insects, particularly butterflies.

I have always felt profound disgust and nausea, revulsion in every living cell in my body, tremors in my innermost fibers for this most innocuous little creature. Even my mother, I've been told, would wordlessly raise a finger against this enemy whose presence her infallible instinct detected whenever she entered an empty room or passed through the courtyard. And she would persist in this until her companions removed the source of her discomfort. As for me, it was impossible to avoid contact with the abhorrent labrenas in the house. Thus, ever since I was a boy, I had fantasized at length about what would happen if some evil twist of fate forced me into more intimate contact with them: I mean, forced me to touch one or to endure its touch; and I cannot recall more anxiety-ridden evenings than those spent there in the courtyard in summer with my family.

We sat in a semicircle in front of the large outer door; above it, on the outer wall of the house was an electric light bulb. An extraordinarily corpulent labrena hiding in the shadows of the bulb's base peered out just as a nocturnal butterfly approached, drawn toward the light. Or else, it waited for the butterfly to settle, at which point it would snap it up and gulp it down. How that spectacle of industriousness made me shiver! While others may have been edified by such a diligent exploitation of favorable circumstances, I was exhausted and horrified. "What would become of me," I asked myself over and over, "if its cold, disgusting flesh grazed mine even for a second?" Would I overcome the test? Would I survive? And I was sure that, indeed, I would die; and I prayed that God would protect me.

But as it happened, I was not to be spared such a terrible and decisive experience.

Labrenas, as I said, occasionally invade the lived-in rooms of our house—where, I might add, they skitter toward the windows and balconies, sneaking up on the rightful inhabitants. And if the latter have closed the shutters, they realize they are trapped and go crazy up there on the walls, searching for a way out. It was precisely in anticipation of such a likelihood that I always kept a long, flexible rod in my room with which I could reach the horrendous intruders wherever they might be and prod them, thereby slowly, slowly pushing them out (I didn't have the heart to squash them against the wall, for I knew the sight of their spilled innards would have made me faint dead away).

Now one night after I entered my room to retire and shut the window, I happened to see one bolt like a swift flash of lightning toward the loom; in that split second, I recognized the labrena out of the corner of my eye. Its obvious intention was to reach safety by way of the window which was already closed (as it then witnessed itself). And turning back swiftly, it began running along the walls chaotically; however, it remained high up and finally took refuge in the vault of the ceiling where my long rod couldn't reach (unless I manipulated it at a perpendicular angle). But then

I would run the great risk that the labrena would fall back down on me. In the end, I had no other choice but to wait for my adversary to move, shall I say, voluntarily, which it soon did. Perhaps it did not feel terribly secure in that topsy-turvy position, for after full reflection, it headed down hesitantly. Indeed, it came so near the floor that I thought the moment to act had come. I avoided walking below it and pushed open the closest window, whereupon I prepared to push it out with the rod.

Man's fate is often given over to some unforeseen incident, to some insignificant obstacle. . . . The sharp, flexible tip of the rod slipped a few centimeters under the labrena's ugly little body, but since those walls are not always perfectly smooth, it got stuck and jammed on a protuberance or bump in the plaster. As a result, the tip jerked back, knocking the labrena down and . . . and propelled it with particular force against . . . against my face.

I had just enough time to feel a chill on my skin that was worse than anything I had ever imagined in my life: the vile creature's touch. And I lost consciousness.

When I came to, I was dazed and, in a word, astonished by the peculiar line of vision I seemed to be subjected to. I was facing the vault of a room, and I managed to glimpse some fore-shortened furniture out of the corner of my eye; I mean I was seeing it from the bottom up. The whole place was plunged in an incredibly fierce, unnatural white light which ate away at the edges of objects and distorted them beyond recognition. I realized too that I couldn't move my eyes.

Anyway, it was with inexpressible horror that I became fully conscious of my situation a moment later. Not only couldn't I move my eyes, but not one of my limbs would budge; nor could I emit any sort of sound or produce any signal. And finally, I *wasn't breathing*. I tried to hear my heart, my heartbeat: *it wasn't beating*.

This, then, was the horrendous truth: I was laid out in a supine position, believed dead by everyone, and with good reason. My life or afterlife was centered only, and certainly uselessly, in my surviving senses. But now, someone was mercifully closing my eyes, just as they do with the dead. And since my remaining senses were utterly useless in such a state, now my only remaining intermediaries with the world were smell and hearing, of which the latter would prove more acute in the long run.

However, I needn't emphasize my sense of anxiety and terror, I needn't indicate exactly how I managed to find the shred of courage that led me to the conclusion that although dead, I was still alive and consequently had some chance of revealing this. Rather I will try to record with some sense of order the course of events: minimal events which I did not participate in but was somehow the protagonist of nevertheless. Understandably, at first my impressions were extremely confused, but soon after, I was able to recognize men and things clearly.

2

The great agitation I had initially sensed around my cadaver soon gave way to a funereal calm. A door was opened and closed at nearly regular intervals; light footsteps came within the proximity of what I assumed to be my catafalque. Then I heard a muffled wail or sob, a murmur of condolence, sometimes broken by weeping; whereupon the footsteps grew distant again, and the threshold restored the pious visitor to freedom.

This coming and going lasted quite awhile, but it too finally ceased, and a heavy silence fell in the funeral chapel. Now and then I heard something like the sigh or hiss of a wax taper bent by the wind, or the sizzling of a wick, but nothing else. . . . A new anxiety! In fact, perhaps in my insane hope of proving myself alive I came to fear solitude above all else. But now suddenly, when my furthest thought was to summon my sense of smell for help, my nostrils were filled with a strong, bitter odor whose identity I would've been hard put to deny: someone was holding vinegar right beside me. And what could that mean? Since my skin was utterly numb, I could only deduce an explanation, but it was pleasant nevertheless. I then remembered that it is a local custom to spread a vinegar-soaked handkerchief over a dead person's face so that the beloved's features remain fresh and firm during the long night of mourning. And, in fact, my hearing was ever so slightly diminished (as if the hand-kerchief were covering my ears), confirming that explanation. But meanwhile, the overbearing odor had all but obliterated my already feeble sense of smell. From that moment onward, I would have to depend on my hearing alone, which was also somewhat diminished. Rather than coming closer, the world was growing more and more distant; by then only an extremely tenuous thread bound me to it, a thread that might break at any moment.

As for time, I must say, I didn't have a very clear idea of it; if I had to refer to my absurd sensations in any real terms, time seemed to unwind rather than to proceed. During this unwinding, several sonorous incidents more or less worthy of note occurred, though none of them held any interest for me; like the unexpected thud of a heavy body (a particularly sensitive female visitor, perhaps?) or later, the sinister moan of a piece of furniture loaded (perhaps) with heavy funeral wreaths. Nor will I forget the horrid prayers and the series of chants recited at my coffin by veiled and muffled voices (nuns, no doubt). These episodes, I repeat, were of little consequence given my situation—save one, which I will now relate.

The usual door opened suddenly for the umpteenth time; but now it was not the usual timid footsteps I heard advancing, but determined, almost arrogant footsteps that sounded at once fa-miliar. Nevertheless, I waited for the newcomer to speak to make sure of his identity: and when he did so in a subdued yet au-thoritative tone, I had no doubt.

"My dear, dear Enrichetta," I heard the voice of my cousin, the Baron S (so it was he after all), "I just found out: I'm so sorry! . . . And you, cousin?"

"Me? What do you mean?" I heard my wife reply in a wisp of a voice.

"I mean, I'm so sorry for you too...isn't there something I can do to help you?"

"Ah, what could you do?" Enrichetta answered between sobs. "Unless you have some power over death?"

"Over death no, but over life, yes," said my cousin in a strange tone.

"Oh, Adalberto, I don't understand you. This is no time for discussions. Yet," she added quickly with feminine curiosity, "what do you mean? How would you...?"

"I love you," he declared peremptorily.

"And I'm grateful for your affection," my wife acquiesced with a tinge of bewilderment or dismay in her voice. "It's a comfort to me in these sad circumstances...."

"Affection nothing," my cousin cut in aggressively. "Enrichetta, I *love* love you, and you've known it all along."

"Shut up! What are you saying?"

"What comes to my lips by virtue of its own power."

"But...you tell me this here? Have you no shame, here, in front of my husband's dead body?"

"There couldn't be a more opportune place or a better witness," exclaimed the other as though overcome. "I respected my beloved kin and friend as long as he was alive. Now that he is dead, what sense is there in my restraining myself?...My friend, you know," he continued, surely addressing me now, "I suffered...if I had only known you intended to assuage the storms of my heart, to suffocate the nightly rebellions of my soul....But now that I have opened my conscience, now that you are dead, why shouldn't I break my vow of silence? Enrichetta, I love you, and you love me."

"I do not."

"Yes, you do, if it's true that one can't love without being loved in return."

"But that's not true either," my wife denied feebly like someone trying to check the heart's ardent reasoning with the futile reasoning of intellect.

"Oh," snorted my cousin, "that's not what I want! Don't conceal your feelings behind useless rationalizations. I want us to swear eternal devotion right here, I want you to accept my offering, as I accept yours with all my heart; as dubious and vague as it might seem to you, it has always been clear to me!... Don't be afraid, darling, you'll have time to prepare for our union. I won't disturb your mourning, however long it takes. I'll wait until you can dedicate yourself wholly to our union. But from now on, you must ... Come here, come."

"Adalberto, what are you doing? Oh, my God, be careful, they can see us. And then—no, no," were my wife's last excited and muffled words.

After which followed a brief pause, brief, and, I might say, swollen. A pause in which I thought I heard the slight, ever so slight (for any other listener) imperceptible sound that might arise when two avid mouths are finally joined.

"Oh, no, that's enough, go away," Enrichetta implored and commanded a moment later.

There's no use in relating what feelings, what profound bitterness that conversation instilled in my soul. But right then, something even more urgent demanded my attention.

From the mingling of varied sounds, but mostly from the chirping of birds that arrived as a window was noisily thrown open, I guessed that morning must have broken. And now the whole house was awakening, other windows squeaking, doors opening ever more frequently and earnestly, sprightly footsteps crossing the room. At the same time, my hearing became crystal clear, as it had been initially. It was then that I deduced that the vinegar-soaked rag had been removed. But then, as though a massive screen were dropped between me and the things and people surrounding me, my hearing was deadened again a moment later, and rather more noticeably. From that point onward, I could only guess: they had arranged me in the coffin. In fact, I heard unfamiliar voices. "He's fine like this, there's nothing else to do; maybe just lift his head back up a bit and straighten the wreath between his hands." "But look how much his beard has grown! Do you think we'll have to shave it again?"

Thus, I was in grave and imminent danger: innocently, they were preparing to bury me, and I could no longer delay my attempts to establish communication with them. I would have to do everything possible to make it known I was alive.

Unfortunately, none of my attempts brought any results. Even worse, I noticed that however hard I tried to emit a shout or a breath, whatever concentration of will I exerted to move my rigid limbs even slightly, only brought about a stronger block. Meanwhile I decided to try to relax, to calm down before I resumed my attempts by taking myself by surprise. But now a new situation threatened, chilling the blood in my veins.

Suddenly, that is, my hearing, which was already greatly diminished by the walls of the coffin, was again muffled nearly to the point of shutting me off from the world. I could hear only the loudest sounds clearly since all others were only perceptible with the greatest strain. And now amid these loud noises, I heard a deep thud, whose meaning (going by my ears, since my body was numb to sensation or stimulus) was immediately clear to me. They had closed the coffin, shutting me inside, and they were hammering the nails into place.

Shortly afterward the coffin began to move, but the labored footsteps and panting of the bearers gave me hope. We went out on the public street, where the pealing of the main church bells, the villagers' comments, the very sounds that the heavens transmit, led me to the correct interpretation of events. They were carrying me to my funeral. And panic overwhelmed me: I already felt the lack of air in my enclosure. On the other hand, I was well aware that any attempt I managed to make in the next few minutes would be useless anyway since the outside noises would overpower my signal. At that very moment, in fact, I heard the tempest of songs and chords that usually mark a man's passing. And I gave myself up for dead. These songs, I thought to myself, will accompany me in my final hour. I'll die with them, if I can hold out that long. But I probably won't make it, I'll suffocate to death first.

The funeral ceremony went on, with a thunder of organs and the silvery voices of children or women while I languished, resigned and awaiting real death. Anyway, strangely enough, I still hadn't succumbed to the symptoms of asphyxiation I was anticipating. I didn't feel that I was suffocating at all and generally felt no better or worse than I had earlier. ... It was then with great relief that I realized my error: the lack of air couldn't harm me at all, since I wasn't breathing. Although my situation was little improved, this realization restored my courage. At least I'd been granted the chance to reserve my greatest efforts for the end of the drama: when, having brought these sacred, sonorous functions to a conclusion, they would carry me in slow procession to the cemetery, and after long rites, place me in the tomb.

Many people, I gathered, were accompanying me to my final resting place. Some among them chattered idly, others wove praises of me with genuine regret, all in subdued tones. Indeed, it was quiet enough for me to hear distant and solitary bird calls and even a rustling of leaves—the opportune moment, therefore, to gather my forces once again and try to transmit a signal to those people on the outside.

Alas, I had no better luck this time than before. On the contrary, that spasmodic tension caused all my faculties (actually my one functioning one) to black out now and then, as if I were falling into what would have been called a swoon or stupor, were I not dead. And I was slow to recover. Thus between those alternate periods of stupor and torturous waking, which were interspersed by my continual, agonizing efforts, some time passed. Meanwhile, my funeral procession crossed the threshold of the cemetery. I heard the huge gates creak and recognized the voice of the caretaker, whom I happened to know.

Along the main path that leads to our family chapel I've often noticed a branch of pitosfora that hangs so low it is nearly impossible not to hit one's head on it. If my pallbearers were carrying my coffin on their shoulders, which I reasoned was likely, now that we were approaching the spot the branch would brush by noisily, which it did punctually. And all the successive, minute events my imagination (or rather my ear) anticipated followed with equal punctuality. First, there was a slight agitation, followed by a sigh of satisfaction (we had arrived at the chapel): the exhausted pallbearers had set my coffin down on the pavement. Then there was a gloomy murmuring of prayers and something striking the lid (perhaps the priest was sprinkling holy water). And, after a long pause, a nasal voice (the mayor's?) enumerating my merits and offering lofty consolations to my loved ones, particularly my wife. Then the priest once again. And finally, a metallic sound (of trowels, no doubt), a clattering and a sinister jockeying about. In short, they were sealing my tomb or the burial niche to which I was destined. So had I needed any further proof, I now began to perceive the noises outside as if they were raining down: that is, the screen of bricks must have now been rather high. Perhaps only a small gap remained open, perhaps the next brick laid in would have hidden any view of my box from my relatives and friends forever. . . . It was now or never! I had to send out my call now or never, if I could.

Gathering all my energies into a nearly unbearable spasm, I sent forth a cry. I figured, I don't know why, that I could shout more easily than I could move, or thaw my frozen limbs. The truth was that in the intervals between every swoon, I had sent out one hundred such cries, and none had brought about the slightest result: the silence within me was the only answer to my desperate and frantic labors. But now, just as I was about to lose all hope definitively, I made one supreme and final effort. And it was with unspeakable jubilation that I heard a sound, weak as it was, responding and corresponding to my agony.

It was too weak, surely. It must have been nothing more than a feeble lament, too feeble for any of the gravediggers to have caught it. But having, shall I say, found a way, I followed the first moan with a second one, and then a third. And then suddenly, the workers' labor ceased, the murmuring stopped, and they seemed to be straining to listen. A moment later, a female voice cried out.

"Dear God, oh, God, I thought... You too?"

"Well, yes, but..." another female voice answered.

"What's the matter?" a man's voice inquired. And learning what it was, he pronounced, "Overly sensitive women shouldn't ever..."

"We must reopen the casket at once," a third woman whom I recognized as my good sister yelled with providential resolve.

"But we can't without permission from the, the..." an unfamiliar voice broke in. "What permission!" my sister burst in: "who cares about permission under these circumstances! Here, here, all of you, pull the casket out of there and get to work immediately! I'll take responsibility for it." Upon which, nothing followed, that is, none of the sounds that a prompt execution of that order would have suggested. I tried to produce one final and even more persuasive moan, but I couldn't. I was mute all over again, that ardent spark in my chest had been spent once again. In fact, I slipped back into one of my swoons, surely never to emerge again.

At last, they seemed to make up their minds, and the sequence of sounds I had been longing to hear rose around me and grew more and more urgent: the thud of my coffin against the earth, hammering, the shock of nails pried loose, the buzz and clamor...

But within seconds, I was unable to hear any of it. The emotion of knowing I was saved had sapped the little consciousness I had left.

3

My new awakening (two days later, they told me afterward) was one of my happiest. Though still extremely weakened I had full mastery of all my movements and faculties; my limbs seemed to be invaded by a pleasurable tingling, by a beneficent warmth portending renewed life. The large flowering almond tree framed in the facing window rustled gently in the spring breezes under an azure sky. The first person to appear before me was my wife, with an attitude of loving concern, but I would have rather seen the devil. My whole being responded to her festive smile with a spasm of horror. If I had actually been able to forget her and all that concerned her during the last phase of my terrible experience (when death seemed inevitable), now all the bitter, atrocious feelings that her sly, ambiguous conversation with my cousin had provoked in me rose up again.

I had been reborn fortuitously, but at what price? Specifically, how had my wife emerged from this situation which exceptional circumstances had allowed me to participate in and witness? My wife, my beloved and loving wife, the keeper of my most secret yearnings, the urn of my faith or (as the ancient saying goes) my resting place? She who never betrayed me or suffered my betrayal, who always sustained me on my earthly journey and comforted me in my vacillating footsteps? My second or perhaps my first spirit, my Enrichetta, after all? I mean was she really a liar, a traitor who had abused my trust and my love? Was there a serpent brooding in her breast, or more generally speaking was she a despicable woman? Such was the problem that plagued me continuously and became more and more urgent as my strength was restored (thanks to her loving care).

Naturally, I began to reexamine that disastrous conversation as I remembered it point by point (I was sure I remembered it well). Aside from the inferences in which I might have indulged in the telling and which may be a matter of my own subsequent appraisal, the first as well as the second exchanges in this conversation seemed to be without bile or flaw; moreover, they seemed straightforward. The bile or poison, and the flaw, always lurk at the end, if at all. But I must be quite clear here too. The fact that Adalberto loved my wife did not present any offense or threat to our conjugal love, although just how inauspicious it was remained to be seen. Whereas there would have certainly been threat and offense if Enrichetta had accepted or even tolerated my cousin's infatuations. The obvious question, in any case, could be boiled down to the following: if the two had truly exchanged a kiss, in what spirit had my wife accepted it? Had she merely endured it or had she really responded with a full heart? And if the first were the case, why hadn't an echo, a concrete echo (the sound of some gesture, some word) reached my ears? In the second, oh, well, the second speaks for itself. And yet, it is certainly true that these are matters of opinion. For example, a legitimate desire to avoid a scandal at such a delicate moment may have held my wife back and induced her not to become overly offended. . . . And yet, yet, that air between them, as though they had an understanding, seemed to allude to a prior familiarity, to prior relations. . .?

And so went an inquiry that was already threatening to become insane.

Finally, it was a new woman who stood before me (or so I suspected), but the man she gazed upon was no less new. I did not recognize my loving companion in her, which is to say I persisted in perceiving a mask of impurity and falsehood on her face. She, in turn, could not recover her mild, kindly mate and friend in me. Frowning, we scrutinized one another like adversaries anxious to break down each other's guard; all peace was lost between us, all abandon denied; Enrichetta was no longer Enrichetta, she was a larva which would only bring me uncertainty and deception.

Despite all these tortuous imaginings, I was able to hold fast to my initial, instinctive plan. That is, not to utter a word to her about the experience I had lived through and certainly not about my discovery, or alleged discovery, concerning her. Indeed, nobody should suspect that I had actually sustained a light of consciousness during the apparent death, from which I'd miraculously returned to life; I thought that by keeping up this pretense, perhaps I'd be more likely to catch the others' secrets. In the meantime, I went on feverishly imagining what sort of evidence I could put to my wife to force her to give herself away. Evidence, or even better, a confrontation: and what evidence could be more convincing or definitive than summoning my cousin in person? As for me, I would keep my eyes open.

Adalberto came, and in his usual bold and arrogantly ceremonious tone, said:

"Oh, my dear, dear fellow, I flew here when you called! I didn't consider it my right to disturb your convalescence. So how are you, survivor? What news do you bring from Acheron? Enrichetta! I didn't see you. Ah, it must have been difficult for you too...."

Et cetera, et cetera; and I observed the two of them attentively and saw nothing. Nothing notable, nothing important. My cousin acted just like a cousin visiting a sick cousin, my wife acted like a wife nursing her sick husband and exhibiting this to the visiting cousin. . . . In other words, everything looked normal again, and I saw nothing unusual, much less sinful, in any of it.

But now, excusing himself and embracing me as he left, Adalberto extended his hand to caress my wife's face: a caress understood to be familial, of course. Indeed, I even admired the facility of his gesture. It was, I must say, more than I'd hoped for. How would Enrichetta react? Focusing my attention, I was able to ascertain two things. First, that the caress lasted a split second longer than necessary; and second, that in response, my wife's eyes widened ever so slightly, a reaction sometimes manifested by women in love, for whom even the slightest touch is a memory and token of intense sensuality.

Oh, God, this too was a matter of opinion, especially since neither vacillated in their outward behavior.

"You're all right, cousin!" Adalberto had concluded. And to Enrichetta, meaningfully: "Take care of things, cousin."

And she:

"Thank you, thank you." Then to me: "You know, sweetheart, Adalberto was very concerned about your . . . your mishap, and I must say, he was very close to me during this horrendous trial. . . ."

But my cousin had already kissed her hand warmly and withdrawn.

Bewilderment, anxiety, terror! These were what my investi-
gations and lucubrations left me with. And the temptation to
openly confront my wife with her lapses grew greater and greater.
A temptation which one day, despite all my plans, I could no
longer resist. I started offhandedly, broaching the subject from
afar:

"Enrichetta, I'd like to put a question to you. Let's say I were
dead. . . . Would you. . . ?"

"What is that supposed to mean?" she replied.

"No, I'm saying—what would you do?"

"Nothing. . . . I'd cry."

"Right, and then?"

"What do you mean 'then'?"

"You couldn't go on crying your whole life."

"So?"

"I'm asking you. Finally, you'd have to find someone else, I
imagine."

"Find someone else!" she repeated, suddenly upset. "Oh, what
a stupid and cruel interrogation," she continued, tears welling in
her eyes. "Don't you think I already cried enough when I wept
over your death? Anyway, how stupid of you to insinuate that I'd
have to find solace in another's affections. That's what you meant,
isn't it? Fine, then, let me tell you, it will never be. Good or
bad, in full command of your senses, or as undone as you are
now—by this terrible experience, living or even dead, you, and
you alone were given to me, and I will keep myself eternally
faithful to you alone. . . . Anyway, what do you know about it? I
could very well cry for my whole life and never bemoan my fate."

And the truth is that she was crying uncontrollably now. And
although I didn't have the courage to persist just then, my probing
disposition kept me from weighing just how consoling her words

might have been. But a week later, I took up the task once again.

"Let's say I wasn't really quite dead during those days; let's say one, just one, of my senses had remained, my hearing or whatever, and it allowed me to maintain contact with the world. . . ."

"What a strange fantasy."

"Don't take it too seriously."

"Okay. And so?"

"Right, I could have heard everything that was discussed around my supposed corpse."

"Not terribly entertaining discussions."

"Not at all, but instructive perhaps."

"In what sense?"

"My God, someone could have opened his heart, thinking I was dead."

"Someone: who?"

Once again I didn't dare answer such a direct question. And my wife walked off shrugging her shoulders, shaking her head and giving me a long look, but not without commenting from the doorway:

"I've been finding you strange for a while; you're going to have to make some effort to become your old self again, damn it."

But there came a third time: one night when my bewilderment and anxiety became too much to bear, I resolved to confront Enrichetta on clearer terms. The incident, or I should say its psychological spur, was provoked by my physical prostration: I was lying on the daybed with three pillows under my head, and I must have appeared quite pallid. My wife was tending to me with her customary solicitude, though it was tinged with suspicion and diffidence. She showed me compassion; she caressed me; and while that picture of domestic affections moved me to the point of tears, it also wore on my self-control, with the unforeseeable outcome of renewing my courage. How could I not then compare her to her other image, the wicked one which my memory brought back to me. . . .

Seeing that I had proved myself incapable of bringing a cir-
cuitous conversation to a useful conclusion, this time I actually
assaulted Enrichetta.

"Poor dear, you're suffering," she'd said to me, leaning over
to adjust the pillows. And I:

"How could I not, Enrichetta? I really did hear you talking to
Adalberto."

"I'm sure you did," she answered looking straight at me without
a cloud in her clear blue eyes. "I've talked to him so many times,
the last one right in front of you. So what?"

"Enrichetta! Not while I was living, I heard you talking while
I was dead: the night in the funeral chamber when you were all
mourning me, or actually doing everything but."

Now her eyes focused, she blinked, seemed to hesitate and
finally said:

"Sweetheart, what pain you're causing me. You persist in this
distressing fantasy of yours, you imagine that you kept a glimmer
of consciousness during that horrifying lapse from which neither
medical art nor a faithful wife could or did resuscitate you; and
you are filling this dark night of your spirit with insubstantial
phantoms...."

"Insubstantial phantoms! You call the voices, the words that
came from your very mouths while you believed me dead, the
words that so clearly revealed the mutual game you were playing
with your feelings and maybe your desire?"

"Your: but whose, my poor friend?"

"Yours and Adalberto's!" I broke in, offended, furious.

"Adalberto's feelings, mine? But when?"

"During the wake, I told you."

"It happens," she claimed, half arrogantly, half disgusted (by
my mental state), "it happens that Adalberto didn't even show
up that night. He was away and still didn't know."

"So I'm crazy both alive and dead?" I screamed. "What I heard
is the mere fruit of my imagination, a nightmare brought on and
fomented by my illness?"

"Calm down," she replied, choosing the path of least resistance now. "I'm not saying that, and you're not crazy. But regardless ... you must admit that mysterious illness might have somehow influenced the workings of your mind. . . ."

"I won't admit anything, and what does my mind have to do with any of this? I remember, I can still hear your words in my ears. No, this—this vivid memory is not a matter of madness."

"And anyway," she went on, completing her thought with particular subtlety, without paying me any attention, "it must have been your return to life that caused those fantasies. They are some sort of retrospective interpretation, though a distorted one. I mean, that night you lay there like a log, so it would have been difficult to attribute the slightest feeling or even the slightest glimmer of consciousness to you."

"You're wrong, wrong!" I screamed again. "There was still a heart beating in the log (as you wish to call it...); I mean it wasn't beating, and... the hell with it! But anyway, even if it wasn't beating, it was suffering, it was capable of suffering. . . ."

"All right, all right," she said with obvious condescension. "But what did you actually hear?"

"Huh, what! I heard you two speaking."

"You're referring to Adalberto—who wasn't there—and me?"

"Without a doubt!"

"And what was said?"

"Nothing much."

"Nothing much? In that case..."

"That nothing much of which important, even decisive discussions are made."

"Go on: be more specific."

"Adalberto was pressuring you, and finally he asked you for a kiss."

"And I gave him one, I suppose?"

"Oh, listen; this lighthearted, tolerant and slightly amused tone of yours is an even worse offense. So my distress is just a laughing matter to you?"

"What do you want from me, anyway," exclaimed Enrichetta, really upset now, "you want me to agree and admit to something that never happened, just to suit you? Watch it," she added, already whimpering in her way, "because it would be easy for me to do it. ... So, yes, then: Adalberto came, he asked me for a kiss; and I, convincing myself that you were senseless or (for all I knew) dead—in fact precisely because your death freed me, I gave him that kiss. ... How's that, are you satisfied now?"

"You watch yourself," I answered, "and don't put too much blind faith in the love I gave you and am still giving you. You dare to confirm that..."

"Certainly I confirm it, I swear it on my life!" she screamed. "But no, to be more consistent, I don't confirm anything. I deny it. Deny it all!" Then, changing her expression and assuming a serious tone: "You're sick, that's the truth. And this isn't the same sickness you had yesterday, or else you're not over it; maybe you just got it now. Let's hope my affection can bring you out of it."

And with that ostentatious remark (the only way she could express herself sincerely), she abandoned me to my thoughts.

My thoughts, my uncertainties, both of which hinged on several points in particular. First of all, as Enrichetta herself had alleged, it was always possible that my illness had so bungled my mind that night that I had misheard. On the other hand, my wife had made a very precise reference, and not without some delicacy, to her only possible justification: which directly or indirectly confirmed my own conclusion. To put it more clearly, she seemed to want to argue: seeing that you were dead, any betrayal on my part, if there were one, would not really have been a betrayal: you can betray the living but not the dead! So be it! But what was that, if not a confession, an implicit but unconscious confession which she had let slip in the heat of anger and sarcasm? And so went the other debates and ruminations, to which I must add one other uncertainty—which I would call fundamental, even if not legitimate.

In the course of reflection, I had often speculated upon the true nature of my prior illness, which seemed vital to any understanding of the situation. Nevertheless I don't know why (or perhaps because in the beginning I had imposed silence on myself) I had avoided the kind of honest investigation that might have clarified it. Enrichetta's vague allusions to my "terrible experience," like all her apparently straightforward comments (which may have well been meant merely as images) were of no use to me whatsoever. Nor were the direct, the reticent or partial responses that I got when I made up my mind to interrogate her. So I decided to talk to our doctor who was also a longtime friend.

"Doctor," I asked him one fine day, "for quite a while I've wanted more precise information about the cause of my illness. Now that I'm nearly cured, I think you can tell me everything with a clear conscience. Exactly what kind of illness was it?"

"My dear friend," he said, "why on earth are you getting all riled up? Why do you really care about knowing all the minute details of your past illness and its development and characteristics now that you are (as you correctly point out) nearly cured? You should tend to recovering all your energy instead."

And then, to my remonstrances:

"Well, your case isn't really all that strange. . . . It's not worth worrying over."

"Oh, Doctor," I exclaimed, "what you say only piques my curiosity even more. I must remind you of your professional responsibility and my right to know everything that concerns me. I'm not a child. Speak up."

"All right, then," he said reluctantly, "precisely what do you want to know?"

"As I said, what were the characteristics and nature of my illness?"

"Come now: I'm not capable of answering such questions. You demand too much of medical science. . . . The characteristics and nature too," he grumbled. "No, sir, your illness is a condition that cannot be easily defined, so there you have it."

"You must admit that your diagnosis is unique. In any case, what can you tell me about my symptoms and manifestations, at least?"

"Oh, that's easy: overnight, from one minute to the next, you fell into a burning cerebral fever and . . . and I don't know what else to tell you."

"Eh, Doctor, how on earth can you not know! How and when did the fatal incident which put me in the tomb and from which I was only saved by a miracle come about?"

"Fatal, tomb?" he repeated, astonished. "Pardon me, I don't get your meaning."

"What are you saying!" I leaped up, becoming excited. "Was I, or was I not struck down by a syncope, or, if you prefer, by a catalepsy that convinced you I was dead? Was I or was I not carried to the cemetery and nearly sealed in my tomb?"

"No," he declared resolutely.

"No?" I screamed, unable to control myself. "Doctor, beware, don't try to deceive me, not even for good reasons. In the depths of apparent death, while all of you believed all my senses snuffed out, I actually sustained a glimmer, or more than a glimmer, of consciousness, and I can easily disprove you all."

"Apparent death," he echoed with a kind of obscure bewilderment. "But I never observed anything of the kind. All I can say is that we had reason to worry seriously for your life at one point. As for the other obscure references you are making, I know nothing whatsoever."

"You know nothing whatsoever," I broke in, nearly enraged. I got up from the armchair in which I had lived out my long convalescence, throwing the covers off my legs and taking several disordered steps around the room. "You know nothing! Then you listen to me. . . ."

And then I caught a strange, almost furtive look in the doctor's eyes, and he seemed to blurt these words:

"In any case, perhaps you're right."

"Right, how?"

"Well, now that I think of it, there was a moment when you nearly appeared dead."

"Nearly, you say?"

"No, no, calm down; completely dead."

"It's about time."

But there was something unconvincing in the doctor's admission, or retraction. Then he took his leave in a great hurry, and I was left with that most unpleasant feeling of having been treated like a lunatic—who will have a temper tantrum if not spared all adversity.

And here I am at the present: although, to tell the truth, I don't have a clear idea about time anymore. It might have been their hesitant or insolent answers to my anxious questioning, it might be this whole thing, some sort of conspiracy carried out in the shadows around me, but there's no doubt that my perspective of time was altered in some way. For example, I always thought and still think that the story narrated here probably happened in a rather distant past. And as long as I don't display any sign of discontent, they keep insisting that it is a thing of yesterday. And they bully in other ways. But ultimately, the question of time is not essential. Let's return instead to the two of us.

I continue to observe and scrutinize Enrichetta's behavior and reactions, I confront her with the conclusions of (what can I call it?) my involuntary eavesdropping; and considering the uncontrollable terror on her face whenever she is near me and, in short, utilizing all the elements at my disposal, I can only reach the following conclusion. My wife, long enamored of my cousin Adalberto, and therefore determined to do away with me, devised this hateful method: she threw me into the hands, if you will, of the labrenas. Indeed, she was fully aware of my aversion, or rather my physical intolerance of the foul beasts, and she hoped that they would carry out her wicked task. So even if things didn't happen as she and her allies had wished, the outcome still wasn't so successful.

Naturally, disputing this outright with her (as I've done) doesn't work: nothing but denials and tears comes of it. And yet I—I repeat and attest to this—I have my reasons and incontrovertible proof, just as four and four are eight. Hell, I've pondered this for a long time, I've reexamined all the most minute circumstances ... That night, for example, a dry, stiff wind was blowing; and yet, in such weather labrenas won't come into the rooms (I've observed it a thousand times). So if there was one in mine, it means someone put it there.

Whatever the case may be, what should I make of the numerous labrenas that have assailed and pursued me ever since that day? I now discover one in my room nearly every day, though it is difficult to figure out how they are getting in since I keep the doors and windows sealed. But my wife comes, she comes into my room—and thus I explain the conundrum: ah, she's trying again, knowing full well that I would not survive a second time. I wouldn't survive, I might add, because they are becoming bolder by the day, inching closer and closer to me where I lie, still weakened, and without my rod to defend myself. ... And why, for that matter, don't I have the rod anymore? I think it might be connected to some intemperance of mine, to which I will gladly confess, even if it was largely justified by the state of exasperation into which Enrichetta and the rest of them often cast me. But I'll try to reconstruct the episode.

The only thing one can do is not let on and keep quiet, at least until the others have the dagger up their sleeve. And yet, the moment comes when one can no longer bear it, and then maybe (yesterday):

"Enrichetta, come here and look me straight in the eyes. ... No, no, don't look away: straight into my eyes, I said. So, why are you trembling, fool? Don't test my patience. So then, Enrichetta, I already told you once that ... yes, I've seen through you. I've seen through your designs. And I know the part you played in my horrendous illness, your present intentions, your reprehensible feelings for another man, in other words, I know everything. And you, you actually deny it all. But I won't allow myself to be fooled by your impudence. . . . Ah, what's this, now your teeth are chattering too? Perfect, it must be a sign you understand what I want from you now, right away. I want a full, detailed confession of all the wrongs you've committed. So don't waste time, speak up, tell the truth, ease your conscience: you wanted to kill me. You still do, don't you. So you'll be free to give yourself over to Adalberto, the man you're madly in love with? Come on, I'm waiting. And listen, I'm not necessarily planning to oppose you in this, perhaps I'll decide to sacrifice myself for your happiness. You don't have to be afraid. All I'm asking is that you bare your soul to me, without any more subterfuge or pretense. But go on or I'll lose my patience."

But she slid her hand across her forehead with an expression of bewilderment . . . one that couldn't fool a child; and she continued to tremble, seemingly unable to find words. And then, naturally, I began to raise my voice.

"Enrichetta, if I ask you to speak up, you must speak. What's gotten into you?"

"But I," she finally blurted, "but I never wanted, I don't want to kill you. . . ."

Oh, right, now this, this playing the innocent was too much! What would you all have done?

"You don't want to kill me?" I screamed, beside myself. "Then try to explain the presence here of that, that thing up there."

"What?" she had the nerve to ask.

"That labrena," I yelled, with what little breath I had left. "That thing up on the wall: do you see it or are you pretending not to?"

"I, oh, Lord, I don't see anything," she said, pulling a little, ugly tear out of her apron pocket.

And in the face of such duplicity, such wicked obstinacy, such criminal cunning, I could no longer see straight. I grabbed hold of my flexible rod and went at her legs to beat the skin to a pulp;

she fled with me at her heels. But then she stumbled, and I jumped on top of her.

Well, surely if they hadn't dragged her away from me . . . Perhaps I regret it now, but I must repeat, is it any wonder then that I lose control if they put me in such a rage? That, in any case, is why they took away the rod.

I flew into a rage at the doctor too, and even at my good sister, the same one who brought me back to life when I lay moaning inside my coffin at the cemetery.

As I said, it's some sort of plot.

On the other hand, it's not even that; it's . . .

My convalescence seemed all over, but now . . . There's no question, this must be a serious relapse. I've begun to fantasize, to see strange, terrifying things. . . .

This morning when I woke, I even had the impression that I was not home, but in a horrible, unfamiliar place; it seemed, but I hesitate to say this . . . that the sky framed within the window was not open and pure, but marked and divided, as if by a sinister black shadow. . . . God! A grating!

And why is this room empty of every kind of furniture whatsoever? And why is the bed I just stepped out of a mere cot? Why, why do the dulled walls seem . . . Oh, God, save me from the horror, padded? Why, why, why is it impossible for me to move my arms and hands, as if they were bound across my chest? A mocking or perhaps compassionate face—though it makes no difference—is observing me from a peephole in the door. If only I could reach it, I swear that person would never scoff or pity anyone again. . . . Or perhaps the face belongs to Enrichetta herself, come to relish her triumph? . . .

And above everything, dominating everything, the mover of it all, this labrena . . .

Once again, how did it get in if no one ever enters this room, not even my wife? . . . And how can I protect myself from it, in this condition?

It watches me with its round, bulging, glittering eyes. It scans for the opportune moment to come to me, to come face to face with me. . . . It watches me with its round, bulging, glittering eyes. It scans for the opportune moment to come to me, to come face to face with me . . . It knows its own gaze, its tremendous power. . . .

It holds within all the world's evil, all the world's suffering. . . .

My God, save me.

CHICKEN FATE

"Well," muttered Ted, scratching his head and then thrusting his large hand under his sweater to scratch his back, "I don't want to say anything, but let's face it, ever since we've been feeding them this damn stuff, hormones or whatever the hell it is, they're not the same, not one bit."

"You bet they're not the same, they grow up better and quicker," Joe answered, yawning, "and we make a little more dough."

"Sure, there's no doubt about that, but still . . . Have you seen, for example, how hard it is to catch them? They seem to know where they're going to end up; we have to outwit them and sometimes run behind them, one of them, for a quarter of a mile."

"Tsst, when did a chicken ever like having its neck yanked off?"

"All right, joke all you want, but this is different. Do you see how big they've grown?"

"So what? I mean, so much the better."

"Ah, no, there's something else, something wrong going on here."

"Come on, what do you mean?"

"How should I know! . . . Look, look at that one back there coming up to the front of the line; doesn't he look like he's spying on us?"

"Let him go right ahead."

"No, don't you see the way he's looking at us with that face of his!"

"Face, now that's a good one. Chickens don't have faces."

"Right, that's what I thought until recently; but now they do and when you finally catch one, he looks at you with that expression of..."

"Oh, you see an expression too?"

"Cut it out, Joe; yeah, he looks at you so... so you get the willies sometimes."

"Admit it, Ted, what you need is a good cup of coffee."

"And you, great man, you've never thought chickens had any intelligence?"

"Me, no; there's even an expression: 'birdbrain.'"

"Well, now... I'm not saying they've become intelligent, but I mean they actually seem to do everything with forethought, even if we do end up with their feathers."

"Uff, do you take me for a sucker?"

"Think what you like, but I have more contact with them and I've had time to observe them."

"And what have you observed?"

"Everything and nothing, a lot and nothing, if you get my meaning."

"So, everything's fine. Why don't you let God take care of things?"

"Then why are they leaving?"

"Leaving? Who?"

"Them. I can't swear to it, but it seems to me a lot of them are missing."

"And where are they going, Mr. Seeitall?"

"How should I know?"

"And tell me, how can they leave if there's a fence all around?"

"How should I know what they've cooked up: they must've found a way. Anyway, how long has it been since you checked the fence down in the overgrowth?"

"But don't you see, they couldn't find a better place than here, where they can eat themselves sick and all. That's why they can't possibly be escaping."

"Right, maybe they're not escaping just for the sake of escaping; maybe they're going somewhere special with something special in mind."

"Ah, you're really serious, then? Come off it, it's obvious that you're weak, you're seeing things: Let's have dinner."

"Don't get me mad, Joe. I'm not saying anything definite, it's just a suspicion; but how, how can you be so sure?"

"Hell. . . ."

"Answer me: how many are there in all?"

"Hmm, about fifteen hundred, I think."

"You see, you said, 'I think': We don't even know exactly how many there are, so how could you prove that none are gone? But in any case, we know for sure that there are no less than fifteen hundred, I mean there shouldn't be. Now, look around, just glance quickly: does that look like fifteen hundred chickens to you? And they should all be back home at this hour, you know. Do you want to count them?"

"What, are you dreaming? It would take until midnight."

"Then trust what I'm saying, trust my suspicions."

"This is a new one: even if it were true, it would be a hell of a job: it would eat up most of our profits."

"That wouldn't be the worst of it."

"Ah, there's more too?"

"Hmm, as I said before, there's something wrong; aside from the profits."

"There you go again with that rubbish, excuse my honesty. Tomorrow we'll start if there's time; come on, come on, let's go and eat."

"And what if there's some danger, some threat?"

"Danger too! For Pete's sake, cut it out, Ted!"

"Yeah, there's something in the air, I feel it!"

"Listen, greenhorn, you're just hungry: let's go."

"Listen, Joe, I know I'm being foolish, but . . . But don't you want me to try to explain it? I have some feeling that they're plotting to harm us, and maybe not only . . ."

"The chickens, huh? Okay, okay, kid, but whatever they might be 'plotting,' I'm going to eat on it. What about you, you coming or not?"

"Joe!"

"What is it?" he yelled, waking suddenly and bolting to a sitting position on his cot.

"Listen."

"I don't hear anything."

"That's strange: and yet I thought . . ."

"What, what did you think, will you tell me?"

"I don't know, it seemed like . . ."

"And will you stop with the 'I don't knows' and the 'likes'! What an imagination! Good God, people like you should go around with a bell on the end of their noses."

"There, there, it's starting again."

In fact, an earsplitting sound, distantly reminiscent of a steam engine or a factory siren, began: began and within seconds reached a nearly intolerable level. But the peculiar thing was that it was impossible to figure out, to pinpoint its source in that expanse— nature. It filled the air and seemed to originate from every point on the horizon at the same time. Now and then it would abate, but only to start up again with renewed intensity, as if it followed a rhythm of its own, much like a sort of implacable hammering. The windowpanes in the barracks began to clatter, and every time the sound started up, the two felt their hearts leap from their chests.

"What the hell is it?"

"That's what I asked you."

In any case, the one thing they could not do was stay inside, doing nothing; so they threw their clothes on and rushed outside.

The night was dark and humid; outside the sound was so loud

that it swallowed up their words. But there was nothing, nothing to be seen; everything seemed normal except for that sound. At first they ran toward it, as if they knew where they were going; then suddenly, as if by mutual agreement, they both stopped.

"Where are we going, anyway?"

"Eh, I don't know, it's coming from down there."

"But, no, I mean why are we going toward it?"

"What do you mean why? Do we have any choice? My head is spinning; we have to go and see, make them stop."

"Who?"

"Someone must be making a racket just for fun, and damn it, I'm going to give him a piece of my mind. Why, do you have a better idea?"

"I'll go in the opposite direction: there could be something... something dangerous."

"Don't start that foolishness about danger again. Anyhow, smarty, which is the opposite direction? Come on, come."

They ran one way: the sound neither increased nor diminished. They ran the other way, and it was the same thing. Then they finally seemed to realize that the center or epicenter of that terrible din was coming from a dark wooded hill which rose a half a mile away: stunned and seemingly blinded, they set out toward it, and actually, after about one hundred feet, the sound seemed to increase in intensity, if such a thing were possible, and become more distinct. Now it seemed more like a man or perhaps an animal howling, that is, if one could imagine a being so gigantic lamenting or moaning in such a thunderous voice. And then, it had a curious attraction, a magnetic force; yes, it was like a drawn-out, irresistible call. And if it were indeed a call, now they were running toward it.

"Let's stop, I'm scared now."

"Rubbish: you'll see, I'm going to give them a piece of my mind."

"But who, who?"

They reached the foot of the hill; the sound seemed to be

hanging over them now, as if a thousand heavy bombers were passing overhead at a low altitude. And though it could be heard very clearly now, it wasn't vibrating like a motor; nor did it seem to be coming from any sort of machine at all; rather, it became more and more apparent that it was the voice of an animal.

"It's here, up here, it can't be far now."

"Joe..."

"Let's go, come on."

They began climbing the hill breathlessly; it was so dark beneath the thick shrubbery that they were almost groping for their way. On the other side of the hill, they came to a fairly flat clearing, which they crossed, reaching a slope again; and as soon as they entered the woods once more, they came face-to-face with a metal netting.

It wasn't their netting: theirs didn't extend that far and anyway, they had let themselves out of one of their own gates, quite a ways back. Nevertheless, it looked exactly like a chicken coop net. Meanwhile, the sound quickly changed rhythm and tone, transforming above them into a sort of thunderous, hoarse laughter that stopped abruptly, leaving them more stunned than before.

"In God's name, Ted, what is it?"

"I... I don't know...."

"And this net, what does it mean?"

"How should I know? I can't figure it out," Ted answered, shuddering.

They felt the net: it was well grounded and more solid than they had imagined, and it vanished above them, so that it seemed as impossible to climb over as to break through it. Therefore, they ran back and forth, reaching out blindly in an attempt to get around the obstacle or find a way through it. But the net was solid to the left and to the right and it looped back, leading them to where they'd started. And meanwhile, that horrendous, high-pitched laughter exploded violently, repeatedly, above their heads, as if to comment upon and mock their futile efforts.

"Joe, why keep trying to get through there, what are we looking for? Let's turn back instead. Joe, do you hear me? Let's go back now!"

"What: turn back!" Joe blurted, hesitantly. "I want, I have to..."

But a louder and even more atrocious roar followed, as if in response to Ted's words; a deafening and drawn-out roar that went on and on, interrupted by a sinister and earshattering gurgling, similar to the kind of gobble gobble some monstrous turkey would make. The air quavered, and their guts quavered; their eardrums, their skulls, were literally on the verge of exploding.

"Yeah, maybe you're right: let's get out of here, fast, run!"

"It's unbearable."

They ran down the hill, thinking only of escape, the frightening laughter pursuing at their heels. In a matter of seconds, they covered half the path they'd just taken, and suddenly they came upon another net, as solid, high and unbroken as the first.

"How... how is this possible?" blurted Joe, shivering. "We're actually lost!"

"That's impossible."

They tried frantically, unsuccessfully, to overcome the new obstacle; and the roars, the howls, the gobble gobbles, the whole acoustic earthquake which had stopped for a moment began again. They tried on the other side and here and there under the shrubbery, but wherever they went they found the net. So, they were prisoners! Prisoners in a corral, however vast: just like the chickens they raised.

Finally, they began hurling themselves this way and that, like crazed mice in a trap.

"But how could this happen, what's going on? Come on, Ted, help me, let's try to knock down this damn net."

"It's useless."

"Why are you saying that? Come on, maybe if we push... No matter what, we have to get out of here, we can't stay, we can't! Listen, be brave."

"Ah-ha," Ted yelled suddenly, "ah, I knew it all along: it's them!"

"Them? Ted, Ted, now what's got into you?"

Ted was rolling around on the ground, laughing, crying, roaring, biting his fists, overtaken by violent convulsions; and between sobs, he kept repeating: "It's them; it's them."

The air above them seemed to sneer.

One, two gigantic swollen shapes, distinct from the surrounding darkness, passed in the near distance and vanished. Their feet, if they had any, made no sound; or if they did, it was the sound that a puppy or a chicken makes.

Joe was wakened by a confused clamor, or perhaps only by the light; it was dawn. Ted was still lying beside him motionlessly, in a contorted position; he too must have been overcome, more by terror than by sleep. He was nauseous, he had a headache and his eyes were blurry. Or was something overshadowing him, blocking his vision? He looked again.

The thing in front of him, or rather above him, was surely a chicken, but a gigantic one of unimaginable proportions; its relatively small head reached the top of the nearby trees.

The monster, flapping its wings slightly, looked down, observing him alternately with one eye and then another, as chickens do. Joe was stunned by the expression in those eyes: there was nothing fierce in them, only a sort of bemused, almost kindly curiosity. Anyway, poor Ted had been right: what an intelligent face a chicken could have! But none of that prevented this one from preparing to drive its terrible beak into him, Joe could see this well. But aside from his headache, his exhaustion and all the rest, why should he have tried to flee, flapping headlong here and there, exactly as their chickens did every time they had to be caught for...? Therefore, there was no escaping, just as not long ago, though that time already seemed remote, their chickens could not have hoped to escape from the two of them.

Well, obviously this was his fate, a chicken's fate. Or maybe the monster would finish him off with that look, or somehow or other; after all, this chicken and the others had actually led them into the trap.

Anyway, it made no difference. He picked his head up, let it fall back to the ground again, relaxed his limbs and waited. Out of the corner of his eye, he saw more of those gigantic creatures moving around the barren slope, and he understood where the clamor was coming from: there were people there, a lot of people. Some were lying down, others were moving about; one disheveled girl was running, shrieking hysterically (a real hen, Joe thought) as one of *them* pursued and soon overtook her.

The first time the beak struck, it took off a whole leg, but he didn't move. Not that he lost consciousness: he still saw the terrible face descend dizzyingly. And this time it seemed to be right on target.

TWO WAKES

1

My lady, what shall I say to you now? You are about to descend to the cold tomb, and all my affection, all my worth, all my hope will be shut down there with you, everything that is pure, noble, trusting in me, all my worldly good, all my joy, and in short whatever can make a man's solitary life beautiful. I love you now, lovely creature, now more than ever before, I who met you after long years of melancholy, after a long journey through an arid desert; and you have been taken from me. I who saw all perfections and delights in you, who vowed all of my heart to you, every blood rush. And you were taken from me so cruelly, so soon that our wedding and these funeral rites blur together as one. And you loved me too, no other could have loved me as you did; I can surely say that not only my love but also what your love brought me, my paradise, will be shut in your tomb. And what will become of my life now if that which made it what it is, its living spirit, is torn from it? Ah, I'd gladly give all my blood, save the one drop that I would need to go on relishing you, so that yours might flow again; ah, I would gladly follow you—for how could I do otherwise?—on that dark journey, if I weren't afraid of hurting you, tender lover, you who would still protect me with your light or your shade! And yet, who will restore you to me—you yourself? You're beautiful and you're good; but alas,

I have to say you were. Genius and every other grace of the spirit shone in you, shedding light upon loveliness and goodness while they received your warmth in return. And that, all that was taken from me. . . . And you, little mouse, climbing watchfully up the leg of the chair, what are you looking for in this sorrowful house? Little creature, I must kill you or cast you out, but come here fearlessly and keep me company! Oh, but my voice frightens you and you bound across the room in your little gallop; can I blame you for rushing happily toward the secret hole where your mate awaits you. . . . And you too are happy, melodious nightingale: your trills fill the distant night, and thus, as the poet says, your little bride lives in your nest with you. "Lives": sweet, singular word. . . . But am I seeing things! A delicate pink is suffusing her cheeks. . . . Ah, no, it's my tired eyes' cruel deception. . . . Ah, but yes, it's no deception: most jubilant miracle, she lives again, oh, this inexpressible joy brings me back to life too! Wait, she's starting to murmur something. . . .

2

"My lovely crystal vase on that unsteady shelf: the slightest push and it will fall."

She's speaking distinctly: oh, be gone forever, stay in the past, horrendous nightmare, horrendous grief!

"Take it down from there. And what are these candles and these flowers doing here?"

"They're to light and to celebrate your reawakening. My dearest, you have returned to your lover's arms, to all of nature's jubilant reception, you . . ."

"Goodness, tomorrow must be the fifteenth! Besides the installment on the vacuum cleaner . . . God knows how we are going to make it until the end of the month. There's never enough cash these days; tell me, do you know what spinish costs now?"

"Spin . . . ? Really, I already told . . . we say spinach and not spinish. But anyway, look out the window, the stars are growing pale now under the setting moon, they seem to be glancing into this room which only moments ago was the seat of evil terror..."

"Servants are truly God's revenge: ours robs from the cupboard and the house and gets away with it, and that certainly doesn't help matters. No, I must say, I sometimes feel discouraged."

"... as if they wanted to take part in our feast of love!"

"You should confront her and teach her a lesson; oh, right, you don't care about anything."

"Oh, my delight, breathe the night's reviving exhalations!"

"And not only that, how many times have I told her that bleach ruins the laundry, but she wants to use it. Ah, obviously she figures 'It's my whip and someone else's horse.'"

"But finally..."

"And then that Ada, what does she think, coming here like that, dressed to the nines and garlanded like a young girl? That she can humiliate me, maybe? Well, it would take more than that! It's simply ridiculous at her age. And for starters, she needs a better dressmaker. How could you not realize where she gets her money. Ah, poor husbands! But then you take a shine to her, so it's useless to talk to you about it."

"But no, I swear to you..."

"I will absolutely need a new little sundress for this summer: the old one's in such a state and anyway, it's out of style now."

3

Oh, you're really dead this time if God so wills it. Many years have passed since that first wake when you suddenly came back to life. Then I "would have gladly given all my blood," et cetera; and "in response to my ardent pleas, the heavens willed you to wake from your mortal lethargy," et cetera, et cetera. (I used to express myself and even think in those terms then.) And by the way, what was afflicting you? Bah, I don't remember exactly what they called it, some sort of catalepsy, I think. But that doesn't matter.... Such long years.... What a luminous image you would have left, you were leaving me then! And what can I say to you now? Well, let's not exaggerate: you are basically as blameless

as anybody else; so, may your soul rest in peace. All right; but
... but what have all these years given me (or given us, if you
prefer, because looking back now, the discussion could always
be reversed). I believed you were sweet, beautiful, good, intelligent—agreed—but I had to convince myself that you were also
sulky, nasty, stupid and vulgar, not terribly, but vulgar enough.
Therefore instead of giving, you took something from me. I mean
(to be precise) you took what you could have given me before
plus a little, a trifle: the possibility of hoping to be happy and of
being happy because the person who has been disappointed once
cannot delude himself again. Uhm, the very thing you were taking
away from me could have, and perhaps should have, made you
dearer to me, I understand that perfectly. Or to put it more clearly,
I understand that I should understand it, but in reality I don't
understand it at all.

How could you be dearer than on that day the first time you
died? Ah, no, nobody could make me believe such a lie: those
who hide from disappointment, who nurture themselves only on
satisfaction and happiness, are a sad humanity with sad emotions,
sick emotions—an alternative for desperation, a confession of
our vulgarity which they would ennoble proudly, like so many
other sick and abject things, like the revolting pain we suffer as
human creatures, et cetera. "She was a woman, no more than a
woman, and I loved her precisely for that": so goes a certain
rhetoric ... and hence our impotence. But leaving those points
aside, what was our life after all (perhaps simply because it was
shared, or because life in two can be nothing but what it is) if
not a kind of dialogue (when it wasn't an argument) with no end,
or rather no beginning or end, a buzzing, persistent and grim
dialogue, about God knows what? If not a sordid sequence of
pointless preoccupations, deprived of all light? And, of course,
I, for my part, "ignored your most awesome bouts of melancholy,"
and all the rest of it. To put it briefly, am I not perhaps justified
in retrospectively wishing that ... —what a hell of a sentence!—
I mean to regret that you didn't die in time, I mean that time

when you made believe? Yes, happy is he whose bride dies the same day of the nuptials, if possible, because he is left with a pure image that anything afterward would only sully. Ah, that first night! If I had had enough good sense, I would have screamed, "How lucky I am that you are dead!" instead of despairing! And later, instead of rejoicing, I should have put a mourning ribbon on my hat. But in fact, you came back to life, and the difference between the first and second time is precisely the difference between life and death; but let it be clear, death was this, this here. True, it may be that we can hope for life only from death, unless it too betrayed us; or to put it differently, what if our only enemy is life itself? But there I go again with my rationalizations! And you there, little mouse peering out from behind the credenza, is it possible that this house cannot be free of you? Yes, yes, go on, run away: I'll find a way to get you. I'm going to try poisoned grain. And you too, damn petulant nightingale, exploiting this tatter of a garden, are you? This time you've come to the window to let your pearls fall like little silver kisses, or whatever the poets have come up with now! When will you cut it out? A good shot, just to scare you off, that's what we need for you.

THE KISS

The notary, D, a bachelor who was still in his prime but hopelessly timid with women, turned off the light and got ready to sleep, when he felt something like a breath or rather a wing grazing his lips. He didn't pay it much attention—perhaps the blankets or a moth had stirred the air—and he soon fell asleep. But the following night he was aware of the same sensation; indeed, it was even more distinct: instead of slipping away, whatever it was rested on his lips for a moment. Rather shocked, if not alarmed, he turned on the light, but in vain; then he shook his head and fell asleep once again, though not as easily. Finally on the third night, it was even more distinct and revealed itself for what it was: a kiss, without a doubt! One might have said it was a kiss from the darkness itself, as if the darkness had gathered on the notary's lips. However, he didn't take it that way; a kiss is always a kiss, and even if this one was slightly dry, not damp and sweet as he had always fantasized, it was still a gift from the heavens. It was probably no more than a projection of his innermost desires, a hallucination—and a welcome one. Disturbed, delighted and dismayed, our hero remained splayed out like a log in the dark (which he rightly considered a matchmaker); and a little later, he had the pleasure of another kiss.

As the nights passed, the kisses became more frequent and

43

more substantial, although the notary didn't discover or uncover the slightest scent of a female mouth in it. And now, despite the fact that his old-fashioned reason told him better, the notary was overwhelmed by a longing to somehow evoke the creature who was lavishing kisses on him: he was tired of grabbing at the air, and didn't a kiss presuppose some creature who gave it? However ethereal or subtle she was trying to be, there had to be some way to gather her up, to squeeze her in his arms. My God, it wasn't that he had already lost his sense of all relationships, but at first he imagined or pretended that his longing was nothing more than a desire for his own hallucination to be more corporeal; but he soon ceased doubting that the kissing creature actually existed.

Still, upon closer consideration, how could he induce her to manifest herself less exclusively, to lead her toward corporeality? The notary realized full well that in such a situation the only means at his disposal were psychic ones; so each time he was kissed, he began to concentrate, to project his will and energy, as if to force himself to intercept some of the illusive creature's particles, her fluid or substance; all together, those particles should have added up to some sort of being. That was followed by another step which generally was intended to evoke and urge on the darkness. And whether this was indeed the right method or there were other reasons, before long he began to reap the fruits of his labors.

To begin with, the room gave onto a narrow courtyard, even though it did not enjoy any light from the outside during the night; in any case, the blinds whose slats, oddly enough, fit together properly, would have shut it out. Nevertheless, one night in that pitch-dark, the notary thought he glimpsed another darkness, a blacker one, a shadow, as absurd as that may be, except that he couldn't figure out where it was or make out its silhouette. And even more peculiar, on another night a sort of bloody dawn came up in the room, a frail and sinister luminosity, like an aurora borealis that loomed up from the floor and took the shape of a fringed sash as it rose, quivering, fluttering and slowly fading out altogether. And finally, to move on to things of a different nature, one evening he distinctly heard muffled laughter in a corner, not a merry laugh, but an icy, unnatural one.

The notary didn't know whether to feel cheered or horrified by his results: the creature was turning out to be something altogether different from what he had imagined, and furthermore, it didn't seem willing to make any more concessions. Thus, he decided to stop performing these evocative exercises for a time, but that didn't mean that she stopped appearing in her various guises. As for her kisses, they had become devouring. And he, emaciated, exhausted, empty, lacking sleep and appetite, wondered if this wasn't going too far. His work went to the dogs, his health was gravely threatened, he couldn't go on like this. At last, he decided belatedly upon something that probably would have helped from the very beginning: to sleep with the light on. His decision to give up the game, to give up on the whole thing, cost his romantic inclinations dearly; but in reality, for some time since he had become the object of those mysterious attentions, his initial ecstasies had given way to a sense of impending danger. Whatever the case, he began to sleep with the lights blazing; to sleep, at last!

For a while everything was fine; he caught his breath a little, and yet he felt something was missing. But in the blazing light one night, he got or was subjected to a kiss again. The truth is that he was sleeping (as best he could) when it happened, and, as he leaped awake, he might have thought he was dreaming. Nevertheless, when he dozed off again, or rather while he hovered between waking and sleep, another lusty kiss was planted on his lips. "Planted," as they say, but in reality that kiss was more like a whirlwind. In short, the notary understood that the creature, unable to count on darkness now, was taking advantage of his sleep, and nothing could stop her. And at the same time, the atrocious suspicion he had denied for so long became a certainty: the creature was feeding on him, growing big and strong on his blood, on his life, his spirit.

This certainty only sapped what was left of the notary's strength, casting him into a state of dull resignation; from this point onward, his life would be no more than a long, but not too long, wait for his inevitable death.

His situation was idiotic and grotesque, yet there seemed to be no defense against it; grotesque and tragic, as is so often the case. Perhaps he could escape? But where? And how, if he himself had invented the creature? And if indeed he had, where were that same strength and will now? No, it would be better to facilitate her work so it could be carried out as quickly as possible and to try to get a look at her, a glimpse, now that she'd grown robust. Yes, he now only felt a sort of dreadful curiosity, which he could not overcome, ashamed as he was. He began turning off the light again: what better way to restore her confidence and audacity?

During those nights of agony, he saw and experienced so many things, all of them horrendously absurd. At first a sort of immense mass that was strangely vacuous and distinct from the dense surrounding darkness seemed to occupy the whole room, an emptiness within an emptiness, like certain gaps in the black cosmic ether. It swarmed with appendages, paws or tentacles that waved up and down as if blown by a hidden wind. Then all of a sudden, this negative mass, this bubble of emptiness, was transformed into something extremely meager and sharp that broke into a thousand rivulets like capillaries and pervaded everything, even him. Or sometimes, a sweet, putrid odor spread through the room, evoking incomprehensible images and landscapes that he'd never seen. Or it was simply a sense, like a fleeting memory, which itself was anticipated by inexplicable terror, or hovered behind everything, every plausible experience, or came up against shapelessness and nothingness. And once again, muffled laughter, frozen cackling; something like shivers grazed his skin, and the bitterness in his mouth pervaded his whole body.

But the notary's hours were already numbered. On the last night, a gigantic, overturned chasm opened before his eyes—his body and soul—a grayish whirlpool like a matrix or a conch; it loomed, and from the apex of its spiral, it beckoned to him. Meanwhile, his skin, shrunken to arid scales, shone with a dull phosphorescence—not a sign of life but of putrefaction, the kind that gives rise to will-o'-the-wisps. He imagined himself a fish in the depths, weakly luminous in the black abyss: yes, he was drained of blood now, and this tenuous light would soon be spent too. It was over. He let himself go; and perhaps in that last instant, in return for his abandon, he was allowed to look her in the face, to glimpse the creature who had sucked away his life, who now ripped the ultimate kiss from him.

That was it, the end. And the unknown creature rose from the empty spoils and made its way through the world.

GOGOL'S WIFE

Thus confronted with the complex question of Nikolai Vasilyevich's wife, I am overwhelmed by hesitation. Do I have any
right to reveal something that nobody knows, something that my
unforgettable friend himself kept hidden from everyone (and with
good reason) and that will undoubtedly serve only the most evil
and foolish interpretations? Not to mention the many sordid,
sanctimonious and hypocritical souls who will be offended, and
perhaps some truly honest souls too, if they still come that way?
Do I have any right, finally, to reveal something before which my
own sensibility shrinks, when I am not inclined toward a more
or less open disapproval? But, after all, precise duties are in-
cumbent upon me as a biographer: and seeing that each and every
piece of news about such a lofty man might turn out to be precious
to us and to future generations, I would not wish to entrust it to
transient judgment, in other words, to conceal something that
could only eventually, if ever, be judged sanely. Because who are
we to condemn? Have we been granted the right to know not only
the needs of these outstanding men, but also the superior and
general ends to which their actions (which we may consider vile)
correspond? Certainly not, since fundamentally we understand
nothing of such privileged natures. "It's true," a great man said,
"I pee too, but for altogether different reasons."

But dispensing with all that, I will come to what I know undeniably, what I know without a shadow of a doubt about the controversial question, which I can prove in any case to be otherwise, at least I dare hope; thus, I will not summarize any of that, since at this point it is superfluous to the current phase of Gogol studies.

Gogol's wife, it must be said, was not a woman, nor was she a human being, nor a living creature of any kind, nor an animal or plant (as some have insinuated); she was simply a doll. Yes, a doll; and this well explains the bewilderment, or worse, the indignation of some biographers, who were also personal friends of our Man, and who complained they had never seen her although they frequented her great husband's house quite often; not only that, they had "never even heard her voice." Hence, goodness knows what dark, disgraceful and perhaps even abominable complications they may have inferred. But no, gentlemen, everything is always simpler than one might believe; you never heard her voice simply because she could not speak. Or more precisely, she could only speak under certain conditions, as we will see, and in all those cases, except one, only to Nikolai Vasilyevich. But let me dispense with useless and facile refutations, and let us work toward the most precise and complete description possible of the being or object in question.

Gogol's so-called wife, then, looked like a common doll made of thick rubber the hue of flesh, or as it is often called, skin color, and was nude regardless of the season. But since women's skin is not always the same color, I should specify that hers was generally somewhat fair and smooth, like that of some brunettes. It, or she, was in fact (but must this be said?) of the female sex. Indeed, let me add immediately that she was highly fickle in her characteristics, although obviously, she could not change her sex. Yet without a doubt she could appear thin, almost flat-chested and straight-hipped, more like an ephebe than a woman, on one occasion, and on another, exceedingly buxom, or to put it plainly, plump. She frequently changed her hair color as well as the other

hair on her body, sometimes to match and sometimes not. Thus
she could also alter other minute particulars, such as the place-
ment of moles, the color of her mucous membranes, and so on;
and even to a certain extent, the actual color of her skin. Therefore, ultimately, one must ask oneself what she really was, and
if he should speak of her as a singular being; yet, as we shall
see, it would not be wise to insist on this point.

The reasons for these changes were, as my readers must already
have guessed, none other than the very will of Nikolai Vasilyevich.
He would inflate her accordingly, change her hairstyle and other
body fuzz, anoint her with oils and touch her up in various ways
in order to obtain the closest possible version of the type of woman
that suited him that day or that moment. Indeed, he sometimes
amused himself by following the natural inclination of his fantasy,
manipulating her into grotesque and monstrous forms. Because
clearly, beyond a certain air capacity, she only became deformed,
but she would appear equally hideous if the volume remained too
low. But Gogol soon tired of such experiments, as he considered
them "basically disrespectful" of his wife, whom he loved in his
own way (as inscrutable as it might be to us). He loved her, but
one might ask precisely which of her incarnations he loved? Alas,
I have already indicated that the rest of the present account might
provide some sort of answer. Oh, dear, how could I have just
stated that Nikolai Vasilyevich's will governed that woman! In a
limited sense yes, that is true, but it is just as certain that she
soon became his tyrant rather than his slave. And this is where
the abyss, or if you will, the jaws of Tartarus, open. But let us
proceed in an orderly manner.

I also said that Gogol obtained an approximation of the woman
that suited him from one occasion to the next. I should also add
that in those rare cases when the resulting form completely in-
carnated his fantasy, Nikolai Vasilyevich fell in love, "in an
exclusive manner" (as he put it in his native tongue), which
actually created a stable relationship for a certain period, that
is, until he fell out of love with her appearance.

I must say that I have only come across three or four instances of such violent passions, or as the unfortunate expression goes today, crushes, in the life, or might I say the married life, of the great writer. Let us add right away for the sake of expedience that several years after his so-called marriage, Gogol even gave his wife a name; it was "Caracas," which, if I'm not mistaken, is the capital of Venezuela. I have never been able to comprehend the reasons for such a choice: the eccentricities of lofty minds!

As for her overall shape, Caracas was what is known as a "beautiful woman," well-built and proportioned in all her parts. As remarked earlier, even the smallest characteristics of her sex were where they should have been. Particularly noteworthy were her genitalia (if this word can have any meaning here), which Gogol allowed me to observe one memorable evening; but more about that later. This was the result of an ingenious folding of the rubber. Nothing had been overlooked: the pressurized air inside her and other clever devices made her easy to use.

Caracas also had a skeleton, though a rudimentary one, made perhaps from whalebone; special care had been taken in the construction of the rib cage, the bones of the pelvis and the cranium. The first two systems were more or less visible, as one would expect, in proportion to the thickness of the so-called adipose tissue which covered it. If I may quickly add, it is a real pity that Gogol never wanted to reveal the identity of the artist behind such a beautiful piece of work; indeed, I never understood the obstinacy of his refusal.

Nikolai Vasilyevich inflated his wife through the anal sphincter with the aid of a pump of his own invention, somewhat similar to those that are held in place by the feet and which are commonly seen in mechanics' garages; in the anus there was a small movable valve, or whatever it is called in technical jargon, comparable to the mitral valve in the heart, such that once the body was inflated it could still take in air without losing any. To deflate it, one had to unscrew a little cap located in the mouth, at the back of the throat. And nevertheless . . . But let's not jump ahead.

And now I think I have covered all of the notable particulars of this being—except to remark upon the stupendous row of little teeth which graced her mouth and her brown eyes which, despite constant immobility, feigned life perfectly. Good Lord, feigned is not the word for it! Indeed, one really cannot say anything legitimately about Caracas. The color of those eyes could also be modified through a rather long and tedious process, yet Gogol rarely did this. And finally I must speak about her voice, which I had occasion to hear only once. But first I must touch upon the relationship between the spouses, and here I can no longer proceed randomly, or answer everything with the same absolute certainty. I could not do that in good conscience, for what I am about to relate is too confusing, inherently and in my own mind. Here nevertheless are my memories, as chaotic as they may be.

The first and indeed the last time I heard Caracas speak was on an intensely intimate evening spent in the room where the woman, if I may be allowed this verb, lived; nobody was permitted to enter. The room was decorated in somewhat of an Oriental style, had no windows and was located in the most impenetrable corner of the house. I had not been unaware that she spoke, but Gogol never wished to clarify the circumstances under which she did. There we were, you see, the two, or three of us. Nikolai Vasilyevich and I were drinking vodka and discussing Butkov's novel; I remember that he digressed from the topic a bit and was insisting on the need for radical reforms in the inheritance laws; we had nearly forgotten her. And then in a hoarse, meek voice like Venus in the nuptial bed, she said point-blank, "I have to go poop." I gave a start, thinking I had misheard, and I looked at her: she was sitting propped against a wall on a pile of pillows, and on that day she was a soft, gorgeous blonde, and rather fleshy. Her face seemed to have taken on an expression bordering on maliciousness and cunning, childishness and scorn. As for Gogol, he blushed violently and leaped onto her, thrusting two fingers down her throat; and as she began to get thinner and, one might say, paler, she took on that look of astonishment and befuddlement that was truly hers; and at last she shrunk to nothing more than a flabby skin covering a makeshift framework of bones. In fact, since she had an extremely flexible spine (one can intuit how this made for more comfortable use), she nearly folded in half; and she continued to stare at us for the rest of the evening from that degrading position on the floor where she had slid.

"She is either being nasty or joking," Gogol muttered, "because she doesn't suffer such needs." He generally made a show of treating her with disdain in the presence of others, or at least with me.

We continued drinking and conversing, but Nikolai Vasilyevich seemed deeply disturbed and somehow removed. Suddenly he broke off, and taking my hands in his own, burst into tears. "Now what," he exclaimed. "Don't you see, Foma Paskalovic, I loved her!" It must be mentioned that, short of a miracle, none of the forms Caracas took was reproducible; she was a new creation each time, and any attempt to recreate the particular proportions, the particular fullness and so on, of a deflated Caracas would have been in vain. Therefore, that particular plump blonde was now hopelessly lost to Gogol. And indeed, this was the pitiful end of one of Nikolai Vasilyevich's few loves which I made a reference to earlier. He refused to provide any explanation, he refused my consolation, and we parted early that evening. But he had opened his heart to me in that outburst; from then on he was never as reticent, and soon he kept no secrets from me. This, parenthetically, was a source of infinite pride.

Things seemed to have gone well for the "couple" during the first phase of their life together. Nikolai Vasilyevich appeared to be content with Caracas and slept in the same bed with her regularly. He continued to do this up until the end as well, admitting with a timid smile that there could not be a quieter or less tiresome companion than she; nevertheless, I soon had reason to doubt this, judging mostly from the state I sometimes found him in when he awoke. Within several years, however, their relationship became strangely troubled.

This, let me caution once and for all, is merely a schematic attempt at explanation. But it seems that around that time the woman began to show an inclination for independence, or should I say, autonomy. Nikolai Vasilyevich had the bizarre impression that she was assuming a personality of her own, which, although indecipherable, was distinct from his own, and she seemed to be slipping, if you will, from his grasp. It is true that a continuity was finally established among all her diverse and varied appearances: there was something in common among all those brunette, blond, auburn and red-haired women, among the fat, thin, withered, pallid and ambered ones. In the beginning of this chapter, I threw some doubt on the legitimacy of considering Caracas a single personality; nevertheless, whenever I saw her I could not free myself of the impression that, incredible as it may seem, she was essentially one and the same woman. And perhaps it was precisely this which prompted Gogol to give her a name.

It is another thing again to try to establish the nature of the quality common to all those forms. Perhaps it was no more and no less than the breath of her creator, Nikolai Vasilyevich. But truly, it would have been too peculiar for him to be so detached from himself, so conflicted. Because it must be said immediately that whoever Caracas was, she was nonetheless a disturbing presence, and let this be clear, a hostile one. In conclusion, however, neither Gogol nor I ever managed to formulate a vaguely plausible hypothesis concerning her nature. I mean to "formulate" one in rational terms that would be accessible to everyone. I cannot, in any case, suppress an extraordinary incident which occurred during this period.

Caracas fell ill with a shameful disease, or at least Gogol did, although he had never had any contact with other women. I will not even try to speculate on how such a thing happened or from whence the foul illness sprung: I only know that it happened. And that my great unhappy friend sometimes said to me, "So you see, Foma Paskalovic, what was in Caracas' heart: the spirit of syphilis!" But at other times, he blamed himself quite absurdly (he had always had a tendency for self-accusation). This incident was truly catastrophic for the relations between the spouses, which were already confused enough, and for Nikolai Vasilyevich's conflicting feelings. He was thus obliged to undergo continuous and painful cures (as they were in those days). And the situation was aggravated by the fact that in the woman's case, the disease did not initially appear to be curable. I should also add that for some time Gogol continued to pretend that by inflating and deflating his wife and giving her a great variety of appearances, he could create a woman immune to the infection; however, as his efforts were not successful, he had to cease.

But I will shorten the story so as not to bore my readers. Besides, my conclusions are only becoming more and more confused and uncertain. Thus I will hasten toward the tragic denouement. Let it be clear, I must insist upon my view of this: indeed, I was an eyewitness. Would that I had not been!

The years passed. Nikolai Vasilyevich's disgust for his wife grew more intense even though there was no sign that his love for her was diminishing. Toward the end, aversion and attachment put up such a fierce battle in his spirit that he came out of it exhausted and ravaged. His restless eyes, which normally reflected a myriad of expressions and often spoke sweetly to the heart, now nearly always shone with a weak light, as though he were under the effects of a drug. He developed the strangest manias accompanied by the darkest fears. More and more frequently he talked to me of Caracas, accusing her of unlikely and astonishing things. I could not follow him in this, given my occasional dealings with his wife, and the fact that I had little or no intimacy with her; and above all given my sensibility (which is extremely narrow in comparison to his). I will therefore limit my references to some of those accusations without bringing in any of my own personal impressions.

"You understand, don't you, Foma Paskalovic," he often said to me, for example, "you understand that *she's getting old?*" And, caught between unspeakable emotions, he took my hands in his, as was his manner. He also accused Caracas of abandoning herself to her own solitary pleasures although he had explicitly forbidden it. He even began to accuse her of betrayal. But his discussions on this subject ultimately became so obscure that I will refrain from reporting any others.

What appeared certain is that toward the end, Caracas, old or not, was reduced to a bitter, argumentative and hypocritical creature who was subject to religious obsessions. I don't rule out that she may have influenced Gogol's moral attitude during the latter part of his life, an attitude known to all. In any case, the tragedy befell Nikolai Vasilyevich unexpectedly one evening while he was celebrating his silver anniversary with me—unfortunately one of the last nights that we spent together. Exactly what had brought it on just then, when he already seemed resigned to tolerating just about anything from his consort, I cannot, nor is it my place to, say. I do not know what new occurrence may have come about in those days. I am sticking to the facts here; my readers must form their own opinions.

Nikolai Vasilyevich was particularly agitated that evening. His disgust for Caracas seemed to have reached an unprecedented pitch. He had already carried out his famous "vanity burning," that is the burning of his precious manuscripts—I dare not say whether or not at his wife's instigation. He was in an agitated state of mind for other reasons too. As for his physical condition, it grew more pitiful by the day, reinforcing my impression that he might be drugged. Nevertheless, he began to speak rather normally of Belinskij, whose attacks and criticism of the *Correspondence* was causing him concern. But then he broke off suddenly, crying out, "No, no! It's too much, too much. . . . I can't stand it anymore . . . !" as tears streamed from his eyes. And he added other obscure and disconnected exclamations which he failed to clarify. He seemed to be speaking to himself. He clapped his hands together, he shook his head, and after having taken four or five faltering steps, he leaped up only to sit back down.

When Caracas appeared, or more precisely, when we moved

to her Oriental room late that night, he began to behave like an old, senile man (if I may make such a comparison) whose fixations have gotten the better of him. For example, he kept elbowing me, winking and repeating nonsensically "Look, there she is, there she is, Foma Paskalovic!. . ." Meanwhile she seemed to be watching him with scornful attention. But behind these "mannerisms," one could sense genuine repulsion, which I suppose had surpassed tolerable limits. In fact. . .

After a time, Nikolai Vasilyevich seemed to pull himself together. He burst into tears again, but I would almost call these more manly tears. Once again, he wrung his hands, grabbed hold of mine and walked up and down muttering: "No, no more, it's impossible!. . . How could I. . . such a thing? . . . Such a thing . . . to me? How can I possibly bear *this*, endure *this*. . .*!*" and so on. Then, as if he had just then remembered the pump, he leaped on it suddenly and made for Caracas in a whirl. Inserting the tube in her anus, he began to inflate her. Meanwhile he wept and shouted, as if possessed: "How I love her, my God, how I love her, the poor dear. . .! But I must blow her up, wretched Caracas, God's miserable creature! She must die," alternating these phrases endlessly.

Caracas was swelling. Nikolai Vasilyevich perspired and wept as he continued to pump. I wanted to restrain him, but I didn't have the courage, I don't know why. She began to look deformed, and soon she took on a monstrous appearance; yet up until then she hadn't showed any sign of alarm, being used to such pranks. But when she began to feel unbearably full, or perhaps when she realized Nikolai Vasilyevich's intentions, she assumed an expression which I can only describe as stupid and befuddled, and even imploring. But she never lost that scornful look of hers; though she was afraid and nearly begging, she still did not believe, could not believe, the fate that lay ahead for her, could not believe that her husband could be so audacious. Moreover, he could not see her because he was standing behind her; I watched her fascinated, not moving a finger. Finally, the excessive internal pressure forced out the fragile bones of her cranium, bringing an indescribable grimace to her face. Her belly, thighs, hips, breasts, and what I could see of her behind had reached unimaginable proportions. Then suddenly she belched and let out a long whistling moan, both phenomena that could be explained, if you will, by the increasing air pressure which had suddenly burst open the valve in her throat. And finally, her eyes bulged out, threatening to pop out of their sockets. Her ribs were spread so wide that they had detached from her sternum, and she now looked like a python digesting a mule. What am I saying? Like an ox, an elephant! Her genitals, those pink and velvety organs so dear to Nikolai Vasilyevich, protruded horrendously. At this point, I deemed her already dead. But Nikolai Vasilyevich, sweating and weeping, murmured, "My dear, my saint, my good lady," and continued to pump.

She exploded suddenly, and all at once: thus, it wasn't one area of her skin that gave out, but her whole surface simultaneously. And she was strewn through the air. The pieces then drifted back down at varying speeds depending on their size, which were very small in any case. I distinctly remember a part of the cheek, with a bit of mouth, dangling from the corner of the fireplace; and elsewhere, a tatter of breast with the nipple. Nikolai Vasilyevich was staring at me absentmindedly. Then he roused himself, and possessed by a new mania, went about the task of carefully collecting all those pitiful little scraps that had once been the smooth skin of Caracas, all of her. "Good-bye, Caracas," I thought I heard him murmur, "good-bye, you were too pitiful..." And then he added quickly, distinctly, "Into the fire, into the fire, she too must burn!" and he crossed himself, with his left hand, naturally. Once he had gathered up all those withered shreds, even climbing onto all the furniture so as not to miss any, he threw them straight into the flames in the fireplace, where they began to burn slowly with an exceedingly unpleasant odor. Indeed, Nikolai Vasilyevich, like all Russians, had a passion for throwing important things into the fire.

Red in the face, wearing an expression of unspeakable desperation and sinister triumph, he contemplated the pyre of those miserable remains; he grabbed my arm and clutched it violently. But once those shredded spoils had begun to burn, he seemed to rouse himself once again, as if suddenly remembering something or making a momentous decision; then abruptly, he ran out of the room. A few moments later, I heard his broken, strident voice addressing me through the door. "Foma Paskolovic," he shouted, "Foma Paskolovic, promise me you won't look, *golubcik*, at what I'm about to do!" I don't remember clearly what I said, or whether I tried somehow to calm him. But he insisted: I had to promise him, as if he were a child, that I would stand with my face to the wall and wait for his permission to turn around. Then the door clattered open and Nikolai Vasilyevich rushed headlong into the room and ran toward the fireplace.

Here I must confess my weakness, though it was justified, considering the extraordinary circumstances in which I found myself: I turned around before Nikolai Vasilyevich told me to. The impulse was stronger than me. I turned just in time to notice that he was carrying something in his arms, something he hurled into the flames, which then flared. In any case, the yearning to see which had irresistibly taken hold of me, conquering every other impulse, now impelled me toward the fireplace. But Nikolai Vasilyevich stepped in front of me and butted his chest against me with a force I did not believe him capable of. Meanwhile, the object burned, giving off great fumes. By the time he began to calm down, all I could make out was a heap of silent ashes.

Truthfully, if I wanted to see, it was mainly because I had already glimpsed, but only glimpsed. Perhaps I best not report anything else, or introduce any element of uncertainty in this veracious narration. And yet, an eyewitness account is not complete if the witness does not also relate what he thinks, even if he is not completely certain of it. In short, that something was a child. Not a child of flesh and blood, of course, but something like a puppet or a boy doll made of rubber. Something that, in a word, could be called Caracas' son. Could I have been delirious too? That I cannot say; yet this is what I saw, however confusedly, with my own eyes. But what sentiment was I obeying just now, when I refrained from saying that as Nikolai Vasilyevich entered the room, he was muttering, "Him too, him too!"

And now I have exhausted all that I know of Nikolai Vasilyevich's wife. I will relate what became of him in the next chapter, the last chapter of his life. But any interpretation of his relationship and his feelings for his wife, as for all others, is another matter altogether and a good deal more problematical. Nevertheless, I attempt that in another section of the present volume and refer the reader to it. In any case, I hope that I have cast sufficient light on this controversial question, and that even if I have not laid bare the mystery of Gogol, I have clarified the mystery of his wife. I have implicitly refuted the nonsensical accusation that he ever maltreated or beat his companion, and all the other absurdities. And fundamentally, what other intention should a humble biographer like myself have if not to serve the memory of the lofty man who is the object of his study?

THE WEREWOLF

My friend and I cannot bear the moon: in her light, the deformed dead rise from their graves, especially women swathed in white shrouds; the air thickens with greenish shadows and sometimes with a sinister yellow smoke. Everything is full of fear on a moonlit night, every blade of grass, every frond and animal. What's worse, she makes us roll around, yelping and barking in damp places like the mire behind the haystacks; and if one of our own stops nearby then there's real trouble. We tear him to pieces in a blind fury, unless he's swifter and wounds us with a gimlet. And even then, we stay stunned and torpid all night and the whole next day, as though we are coming out of a dreadful dream. So you see, my friend and I cannot bear the moon.

Now, one night I happened to be sitting near the hearth in the kitchen, which is the most sheltered part of the house; moonbeams filled and suspended the air outside, but I had shut doors, windows and shutters to keep the merest ray from penetrating. And yet, I felt a sinister impulse rising inside me when my friend burst in carrying a huge round object like a sack of lard, only brighter, in his arms. When you observed it, you could see that it was pulsing slightly, like some electric lamps do; weak currents seemed to be running under its skin, producing slight mother-of-pearl reflections much like the hues of jellyfish.

"What's this?" I cried, attracted in spite of myself by something magnetic in the sack's appearance and what I can only call its behavior.

"Can't you see? I managed to catch her," answered my friend, smiling at me hesitantly.

"The moon!" I cried. My friend nodded without a word.

Disgust overwhelmed us: aside from everything else, the moon was sweating a hyaline liquid which dripped through my friend's fingers. Yet he wasn't ready to put her down.

"Oh, put her in that corner," I screamed. "We'll find a way to kill her."

"No," my friend said with sudden resolve, and he began to speak very quickly. "Listen to me, if we leave this disgusting thing to her own devices, I know she will do everything she can to get right back to the middle of the sky (to torment us and countless others); she can't do otherwise, she's like a child's ball. And she won't even look for the easiest way out, no, she'll go straight up all the way, blindly, stupidly. This evil thing that governs us, she too is ruled by an irresistible power. Do you get my idea then? Let's put her right here under the hood of the fireplace; that way even if we can't be free of her, at least we'll be free of her deadly brilliance because the soot will turn her black as a chimney sweep. There's no other way: trying to kill her would be as useless as trying to squash a drop of mercury."

So we put the moon under the hood, and she rose swift as a rocket and vanished up the flue.

"Oh, what a relief," said my friend, "she's so clammy and fat, I wore myself out trying to hold her down. Now let's hope..." and he looked at his smeared hands with disgust.

Soon after, we heard a cacophony up there, a muffled flatulence, like the rumbling in the stomach that induces a fart; we even heard breathing. Perhaps the moon was struggling to pass through the narrow part of the flue, for she seemed to be panting. Perhaps she had to compress and deform her flabby little body to pass through; foul droplets of liquid fell hissing into the fire, and since she was blocking the passageway, the kitchen filled with smoke. Then nothing happened and the flue began to suck up smoke once again.

We raced outside. A freezing wind was sweeping the polished sky, all the stars sparkled vividly and there was no sign of the moon. Hurray, hurray, we yelled like men possessed, we did it! And we embraced. Then we were gripped by doubt; wasn't it possible that the moon was stuck in the flue of my fireplace? But my friend reassured me that it couldn't be, absolutely not, and anyway, I realized that now neither he nor I had the courage to go inside and see; so, we abandoned ourselves to our joy. I fumigated the house when he left, carefully burning poisonous substances, and that put my mind to rest. That same night we went out to roll around in a damp spot in my garden, but innocently, and almost as an affront to the moon, not because we were forced to.

For several months, the moon did not reappear in the sky, and we were free and lighthearted. Not free: free from the wicked fits of fury, and content, but not free. Because it wasn't the moon's absence that made us feel good, but the fact that she was there watching us; only she was dark, black, too sooty to be seen or to torment us. She was like the black, nocturnal sun of ancient times that used to cross the skies backward between sundown and dawn.

In fact, even that meager joy of ours soon came to an end; one night the moon reappeared. She was jagged and smoky, murky beyond all description. She was nearly invisible, so maybe my friend and I could only see her because we knew she was up there, looking down on us angrily with an air of revenge. And then we saw the damage done by her forced passage through the flue; but the wind of open space had gradually cleansed her of the soot as she traveled, and her ceaseless turning had restored form to her soft body. For a long time she appeared as if she had just emerged from an eclipse, but each night she shone more clearly until she became like this again, as everyone can see.

And we have gone back to rolling in the mire.

But she didn't seek revenge, as we thought she would've. Basically, she is better than one might think, less wicked, more stupid, I don't know! I myself am inclined to believe that ultimately she is not to blame, that it is not her fault, that she is forced to do this and that, just as we are. Truly, I am inclined to believe that. But my friend is not: in his opinion there is no excuse.

In any case, that's why I'm telling you: you can't do anything to the moon.

THE PROVINCIAL NIGHT

Try to imagine (my friend began to say) the heart of one of our provinces. I don't even mean one of those small, melancholy cities which is furnished with a club, or a *club house*, as they call it; imagine, rather, a tiny village, a hamlet secluded between the mountains. At the time of my story I was living down there, and anyway, (he added, smiling) I was born there.

Now, do you have any idea what an evening in such a place is like? I mean when the townsfolk, perhaps even the town secretary and the provincial doctor, gather in one of those hovels to kill time as best they can? I mean if you don't, I hope this story of mine will give you some idea of what it's like. Let me add too, to move things along, that on the night I am referring to there was a storm. For three days, the icy wind from the north had been rattling the house, one might say, to its foundations. I must tell you, not one shutter in our house fit perfectly, so the wind crept in, hissing and groaning through the numerous gaps and crevices, but mainly through the wide flues of the fireplaces. I remember too, there was a shutter or shade somewhere or other that banged deafeningly with every gust. No one in our house could ever discover exactly which shutter it was, so it was never fixed.

There were many young people, along with the old. There were plenty of girls too, and they were eager and tainted, as is their nature down there. One among all of them had captured my attention for some time, a slight girl with the look of a supple reed. Her hair was chestnut with green undertones, her deep, dark eyes looked somehow astonished and yet bright. She always seemed to be standing (or at least I remember her) near some light, talking or laughing, yet her lips seemed to hold the slight glimmer of gold lost in the sun's daily passage. The breath that emanated from her mouth was fiery, light, full of the most wild and delicate scents. I must say that this girl often seemed to be burning in her own ardor. Her clear forehead was often shadowed, as if by a troublesome thought, and sometimes she was quiet for a long time, prey to some unknown pain. She had the habitual gesture of raising a hand to her small breast, as though she wanted to calm an impetuous heartbeat (in any case, she was prone to breathlessness). Indeed, she was still a child then. She was probably fourteen years old. As for me, at the time I was only eighteen. And if you think my description too effusive, let me say quickly that this girl was very dear to me.

We played all the popular games, I mean proverbs, telegram, mail and others too. And amid my "mail," I remember, I received a note from her, written on the torn edge of a newspaper. Forgive me, I've got it memorized. It said, "Beauty and summer love quickly fade, and no wise girl would dare trust such a fragile gift" (it was then the beginning of autumn).

The games were popular, yes, but also abused. To tell the truth, they weren't terribly successful, and we were soon overcome by boredom. We young people were in a constant state of frenzy. When the games were over, a moment of suspense set in and everyone listened to the steady wind. Then one of the old men suggested the game assassin, which hadn't been played for so long that it could pass for new. We agreed enthusiastically, gripped by frantic gaiety once again.

I will describe briefly how it went. The game is preceded by a secret drawing of lots; a bunch of index cards, one for each player, is well mixed in some container, from which everyone fishes one out and looks at it privately. All the index cards are white, except two, which are labeled respectively, "assassin" and "cop," or one might say, inspector. Thus, these two main figures play their roles, unbeknownst to the rest of the players and to each other. Now the lights are turned out and the actual game begins: silently the participants wander here and there in the pitch-black of the house until one screams out and plunges to the floor, or if it's an old person, onto the sofa. This is the victim, whom the assassin has pretended to attack violently and who has been chosen to play dead. Afterward, when the lights are turned on, the policeman must identify the assassin, availing himself of all the clues and evidence that he manages to gather from the others (except, of course, the victim) or that he has picked up himself while circulating incognito in the dark. The end is typical: the assassin pays a penalty if he is discovered, and in the other event, the policeman pays.

Hopefully, you can see that such a game lends itself to a wide range of combinations. From an objective point of view, it has only one drawback: it generates constant suspicion, among companions and peers, which is rather unjustified, as you will see when I'm finished. The game is much more useful for those who want to exchange furtive kisses in the dark.

But at this point, it is my duty to admit that I've botched my best narrative devices. In fact, I've gotten lost in preambles, and here I am at the end of the story before I've even begun. So now I've little left to say. I wandered groping on tiptoe (so as not to give the unidentified inspector any clues) through the huge room, looking for some victim. As luck would have it, the role of assassin had fallen on me. Meanwhile, I felt two convulsive arms grab me around the waist. It took me no time to recognize the soft burning lips that barely grazed mine. I tried to hold the girl, but she quickly wriggled away and vanished into the darkness, murmuring some words of affection that I didn't catch. She had never done that before. It didn't even occur to me to kill her. Stunned and happy, I went back to wandering, aimlessly now, and thus without any intervention on my part, the game lasted longer than usual. Confused, I heard muffled, girlish laughter and squealing all around me. Everybody was knocking against the furniture, coughing and clearing their throats loudly to catch the assassin's attention and to provoke him to act.

Then inadvertently I must have come close to the squealers. Hearing me (since I wasn't bothering to muffle my footsteps) and not knowing what role I was playing, they fell silent and their shuffling ceased. There was a total, earsplitting silence, except for the moaning wind and the shutter, which was banging rhythmically somewhere. Suddenly, I was seized by a great anxiety, in sharp contrast to my previous state of mind. And I heard a loud scream on the opposite side of the room. Though the voice sounded genuinely contorted by pain, I recognized it; and practically at that very instant, the lights were turned on.

It occasionally happened that someone took the assassin's duties upon himself, without having been chosen for the post by fate, just to create more confusion. I thought that must have happened now too, and, protesting, I made my way toward the place where her body lay on the floor. But before I even got there I saw the deadly dismay, or actually the utter shock, on the faces of the first rescuers. Everybody wore the heartbroken expression of violated and stricken innocents, of betrayed creatures. We were silent, almost gasping, and it wasn't until minutes later that shouts rang out.

The girl lay on her back, a ghostly white, her eyes closed. One hand was resting on her chest, her usual gesture. Someone had plunged a dagger or rapier, a weapon of quite some proportion, into the hollow of her collarbone, a little to the left of the fontanel of her throat. Sticking up, the handle cast a slight shadow over the now bluish eyelids of the stricken girl. When the knife was removed, blood gushed from the wound.

This is the real ending of the story. There's no point in adding that the real killer was never discovered. Neither the policeman in charge, nor any of the others, knew what to do or say. In any case, who among us, among all humanity, could have wished to kill a girl like that? The real assassin left no traces and provided no clues whatsoever.

I still have that weapon (concluded my friend, wiping his perspired brow and finally looking us straight in the eyes). Its long sharp blade is fine damask steel. The haft could be made of horn and mother of pearl, with its reddish-green reflections, rather murky ones. And yet... well (my friend smiled timidly), it could be some unknown material. And the blade? Oh, yes, it glitters like polished steel... but why are the tiny clots of blood on it still a bright red, even now, after so many years?

OBSESSIVE
STORIES

MARIA GIUSEPPA

Whenever I take a walk up in the high part, as they say in my village, and I pass the churchyard gates, I always think of Maria Giuseppa. Who knows, maybe Maria Giuseppa died because of me, twelve years ago. Ha, ha, if any of you happen to know me, you must be laughing: "A woman dying for Giacomo? How could that be?" Because whoever you are, you surely remember my nose like a green pepper and my idiotic demeanor, as some have called it. And in fact I must certainly be an idiot— because I don't consider myself one and I've often heard it said that I'd be less idiotic if I did. But, by God, do you think it is worthwhile to ponder this?

Gentlemen, I want to tell you how Maria Giuseppa died because of me. Because, be that as it may, I feel I must tell someone, must unburden myself of the peculiar guilt I felt whenever I heard her wheezing over the gas lamp in that windowless room of hers, the one we call the "dark room" in our house. There was always a horde of people outside: sisters, aunts and I can't remember who else anymore. But, really, why should I feel guilty? It isn't a sin to be overcome by a woman's graces . . . but judge for your-selves.

Maria Giuseppa was a woman I kept with me in the large, then uninhabited house where I went to spend a part of my summers.

Maria Giuseppa stayed shut inside there the rest of the year, digging the orchard and selling our greens, and she always gave me a little nest egg when I came back, a very little one, yes, but enough to pay her small monthly wage and food for the year. All my relatives said that Maria Giuseppa was stupid, an ignoramus without a thought in her head, and truthfully, I cannot judge whether she was or not, but I do know that I was always very upset by Maria Giuseppa who wanted to do things her way and never obeyed me, et cetera.

Look here, I wanted to be all alone in that house, but why I wanted that, why I went there or what I intended to do, I swear I have no idea. I only went out around evening to visit my relatives, but during those long summer days I was always alone. But really not alone, I was with Maria Giuseppa.

I sleep very little, so in the morning I was often in my shirt-sleeves and pajama bottoms in the courtyard, getting some air, or throwing stones down at the cats in the orchard, when Maria Giuseppa returned from church. She always woke up in time for the early Mass at the main church in town. I would watch her meekly open the large outside doors, cast me a little timid and mortified look because she knew I wanted coffee as soon as I got up. Without returning her greeting, I would go on throwing stones at the cats and teasing the dog, who knew the game and pursued those swift black objects that turned into frightened cats. I've often noticed that dogs have their owners' personalities; it's easy to mold a dog's spirit without even meaning to. That is why my dog lacked that cocksure air of some dogs owned by intelligent men; and when he came upon one of his own kind, he would either try to avoid him or let him sniff, peering all the while not with a calm but with a foolish look like my own, at least when I look in the mirror. But like his master, who sometimes wasn't a coward, and I mean in his own home, with the cats and Maria Giuseppa, the dog also seemed to take on the courage of a lion.

But sometimes when I was in a nasty mood, I would attack that woman with a flood of strange and even lewd words, with a few Arabic expressions thrown in (I studied Arabic as a boy but after ten years I threw out all my books and grammars, and I don't know Arabic at all anymore). Maria Giuseppa shielded herself as best she could from the tirade and the slaps that I sometimes let her have, but rarely, of course, and I would watch her hurry across the courtyard to warm my coffee, uncovering the burning coals that she had buried beneath the ashes the night before. Maria Giuseppa was so ugly! In truth, to look at her fixed up like that with her oily pigtails poking out of her kerchief, she could have been any woman in the village, but I knew that she was ugly because several times I went up to her room unexpectedly to find her without a smock or slip; and I had discovered that she was a flat thing with no hips, no breasts and thick peasant's legs. And whenever I pulled off her kerchief for fun, that narrow, narrow head of hers, that forehead but four fingers wide and those two bands of oil-slicked hair nearly brought pity to my heart. Maria Giuseppa had large hands and feet and made a noise when she walked that would scare you to death. But anyway, when I had brought her home from the countryside that first day, she couldn't even break an egg and if I hadn't taught her how to make an omelet, I wouldn't have had lunch. She said that she was a country girl and that she only worked the fields and never did any cooking there. But why should you care, after all? I've lost my train of thought... oh, yes. So then, gentlemen, I was saying that I don't know why the devil I went to that house. In the city, sure; I got up, went to the café with certain fine characters who insulted me and probably despised me, but then played cards with me. And in the end, it was hardly a rough life considering the small private income I still get. But there...

I got up early, practically at dawn, and fooled around with the dog or tormented him, if you will, until Maria Giuseppa came back; then I began to torment her too, but gently, of course. Because how can you call all those harmless jokes I played on her torment? It is true that she was tormented by them and wept most of the day; some days, in fact, she moaned and screamed that God only knows what sin made the Madonna give her this cross to bear and that she would rather leave than bear... et cetera. But by God, this is what I couldn't stand: in the first place, what she screamed when she was screaming, so that people probably thought God knows what I was doing to her. And in the second place, if she didn't feel all right, why didn't she leave? Who obliged her to stay? The truth is that she said she was fond of the house (and indeed, she did her best to do everything right and she never robbed me of a dime) but that's a lot of idle chatter, obviously. How can we be fond of a house that isn't our own? I don't know how we can even be fond of our own. And anyway, gentlemen, what afflicted her? Look here, I have always followed the principle of hitching the ass where the owner wants, as the old proverb goes. Now if I told her, for example, to put all the chairs in the room up on the table, or I called her to play catch with the rag ball, what right did she have to refuse and resist and groan that she had too much to do? If I called her, the task at hand was obviously whatever I wanted. I paid her, so tell me, gentlemen, what should an employee do if not what the master wants, and nothing else? But Maria Giuseppa didn't understand that. And yet it's true, by God, that I always managed to get her to do what I wanted: all I had to do was scream some insult right into her ear, or else pick up a crude walking stick that I kept for just that purpose. I hardly ever beat her, but sometimes I prodded her, and in any case, the sight of the stick was enough to make Maria Giuseppa obey, like a dog. Some tigers I've seen in the circus snarl throughout the entire performance even though they do all the exercises that the trainer commands. That is how Maria Giuseppa did what I ordered; but all the while she would be all gloomy and resentful (say she was standing with her arms folded as the ball flew toward her, or she was sitting when she really wanted to feed the hens), muttering that she wasn't a beast and shouldn't be treated like a dog, and that she didn't have time to waste fooling around with me. It irritated me so when Maria Giuseppa sulked. She seemed to take on that peasant spirit again though she had been in the village and at my house for many years, and she would answer me rudely and make a hard ugly face. Then she would cry more than ever, and over nothing; just instructing her, say, to take a different road than usual and to tell this and that to so-and-so of the so-and-sos would make her cry. And if she cried, she usually talked. And if there was no way to stop her from talking, especially when she was distressed, nothing would make her cease. Her voice was not so harsh as it was high-pitched, and I (who am nervous) was horribly irritated by her harping. So I would run over and insult her savagely, but I never managed to shut her up. I would hit her wherever, on the head, in the chest, in the face, but rather than stopping, she only raged on more vehemently; then after shrieking in accompaniment to a crescendo of sobs, she assumed a flat tone of voice and talked, talked without a stop. Finally, holding my head in my hands, I could only flee, leaving her slumped in the low-backed wooden chair, in a flood of tears, talking. By God, I remember her like that quite often. From the next room, I could hear her soliciting numerous saints, saying she wanted to go drown herself, protesting that she would rather leave than live the rest of her days humiliated like this. But she never left. Many times, it's true, she did go out to visit one of my relatives and make her grievances known, but she always returned before nightfall with renewed patience. That talk of hers, gentlemen! How many times did I try to interrupt her discussions, to get her to express herself differently, to use another method, so to speak. But there was no way; if she was interrupted, she would only begin relating the events over in the same order. In any case, she was incapable of stopping in the middle and leaving. I could feel my hands straining to suppress the swarm of words, and this irritated me greatly. I once tossed a plate at her head for this, may God forgive me, but then I stayed to soothe her for a long time. Because obviously, I am a coward. Who knows what the villagers would have said if she had gone around telling: Don Giacomo was up at the barracks, the police took him...

Truthfully, many things about Maria Giuseppa irritated me, yet I felt, how can I put it, drawn to her in the kitchen, I don't know why. There are plenty of books in the house that my father left, so occasionally I thought of sitting down to read. I would ferret out some bookstall edition of Dumas or Sue, but those didn't interest me either. Basically, nothing has ever interested me. And who can understand all those things d'Artagnan and Aramis say and do? I must surely be an idiot, but I have always thought that life was different, something smaller, grayer. . . . But, by God, gentlemen, I keep losing track! I was telling you that nothing in those books interested me; and even if they distracted me momentarily, suddenly an inner force, a nervous impulse, kept me from sitting still on the living-room divan where I had settled in. But really, why am I bothering to tell you this? The point is that I would start running around the courtyard laughing, I would throw the stone ball down from the balcony at the top of the old stairway to make lots of holes in the ground, I would even roll around in the dust with the dog, who howled with joy, but in the end I always ended up in the kitchen. Who knows why? Maybe I was lonely; but when I found Maria Giuseppa standing at the fire carving the meat so carefully, measuring exact amounts of garlic and parsley, I nearly always threw it all on the floor. And when the cats darted for the meat, I would laugh gleefully. Naturally, Maria Giuseppa would start to cry, but silently now, and that amused me. I don't know how to put it, and there's no point in saying it anyway, but I felt as if I had to make her move, to get her off the track. How can I put it? As I saw it, she, all her energy, was stuck in a rut. And isn't it great to break one of those irrigation pipes that brings water to the orchards, to watch the wretched water running every which way and being sucked up by the earth so it can't flow to the end of the tube? By God, gentlemen, I laugh just thinking of it.

Whatever happened, I always tried different ways to taunt her, to beat her, to make her cry. I mean, I didn't want to make her cry, but after defending herself and pleading with me to leave her alone she would always end up crying. Sometimes I would whip her side with a branch, sometimes I would rip her kerchief off her head and throw it into the air. I found it amusing when she ran after me, trying to catch it in midair; I really can't say why it amused me to see her, with that narrow, narrow head and that oil-slicked hair, reaching tiptoed but never getting it because she was short, Maria Giuseppa, I doubt if she came up to my shoulders! That was a weird game; sometimes I actually felt sorry for her and would give her back the kerchief and go to some other room.

Those days were, I don't know, so long and so short. Occasionally I would spend two or three hours humming certain tunes, always the same ones, over and over like some little children do, but I should tell you what position I was in: I would let myself slip down in the chair until only my shoulders were supported, and then fold my legs so that my body made a bridge between them and my shoulders. I had to look all around me, so keeping my neck upright made it sore almost all the time, but that is how I spent whole mornings and afternoons. Yet generally it seemed that I never knew what to do. Maybe it was that particular boredom that made me do those things. But boredom isn't the right word. Because it was great fun to get the old saber and fence in front of the large shuttered windows on the sort of covered terrace in our house. The dog ran back and forth, barking loudly... but soon this began to annoy me. So I would run and get all kinds of coins and play with them in the middle of the room. I talked to myself, inventing new games and giving them names, rules and nomenclatures. For instance, gentlemen, I'm not ashamed to tell you, I shouted, "Come up craps, come on," and I flipped a coin, and then I changed position and called out, say, "Fours on the left, come up a pretty pair," and lots of other names of plays and combinations that I imagined or invented. Then the dog really looked at me strangely, as if he were frightened, but who cared! I kicked him out, literally, and went on by myself. But soon this got on my nerves too. So I would take some bocce

balls and roll them between the dog's legs to make him jump...
but I tired of that within five minutes. Therefore, gentlemen,
maybe I had to end up in the kitchen with Maria Giuseppa. But
going back to the bocce balls, if you're not bored, I'll tell you
about the great game I played under the front door. There's a
sloped ramp leading from the large front door to the courtyard;
it's coarsely paved with a lot of sharp jutting stones. I leaped
down to the courtyard and hurled five or six balls toward the front
door. They went up, then swiftly came back down; I couldn't let
any of them roll by me, I had to stop them all; and if one happened
to get stuck on a rough spot, I had to get it down by hitting it
with another ball, one that had already rolled down. This was a
game I could stick with a little longer. It was usually sunny in
the courtyard, it's true, and it was a summer sun. But I would
put my hat on and continue... but I could only stand it for two
hours at the most. And then? Then I ran screaming into the
kitchen and grabbing Maria Giuseppa by the shoulders, I would
throw my arms around her and yell something like "Darling,
darling, damn the devil!" enunciating the syllables in time to my
racing heart. By God, gentlemen, I'm pleased with that phrase.
It sounds like the kind of phrase a writer would use: I've hardly
read anything, I've hardly studied anything in my life, but somehow I've picked up a phrase like that. To go back to what I was
saying, I didn't always accost Maria Giuseppa, I mean, roughly.
But basically my manner was the same whether I wanted to
embrace her or smack her for fun. And then even if I happened
to be calm, we always got riled up together. In fact, I am not
religious since I think—but I'll tell you my ideas another time;
anyway, I would curse or blaspheme, which would upset her and
she would try to convert me. Maria Giuseppa always spoke in
dialect, a rapid dialect, and she only understood a few Italian
words, among them those spoken by the archpriest in the church.
And she would repeat them to me, but listen how: if she was
saying, for example, "We must cultivate the Lord's vine," she
came down very hard on some consonants and split them in such

a funny way. The *L* in Lord was especially thick. We almost always had discussions of this kind while I was eating, and I often gave her a sermon, relating the passion of Christ or some saint's life story; then, when I saw that ecstatic look in her eyes, saw that she was moved by our Lord's examples, I would lift my glass abruptly and yell: "To Beelzebub!" or some other blasphemy and drink. How I enjoyed seeing her face drop suddenly. But, gentlemen, what can I say? I'm hardly a wicked man, because it's true that if I saw she was really in pain, I would do anything to try and console her. I said earlier that when I threw the plate at her head, I only soothed her out of cowardice; but that's not true. It really pained me to see her suffering. And it wasn't hard to console her because she went from tears to laughter and vice versa easily; all it took was a play of words, usually crude ones, which I'm good at.

Often, though, I made her sit facing me while I ate at the small table and ordered her to talk; about what, even I can't imagine. But it disturbed me horribly if she didn't say anything. And this was often the case, especially after Maria Giuseppa realized that whatever she said was not to my liking. Sometimes when I let her go on, she told me lots of things about the bakery, about who had died, and she chattered on and on about the shopkeepers and how she had bought, say, a half a kilo of macaroni, or a kilo of rice. Then I would realize that they took her for a fool and had overcharged her, and I told her so. And she would start to cry and scream that she never robbed a dime from me and worked all day long on my account; then she would go into the kitchen and cry as quietly as she could. At first this annoyed me, but then I would go in and shake her, saying, "For Saint Marina's and Saint Rocco's sake, you've got to cut that out," and she would laugh.

She seemed to have a fixed plan for everything she had to do. God forbid that she had to change the order of her movements or substitute one for another. She would just stand there, her hands on her hips and her head hanging like a ram's, and not budge. Actually, she would only move at the sound of the walking stick. Maybe that was why I so enjoyed making her do the opposite of what she wanted. She had a passion for flowers and often went to the orchard; I would watch her from the window watering and watering, and running her hands over certain flowers. I don't know why, but that made me absolutely furious, so I would call her inside; not that I needed anything, I just relished the sight of her climbing up the hill sullenly and the sound of her whining if I ordered her to, I don't know, sit down on a chair and waste time.

Maria Giuseppa couldn't bear sitting with nothing to do; she would protest that she had things to do around the house. And this, as I said before, irritated me greatly. In fact, she never stood still, but though she ran through the house all day, her heavy footsteps like a hurricane, at the end of the day she had still accomplished nothing. I scolded her, but she didn't understand. It sufficed that she was working; whether anything was subsequently accomplished was not her concern. In the village, as I said, everyone considered her a fool. But, don't think that my village is one of those typical peasant villages full of people who are only involved in nasty little quarrels; on the contrary, it has, as they say, evolved, and people's horizons have been broadened by progress. So the environment had little to do with Maria Giuseppa's stupidity. She was like that because she was inherently stupid. Maybe that was why she was with me. Because, gentlemen, I can't understand a woman who would live with me and allow herself to be mistreated without ever leaving. The curious thing, though, is that Maria Giuseppa was not a submissive woman; in fact, she was terribly stubborn, I think I already said that. If you only knew how many times I got upset with her, beat her, so that she would cook without salt, as I'd asked her to. God knows why I wanted this; maybe just to test her, to tease her, who knows? But I never ever succeeded. She always wanted to discuss, discuss, discuss, and she never did anything without first being convinced of its usefulness.

But, by God, gentlemen, if you don't understand who Maria Giuseppa is by now, too bad for you. I only meant to tell you how she died because of me, and as usual, I lost my train of thought. So anyway, one day there was a celebration in the village; Maria Giuseppa had gone to early Mass and had not even changed before coming back. She went dressed in her usual peasant clothes, but she was wearing a shiny polka-dot dress that looked like silk and a yellow smock which was shiny too. She had a blue kerchief on her head and certain jewels that suited her well. That day, as on all celebrations, there was an endless procession of farmhands through our courtyard. I acted serious as I always do in front of other people; I pretended to be interested in the local news, but actually I was watching Maria Giuseppa accepting the things people had brought: two ricotta cheeses, twelve eggs, ripe figs. What can I tell you? I felt as if I were seeing her for the first time; she seemed gay and refreshed. Who knows? It was as if I found her beautiful, as if she had become the celebration. At the end everybody left, and the music from the procession passed in the narrow street below. I had made up my mind not to stand at the window; I wandered aimlessly around the house a bit. Then I looked out. The saint, a little saint dressed as a nun with a waxen face and a tiny wax child at her feet, was already below my window. I could almost touch her with my hand. I didn't know who it was; they had probably told me too, but I'd forgotten. Maybe it was Saint Marina, the one who was blamed for making that nun pregnant ... but why bother saying this? While I was watching the brothers move on, carrying the cross with a white cloth, I noticed that Maria Giuseppa was standing at another window below and seemed to be leaning on something pink. The procession kept moving, but I wasn't looking at it anymore. I could feel the warmth of the singing crowd only five feet below, rising toward me, but I was watching Maria Giuseppa. How strange I felt! Women, uugh, I have always given them—the few that have passed under me in my life (how do you like that double entendre, gentlemen?)—given them what they deserved: has anyone ever seen me enchanted by a skirt? But that's another point. Really, I couldn't give a damn about telling you the hows and whys of all this. Now Maria Giuseppa was throwing down on the passing saint some oleander branches and rose petals that she must have taken from my garden. God only knows how upset I might have been by this at any other time because she hadn't even asked permission to take the flowers; but then I wasn't upset at all. For a moment, I thought about what I would have usually done: I would have come up behind her very very slowly, and I would have taken revenge by grabbing her by the legs and tugging her inside suddenly. How that would have amused me, really! But then I did nothing. I kept my eye on her, and when she pulled her head in and hurried down the wood staircase (maybe she was cooking some meat?), I went down too. I really didn't want to upset her at all, I just wanted to hear her voice, to look her in the eyes. So, I asked her to tell me the story of the saint in the procession, and while she talked I looked at her, looked long and hard. By God, gentlemen, I don't give a hoot whether or not you understand what happened. I surely couldn't explain it, even if I wanted to; but at a certain point, I clutched Maria Giuseppa's head and kissed her furiously all over her mouth. I don't know whether or not she screamed. She wriggled, but then I held her still with one hand, I ripped her smock off and lifted her heavy dress. Who knew how it was going to end! I don't remember anything else, gentlemen, and I don't give a damn about your contemptuous looks. I only remember that after—I mean a moment after *that*—Maria Giuseppa was on the floor. I was revolted by that black, withered breast poking out of her ripped shirt and the metal chain on her saint's pendant; it almost made me laugh. But I got out of there quickly, and I don't remember a thing about what I did afterward.

All right, gentlemen, I'm about to finish. Yes, give me those looks if you want, what do I care! Maria Giuseppa got sick, I already told you, and then she died. But did she really die because of me? And then, if she did die because of me, should I really feel guilty? If she appealed to me for a moment, or even if I actually kissed her, is it my fault? After all, I didn't do anything wrong to her.

Gentlemen, give me a small glass of water, a very, very small one. And you there, what in Christ's name are you looking at? You know, I could throw all this water in your face! Ha-ha, I'm kidding—unless you really want me to do it!

And so, to finish up, now I'm alone in the house, truly alone. A woman comes in for half an hour, rushes through some chores and runs off—*the cow*—I don't know why. But I couldn't give a fuck. Every night I go for a walk, and as I said, sometimes I go as far as the graveyard. I'm thirty-four years old. I'm finished, gentlemen. Good riddance.

UXORICIDE

Murdering people is easy. I have never understood all the fuss murderers make, or why they still haven't brought off or perpetrated the perfect crime; it must be simply that they haven't studied their victims closely enough. Take me: when I decided that I wanted to, indeed that I had to, murder my wife ... Huh, what? Why did I want or have to kill her? Don't play the hypocrites, don't make me laugh: if you take any husband and wife, it's obvious that one of the two individuals is too many. In any case, this is not the place for explanations; you only need know that I had to kill my wife. And here is how I attended to this necessity.

My wife (may her soul rest in peace) was an extremely angry little woman; she would foam at the mouth, drool and wring her hands over the slightest thing. Nevertheless, I enjoyed watching her abandon herself to these excesses: she also suffered a slight heart problem; very slight, but still ... I was already planning to bring my genial yet terribly simple project to a successful conclusion. I mean, I was thinking, though still somewhat vaguely, that such fury and the slightest heart debility couldn't coexist for long; so, if the necessity arose, maybe I had merely to lend a helping hand to one of those conditions. . . .

Then when the moment for action came, having begun to observe my Angela [*sic!*] more diligently, I came to the decisive and more or less intuitive conclusion that she compensated for her heart problems with her senseless anger; and therefore, all I had to do to bring about the fatal outcome was to force her into silence and immobility. And with this, my plan was ready.

So, if the preceding is not entirely clear, the faithful account that follows will give the reader full satisfaction.

"I have to talk to you, Angela," I said, in a tone that vacillated between indifference (so that she wouldn't flee, flinging Parthian insults) and severity (to set her against me).

"Oh, you do, do you?" she screamed, baring her teeth. "What do you know: this swine has to talk to me!"

"Why swine?"

"Because anyone who lets his family languish in a mediocre life and a mediocre..." (a refrain I knew only too well).

"But look..." (Up until that point, I had still imagined that I could spare her. If not for this:)

"Ah, I see everything, and even more!... Uggh, these endless, useless discussions! Where do we get with these discussions? I can't stand it anymore, I'm finished, finished!..."

She grabbed a heavy letter holder almost automatically and then she ran to the window as if to breathe more easily. A rather favorable position, as far as my plans were concerned: passing behind her cunningly, I took a cord which I had ready in my pocket and nimbly wrapped it around her arms and body several times. Her awesome physical strength thus restrained, I was able to drag her to a chair in the middle of the room, which I tied her to securely.

I won't even attempt to give you an idea of how she shrieked and croaked and threatened and spit and tried to bite during this operation. But I was prepared and put an end to it in no time with a gag which I pushed deep into her mouth behind her teeth; so that only a thread of saliva and some inarticulate sounds could emerge from the corner of her mouth. But perhaps I should state the exact nature of my criminal plan more openly now for those who may not have been following closely. And yet, it is obvious: I had no doubt that my wife would die if I cut off her every reaction and accused, challenged and derided her at the same time. And then, on the other hand, who could have blamed me for her death? A heart attack is a heart attack, and God alone knows from whence it comes.

Is that clear now? Let us proceed, then.

"You were saying, my sweet soul? 'Finished.' Oh, oh: and why finished? . . . Forget it, don't try to answer: you couldn't anyway. I'll tell you, if I feel like it. I'll talk since you must be eating your teeth by now."

I circled her, rubbing my hands together. Needless to say, I had chosen a massive and heavy chair, a huge chair, in fact, that could support her wild thrashing.

"So then, finished. All right, I'm going to agree, and I am going to state the reasons for that . . . I mean, not for my admission but for your destruction." I deliberately spoke slowly, with incomplete turns of phrase. I began again: "The first reason is that you're an idiot."

"Mm." (That was her response. I am representing conventionally the deaf-mute sounds she was producing, even though in reality her range was a bit greater and reached the pitch of a whistling teapot.)

"Definitely: an idiot! Maybe it's not all your fault, but then this only shows that you're doubly idiotic. . . . Or doubly culpable. By the way, did you give your mother a new supply of salt batteries?" (I broached this explosive topic deliberately: she was terribly protective of her mother, whom she loved dearly.)

"Mm."

"Stop making those half moans! . . . Oh, yes: whenever some little thing, some word hits that little mother of yours wrong, she faints dead away, so don't you think you'd better get busy with the salt and revive her? You inherited the torturer's character from that insipid little mother of yours; you were made in her image, with a generous dash of the rights of a wife, a woman, a whore, a stray dog and a scabby cat thrown in! What, you say that you're the first to suffer? Eh, I can believe it too: a person who causes trouble always gets it thrown back in his face."

I was losing myself a bit in syllogisms, as often happens to me: good, this time she hadn't even answered me, however she could have. I looked at her: she kept her eyes down or closed and even seemed determined to let my brash, sarcastic remarks against her mother ride.

Aha, so I needed something even more direct, more stinging.

"Anyway, shut up, don't breathe a word; I have no intentions of softening you up," I began again. "You're a wreck? I would say everyone else is a wreck; I'm a wreck! Ha, you certainly calculated everything beautifully, you did, with the help of that witch, that she-devil, that plague of a mother of yours. . . ."

"Mm." (Ah, just as well; she was listening to me, betraying her initial plan. Onward, to the end!)

"Right, right: when it came time to make arrangements for a picky type like you, to shackle a pest like you to someone, there wasn't a moment of hesitation; the choice had to fall on a mild-mannered gentleman, and it didn't hurt if he had some cash put aside. . . . Shut me up if I'm lying." (Being called an opportunist was another thing that burned her up.)

"Mm."

"Ah, no? And tell me, then: what would your fate have been, what would you have become, if I hadn't taken you from where I did and given you my honored name and chosen you to be the mother of my children?" (This too, I mean any reference to one of her mediocre successes, was also intolerable to her.)

"Mm-mm." (Good, she was getting excited again.)

"Since you're not answering in any comprehensible way, I'll tell you what you would have become: a store clerk at best, and not even one of the clever ones; hardly, with that pushy manner of yours.

Because, let's hear it, what else could you have done: with zero culture and natural intelligence, uhm, maybe you could have... but I for my part, I never happened to discover it. ... Huh, what?"

"Mm."

"It's true, maybe you're right: there is something, and between us, you would have ended up doing it without fail. You could have become a whore! Oh, you know, that's not to say you weren't already well on the way. ...."

"Mmm."

"Oh, there, there, you're all upset! Didn't you let me smooch with you before our auspicious marriage?" (This vile discussion always put her in a fury.) "Now we twist our mouths and rip the clothes off our lady friends who slide! And yet, yes, you did the same thing and even worse! I repeat: what would have become of you if you had found a cad instead of a gentleman? Just answer this... am I a gentleman? No, I'm a dope. Go on, take a good look at me: what do I have written across my forehead? 'Sap,' that's what." (I could almost hear the same old furious retorts that she made when we reached this point. I began again, with a deliberate, loud sigh:) "Ah, my parents used to tell me, and the spirit of my forefathers told me: there's nothing worse than a *mésalliance*, than a mingling of old blood and plebeian blood. ... Sweet friend, what profession did your forebears practice? On what clod of earth did they spill their sweat, over what plowshare did they break their backs, what servile jobs did they leave behind?"

Truthfully, I had already been asking myself why on earth the matter at hand was dragging on so, and why she still hadn't given up; but now, finally, this last story of my family's supposed greatness versus the low extraction of hers had done it. She was trembling in frustration and shaking dangerously in a supreme attempt to break her bonds, or to leap onto me with the whole chair on her back. Meanwhile those mm's of hers became one long, earsplitting moan. However, she had abandoned herself to similar intemperances earlier too: instead, what I anticipated and

observed with understandable satisfaction was the incipient red-
dening of her temples and soon afterward, her cheeks; moreover,
if I wasn't hearing or seeing incorrectly, her breathing was becoming significantly labored.

Come on, hurry! Now I needed some excessive offense, something at once atrocious and swift to hurry along the process and
pull off the job. I couldn't risk that she would catch her breath.
Yes, but what? I was inspired just in the nick of time.

"Anyway, let's pull off the merciful mask: after all, it's not your
fault if you're plebeian." (Another convulsive struggle.) "Let's
talk about the kid while we're at it. And tell me, who or what is
the poor creature going to become under your guidance? He'll be
as anxious, fearful, sexually impotent et cetera, et cetera, as you
are crazy. In short, you are a terrible mother, the worst mother."

"Mmmmmmmmmmmm."

"But nevertheless... Huh, I didn't quite hear you?"

"M-m-m."

"Oh, I understand. You supply him with everything he needs:
notebooks, ballpoint pens, felt-tipped pens, ham sandwiches and
even *hell on earth*! And when he comes home, he finds a good
hot bowl of soup, and grilled liver, which is so good for kids,
and so on. And then you assume your job is done. . . . Huh, just
one question. A good governess could give him all that too: so
what's the difference between you and any good governess? What
does your role as his mother add up to? . . . Or do you really
imagine that kids live on cookies and ballpoint pens alone? Ah,
a good deal more is required, my dear: in your role as mother
you should waken a love of the beautiful and good in that simple
little heart, open it to pleasures that are not vulgar, encourage it
to participate in the great natural spectacle and the myriad rhythms
of the seasons and in the creations of human genius; you should
open that soul, in a word, to poetry. . . . And how could you do
all that for the little being entrusted to you by a blind fate, even
assuming you were actually capable of conceptualizing such needs?
How, when rage is foaming at your mouth and you're dealing

blows to his dear little head? . . . Ah, I wanted to delude myself, but now I know: you don't love your son!"

Anyhow, I don't know if or what I could have added to that calculated and stupid rambling; and to be honest, I don't care to go on with this portrayal.

It certainly wasn't a pretty sight. At that point, the woman whom I had loved in distant times was cyanotic; the foam drooling from her mouth had turned greenish; her breath, labored and more and more halting, seemed (so help me God, it did) a death rattle; and her eyes, which, incidentally, I have avoided referring to (the way they shone from the depths of her impotence was so poisonous, so terrible), her eyes had become revoltingly supplicating. . . . She wept, wept before me, proud of herself and her life; she wept and begged me in spite of how I had violated her. But her eyes alone wept because she was weeping and suffocating at the same time, and she no longer had enough wind even to moan. Her breath was going, her heart was about to give out. . . . She was almost black now. . . .

And then she kicked the bucket. Finally!

Okay, I heard that little voice in my ear saying, "Hey, braggart, weren't you telling us about the perfect crime: what about the marks left by your bonds and chains on the flesh of your despised beloved? What can we do about that? Even the stupidest investigators will surely catch on to . . ."

I answer: "No, sir, the bonds and chains, which you so classically refer to and which I too portrayed that way here, were actually soft as velvet, so soft that they wouldn't leave a mark. At least, the doctor didn't find a shadow of a bruise or anything else suspicious."

Hell, that would be all I need; as if I weren't already regretting what I did! Yes, in retrospect, I killed her just for the satisfaction of doing it.

Because, quite honestly, now that she (good or bad) is gone, what will I do on the face of the earth?

DIALOGUES

THE TEST

1

"Well, then, handsome. You've been looking and looking, and you still haven't decided? Did you come here to pass time?"

"Decide just like that, so fast?"

"You've been looking around for a half hour!"

"Well, you know how it is."

"Hmph, we have other clients. If you want me I'm Mantova."

"Modena."

"The Abruzzi."

"Taranto."

"Montecatini."

"All right, go on. If I want you I'll call."

"Hey, what are you doing here?"

"What are *you* doing?"

"You have to ask! I came to ——— (of course)."

"So did I."

"You!"

"Why?"

"But..."

"Go on: but?"

"Huh, I don't know: they say that you..."

"What?"

"The other night in ———'s house everyone went with Mitzi but you."

"Oh, really? Who told you that?"

"I don't know: someone who was there."

"Ah, really?"

"He said that Mitzi herself began to sing: 'Give me, give me, give me a hard-on, Mitzi.'"

"Good for all of you."

"But you really don't have to do this."

"What do you mean?"

"That I don't believe you."

"What don't you believe?"

"That you're like the rest of us."

"Why not?"

"I'm not sure: you've got too much I don't know what, or too little I don't know what else."

"Couldn't you be more clear?"

"Suit yourself!... It's that you don't make it with women. Everyone at the university says so."

"Are you absolutely sure?"

"Absolutely."

"Hmm... all right, you want to make a bet?"

"As many as you want. But no tricks."

"Of course not: you pick the woman yourself and talk to her first."

"Which one?"

"Whichever.... No, wait: Montecatini. She's the prettiest, you know; a bit tall, but the prettiest."

"Fine."

"Hold on: what are we betting?"

"If you win, I'll pay for both of us."

"Perfect."

"No, not so fast! And if you lose?"

"If I lose, I'll pay for you."

"That makes my day, that's how sure I am of winning."

"Huh, slow down. ... What about the exact terms of the bet?"

"Everything must go normally, like with one of us."

"Us who?"

"Us males."

"Yeah, yeah, sure, call the woman over and tell her what you want before we go to the room."

2

"My dear Montecatini... what's your name anyway?"

"Giulietta."

"That's a pretty name. Pretty like you."

"You're handsome yourself. ... Come on, let's not waste time, there are others waiting. Are you going to undress or stay like that?"

"No, listen, Giulietta. ... Do you like dough?"

"I would say so: why would I be here if I didn't? Do you think I like it here?"

"Yes, of course, but listen to me a minute: I made a bet."

"A bet?"

"Yes, and I have to win. Not just for the sake of the bet, you know, it's very important to me."

"Oh, I know, that guy told me."

"What did he say?"

"That you don't make it with women, and he gave me some dough to tell him the truth about how it went."

"Right, exactly: and you have to tell him that it went fine."

"But why? Is it true?"

"That doesn't matter; you see, true or false, under conditions like these."

"What do you mean, conditions like these?"

"When someone is put to the test, he always fails."

"That's true."

"And therefore you'll tell him that everything went fine, and that will be that: okay?"

"So is it true?"

"But haven't we just said that under these conditions . . . Forget it; what do you care, anyway?"

"Ugh, you're confusing me and you're wasting my time."

"I'll pay you double the rate and the half hour too, if you want."

"Uhm. But tell me, why did you ask if I liked dough?"

"Because I want to give you some for this favor."

"He already did."

"But I'll give you much more."

"And you don't even want to give it a try?"

"What's the point? And anyway that's not the question."

"But look, he paid me and I don't want to trick him."

"Come on! I'll pay you better."

"Yeah but . . . Sure. For a little lie that wouldn't cost me anything, I could take your money and his."

"So, then!"

"I'm not like that, though."

"You're a woman of honor, or what?"

"Yes, exactly, of honor, my dear: so don't think it goes without saying just because . . . don't think it's so easy with me."

"But how could it be! Aside from the dough, you said yourself it wouldn't cost you anything."

"No, really, your dough doesn't interest me."

"But why?"

"I'm also a woman besides being a whore."

"And that means?"

"That means, that means . . . Why don't you even want to try?"

"It's hopeless."

"You're saying that because you don't know me. Come on, come here . . . who knows, we might even tell him the truth, your friend (some friend!)."

"But this way, assuming that . . . you'll lose my money, that bonus."

"Be patient! Go on, come here, kiss me . . . right here."

"But it's absurd! How can I?"

"You can, you can; don't talk so much; come on, do it."

"... You're ... you're sweet."

"But look, aside from everything else I like you: come on, get busy, no!... Yes, like that, good... again!... You see, you see you're already..."

"Ah, little one, this doesn't mean anything yet."

"Eh, let God take care of it. Come on, and don't talk: because sometimes if you talk too much... And if you think too much: you get an idea in your head and... Don't you like me? Look, look at all of me."

"Yes, yes, you're pretty. Really! I've never seen a... such a ... a pretty little thing."

"Let's not exaggerate."

"Really, I swear!"

"Good, so much the better. . . . You see it, see, you're almost there already."

"Ah, yes, thank you. Wow, you're good! What a new sensation of power, freedom..."

"Keep quiet, keep quiet, concentrate. . . . Oh, but... what now? Why, so suddenly...? What's happening now?"

"Right, what's happening? I should ask you."

"Oh, my God, you get big, you get small... Look how quickly it came back."

"Ah, you don't want to know: it's always like this; in fact, usually I don't even try; it only happened because you're nice and good."

"And there's no good reason for it!... But why?"

"It must be a tendency: didn't you know that there are men like this too?"

"Sure, I knew, but you didn't seem, you don't seem..."

"But I am."

"Oh, what a shame! So what do we do now?"

"Nothing."

"Let's try again."

"No more, please!"

"You poor thing!"

"Eh, no, not that too: at least spare me the pity."

"But come on, let's try again."

"No, no more!"

"Okay, if that's what you want . . . But I'm sorry; just don't say I didn't give it my best."

"Yeah, sure, sure."

3

"Okay, let's get dressed."

"All right. . . . And tell me: how do we stand on our agreement?"

"What agreement?"

"I mean, do you agree to tell him that everything went well?"

"Tell who?"

"My friend who's waiting outside."

"Oh, right, I forgot all about it: what a fool."

"Come on!"

"What do I have to do?"

"For Pete's sake, tell him that everything went normally. And I'll not only give you what you usually get but also all this dough, all this, you see? . . . . One, two, three, four, five: is that enough for you? That's all I have, but if need be I can bring you more."

"It's really too much! But you know, I told you, I don't like tricking people."

"You're starting that again!"

"I'm starting, yes, I don't see why I should have changed my mind."

"But you're honest, you seem intelligent, don't you understand what you've . . . what you've seen?"

"But he, the fool gave me money to tell him the truth."

"I'm the fool, not him. This matter involves me, not him; and as I told you before, this is very, very important for me . . . and for him? It's a stupid juvenile curiosity; for me it's nearly a question of life and death. Think what a life I would have if everybody had the proof, the actual proof, that . . ."

"But he . . . and I am . . ."

"A woman of honor, yes, I know."

"Yes, and that's why I must..."

"And you wouldn't sacrifice this little honor of yours for the sake of peace, I mean to save a human being's ultimate ignominy, or at least for the sake of ambiguity."

"I don't understand a word you said."

"Naturally! Okay, listen, Giulietta, my friend, wonderful creature of unattainable flesh and incorruptible innocence..."

"But what a talker! Good heavens, now what are you doing?"

"That's right, I'm getting down on my knees to you and begging you like a saint."

"And crying too!"

"Yes, crying too; you see, I'm crying."

"Get up, you're frightening me."

"Oh, I beg of you, Giulietta! Witness of my endless misery, of my terror and impotence, you wouldn't want this atrocious spectacle to haunt your nightmares, would you? I beg you, Giulietta, tell the guy who's waiting down there that I'm the same as everyone else."

"My God, what sad, strange words: I've never heard anything like it. You really think that I..."

"I think so, I'm sure of it: you have such a supremely pious nature, you could be my savior."

"But...but you're saying all this, making me feel like I've never felt before, just so that I will tell your friend... Isn't that too much for too little?"

"Oh, I knew it, Giulietta, you are endowed with such dignity that you pull pure gold out of yourself, you come up with arguments that would make people jealous. You say 'Too little!' But what if it were everything? What if our consciousness, the very consciousness that sleeps, drinks, wears clothes... lived only in the image others have of us?"

"Don't act crazy, I can't understand you... but what do you get out of it if I tell him that you et cetera?"

"Ah, another illumination from your deep and innocent spirit."

"Oh, cut it out! You'll be the same, won't you?"

"Maybe, and maybe not."

"But it doesn't make any difference to me. I love you."

"What did you say?"

"That I love you."

"Me? You really love me?"

"Stupid: you."

"Me, like this?"

"You, like this: all the worse, if you're like this. But you'll see that..."

"Then you'll say that everything..."

"That everything was marvelous, that it went as usual."

"Thank you, thank you!"

"And the dough?"

"Here it is."

"Go away, I was kidding; keep it, I'll even give you more, as much as you want.... You're a gambler, right?"

"How did you guess?"

"My secret; and if you don't turn out to be a loser, you can have some for your game too."

"But I always lose."

"Okay, we'll arrange it."

"But I wouldn't want you..."

"I know what you're getting at; I'm a whore, and you're a gentleman."

"No, no."

"Oh, yes, and one way or another we'll arrange things...but let's go down now."

"Don't forget, now."

"Don't worry."

"Wait.... I'm a clown dripping blood, that's what I am."

"Sure, sure, come on, otherwise the madam will eat me alive."

4

"Ladies, into the room!... And you there, how about it, what have you been doing here for an hour! Why don't you choose?

Haven't you gotten a good enough look? They're fifteen hot ladies. What a slowpoke!"

"I'm waiting for a friend."

"Ah, okay."

"There he is. Over here, here, you two."

"I'm sorry, good friend: pay up."

"No, she's really the one who should tell me; I'll talk to her privately."

"Go right ahead."

"(So then? . . . Remember, I gave you the cash to tell me the truth.)"

"(Everything was fine.)"

"(Fine, really fine?)"

"(Yes, yes, just like usual, like all the others.)"

"(You sure?)"

"(Oh, listen, what could I gain from this?)"

"(How can it be?)"

"(That's right.)"

"(You mean he isn't even manic or lewd? He didn't tie you to the radiator or beat you? Or make you beat him or tell you to curse?)"

"(No: everything was normal, I'm telling you.)"

"Okay then, my dear friend, I surrender and pay. But I'm not convinced."

"What else do you need to be convinced?"

"Bah, I don't know, let's see. But look, she's basically a . . ."

"A whore?"

"Right: and what if you begged, what if you gave or promised more cash than I did? . . ."

"If you think that way, why did you make the bet?"

"Sure, sure, right. . . . Let's go now. But I must admit, I don't feel very certain . . ."

"Certain about what?"

"Certain about what I'm certain of."

"Very amusing."

"Yeah, yeah, you're right. Come on, let's get out of here."

"'Bye, beautiful."

"'Bye, handsome, come back soon: I'll be here."

"Undoubtedly."

"One moment, you; no, you."

"(What is it?)"

"(Your friend who came in the room with me, who is he, a student like you?)"

"(... Noooo, hell, no! He's a famous writer. 'Lorenzo' is his pen name—you must have heard him spoken of.)"

"('Lorenzo': yes, now that you say it, I think... I've probably even read some book of his.)"

"(Sure thing, like hell!)"

"(Oh, now I get it.)"

5

"Ah, finally a bit of fresh air: all the odors in there could suffocate you. . . . By the way, while you were upstairs, the *patronne* came and drew the curtains; so you see, naturally, I started to spy through them . . . and can you believe this, a monsignor came in."

"Oh, really, in his habit?"

"Not really, but you could easily see that he was a monsignor, or a priest in any case."

"What nerve."

"Oh yeah, she asked who you were."

"Who did?"

"Your lady."

"And what did you say?"

"I told her that you're a famous writer: I called you 'Lorenzo.' And she said: 'Right, I think I've read some book of his.'"

"Oh, oh."

....

(She loves me. She's beautiful, kind, good, wonderful; she loves me, or so she says. . . . Of course, I'd better make sure I never see her again.)

THE AMPULLA

"Oh, pardon me."

"That's quite all right."

"You know, I was taking off my coat and I accidentally..."

"It doesn't matter."

"Eh, no, I knocked my glasses off too; pardon again."

"Certainly!"

"If you don't mind I'll sit at this table here."

"Go right ahead."

"I won't bother you?"

"Why should you bother me; not at all."

"Thank you. ... Are you drinking coffee?"

"As you can see."

"Coffee coffee?"

"Sure."

"Aren't you afraid for your heart? At our age ... The caffeine-free is better."

"Yes, but look ... "

"Right, it's a whole other thing. ... Uhm, take a little sniff: haven't you noticed anything?"

"In the coffee?"

"No, no, in the world."

"How's that? What are you talking about?"

"In the world, the world at large."

"You mean political events, international tensions, and so on?"

"No, no: the odor."

"You mean the general corruption?"

"No-o! An actual odor."

"What odor?"

"The odor of the dead."

"The dead?"

"Yes, of the dead: is that so strange?"

"You can smell the dead?"

"I do! I imagine that everybody must."

"I'm sorry?"

"Good Lord, it's not that hard to imagine. I'm telling you again, it's the odor of the dead."

"But there have always been dead people, and they're under the ground, and no one..."

"That's precisely why, because they've always been there. I mean, do you realize that there are many more people dead than living? Every living man has infinite generations of dead men behind him."

"Obviously; so what?"

"Bah, it was fated that at a certain point the earth would be saturated and reject the odor. The earth we walk on is basically made of the dead: therefore, it has to smell on this planet of ours. One could make a rather approximate calculation of the ratio of the dead (men and otherwise) to the earth's expanse; and one would find that underneath us, around us, in the air, everywhere, there's only death."

"But, certainly... if you put it in those terms..."

"What others are there? Anyway, don't you smell the odor?"

"Well, an actual odor, no. . . ."

"Because we're used to it! Or rather, you're used to it (I'm not), so in the end you can't smell it anymore."

"Perhaps, but in any case..."

"'In any case,' huh? We go to the country, we lie down at the feet of old oak trees, we delve deep into the shadows of forests, amid the twittering of warblers (if you will); May is embalmed with saps, with flowers reawakening and blooming; a delicate, or violent and dismaying perfume tickles our nostrils. . . . But do you understand, good sir, that balsam and perfume is, in reality, the atrocious odor of corruption?"

"Right, perhaps; but, in the end the important thing. . ."

"Is that the so-called fragrances seem to us something they're not?"

"Exactly, if indeed they are not."

"Well, no, on the contrary! The important thing is that we distinguish the odor within the perfume, whatever perfume it may be. Otherwise we are sacks of potatoes, rhinoceroses, not men. . . . And besides, we would be deprived of the best thing: accusation."

"Who would be deprived and who would be accused?"

"I don't know: someone, in any case."

"So you want the human race to be miserable?"

"Me, want misery! Don't make me laugh. Men are already miserable, and maybe they are because they don't take a hard enough look at their condition?"

"That's one way to look at it."

"No, it's the only way now that so many others have been invalidated."

"Perhaps, perhaps, but calm down. Look here though, wouldn't it just be easier to forget about it?"

"Easier, you said it! And isn't that just the problem?"

"Please sit down: people are looking at us. . . . Anyway, sure, sure; what you're saying is intriguing after all."

"What do you mean intriguing!"

"Oh, God, I mean, on the contrary . . . I mean, well, ummm . . ."

"What can we do about it, right?"

"Yes, that's right: you, how do you see it, if I may ask? Do you have any ideas?"

"Look, I'm not the only one who has such ideas; or so it seems."

"Oh, no?"

"It seems men have dedicated themselves in body and spirit to the conquest of space."

"And so? . . . Ah, I get it."

"Then get this: why do you think they go to all that trouble if not to escape from this odor?"

"You mean they are searching for a planet, some celestial spot, free of life, and therefore free of death?"

"Naturally. And though they are still taking the first steps, or leaps, and they remain stuck on their native crust, it's not impossible that they'll arrive on the new planet some day."

"It's just as well."

"Not at all! They don't realize that it's all a waste of time."

"A waste of time, but why?"

"Don't you see? Given what we know about the universe in general, can we really be sure that there isn't any life and never has been on that or some other celestial body? And if there has been life, and accompanying death, the odor will remain. Am I explaining myself?"

"Marvelously! But in that case, if we're not at home on earth and we have no hope of being at home in the sky, what can we do?"

"How should I know! I'm not God almighty by profession, I'm only an employee at the land registry. We must bear the odor, I suppose; as long as we know that it is an odor and not a perfume; as long as we're not tricked by the dithyrambs of those who praise earthly fragrances, such as goodness and sanctity."

"What do goodness and sanctity have to do with it?"

"Actually, not much; but some people say that health, for instance, has a certain odor. . . . On the other hand, disregard my last statement completely."

"But I ask you, what's the use of all this? Wouldn't it be more useful . . ."

"To claim that we felt reverence and to give thanks for a perfume that is actually an odor?"

"I don't claim anything; nevertheless..."

"Oh, forget it. But now haven't you begun to smell something?"

"Well, if you really want to know, frankly I think, by God, yes. What an unbearable stench!"

"The stench of a cadaver, that's what it is."

"And I feel a sort of desperation inside me... as if everyday reality, as if my own life... See where your damn talk got me."

"Desperation! Terrific! That's already a big step forward."

"What! That's what you want, then, we're back to that, you want us to live and die in desperation?"

"No, no. Pull your seat closer, look at this."

"An ampulla."

"Yes, I carry it around with me; I'll open it now."

"Ah, what a delicious fragrance."

"Isn't it?"

"Ah, let me inhale it deep into my soul; you're restoring life and hope to me."

"'Deep into your soul'—isn't that a bit much?"

"It's just an expression."

"No, because we must watch our words here."

"Of course. At any rate, it's a delicious and truly inebriating perfume."

"Yes, thank you. But it's just a defense against dying (at least before my time), and giving anyone else satisfaction. But it's a false defense."

"Ah, now what? Your left hand is going to take away what your right just gave me?"

"It has to: the truth is, this perfume is an odor, it couldn't be anything else. Where would I have gotten it, if not from something or other that is, by its very nature, the fruit of corruption? You understand? But nevertheless, this secret essence helps me to hide from other men and get along as best I can, almost in spite of them. But I'm willing to make an exception for you: do you want the recipe?"

"Of course, I do."

"Then I'll write it out."

"One moment, we'll have time for that; and anyway, since you've convinced me, I can pretty much imagine the ingredients."

"That's a consolation."

"Yet . . . you know, for the sake of precision . . ."

"Yes, go on, go on?"

"Why not actually call this odor 'the odor of life'?"

"Magnificent, extraordinary, perfect! Amendment accepted. I can see that you've gotten right to the heart of the matter, and I congratulate you, and myself too. Yes, from now on our odor will be known as—the odor of life."

HORRIFIC
STORIES

A WOMAN'S BREAST

My eyes followed the girl moving hesitantly along the edge of the sidewalk as if she were about to cross the street. She was superb, not so much in the clothes she wore but in the elegance of her body itself: long, tapering, perfectly shaped legs, a narrow pelvis, delicate, slender shoulders crowned by a great head of brown hair which matched a slight, gentle, tawny face. But my eyes followed her mostly because of her breasts, which didn't seem to be compressed into the usual oppressive garment but bounced freely as she walked. There was chirping all around, birdsongs, the fragrances of spring. And watching the girl, all I could think was what breasts! neither imagining nor daring to let my thoughts go further. But I kept on walking until I was beside her.

She had decided, she had stepped off the sidewalk. A speeding car was barreling toward her, threatening to run her down; as I was beside her now, I simply grabbed the top of her sleeve and yanked her backward violently, hoping to rescue her. She turned to look at me, half dismayed, half flabbergasted, still unaware of the danger while I tried in vain to plumb the depths of those eyes.

"My God," she said in a surprisingly full voice, "what, what happened?"

"Nothing special; there was a car coming, and..."

"You saved my life!"

"Don't exaggerate: you might have been run over or you might not have; but just in case..."

"I surely would have been run over!"

"If you say so. But anyway, nothing happened."

"No, no, you really saved my life, I realize it now."

"Fine, I'm glad I did!"

"Wait a minute! I have to thank you."

"You have already, implicitly."

"Ah, no, no, that's not enough."

"Come on! Besides, let's say I really did save your life, are you sure it's to your advantage?... Are you happy?"

"Yes, well, no. But that has nothing to do with it."

"What do you mean it has nothing to do with it: that's the whole point, it seems to me."

"No, it doesn't cancel or pay my debt to you, at least as far as your intentions are concerned."

"As far as my intentions, as you call them, go, that may well be; but so much the worse for them. It would pain me to have saved an unhappy soul."

"Oh, but who would prefer death to an unhappy life?"

"Lots of people."

"Yes, maybe, but I'm not one of them; and anyway my life isn't really unhappy."

"All the better, then."

"Ah, it's simple for you to say. But don't you understand? My debt doesn't need your good intentions to exist."

"Let's face it, it's not such a serious matter; or if it is, forgive me."

"You still don't understand! I can't stand debts, they make me feel guilty and upset in all kinds of ways."

"How ungrateful!"

"Maybe; but the fact is I have to repay them as quickly as I can and get them off my mind...."

Though our conversation was a bit peculiar, it wasn't that

different from the usual more or less pleasant banter with which
men and women flirt. But I, for my part, had no intentions whatsoever; basically only one thing about the girl interested me; I
had only one objective.

"Ah, if there were only something I could do for you," she
began again.

And then, as if compelled, I answered:

"Well, if you really want to, there is something."

"Oh, really, really? What?"

"I'm embarrassed to say it."

"What, why? Is it so terrible?"

"Not at all, it's beautiful."

"Say it, then, be brave."

"Uh, no, I can't."

"Oh, please, I beg of you. Just think, you'd free me of all
obligation. . . . And anyway, you're piquing my curiosity, and that's
unfair: I'm a woman."

"You really want to give me an IOU, don't you?"

"Of course, that's exactly what I want."

"No matter what I have in mind?"

"Well, as long as it's not dishonest or unreasonable."

"Dishonesty depends, you know, on how you look at it."

"Oh, you're driving me crazy! Go on, all right: no matter what
it is."

"But what if . . . ?"

"Oh, God, are you trying to kill me? Tell me already."

"Fine, but don't forget, you asked."

"Yes, sure, I'll accept anything, promise anything, are you
satisfied? Just go on."

"Anything?"

"Yes, yes, yes!"

"All right, in exchange for this supposed rescue, you should . . ."

"I should . . . ?"

"Let me . . ."

"Let you? . . . I can't stand it anymore!"

"Kiss one of your nipples."

She whitened, she stared at me darkly, and said:

"Which one?"

"Huh, what did you say?" I said, disconcerted.

"I said which," she repeated, "the left or the right?"

"But, in the end, for me..."

"It's not the same thing."

"Oh, no? Why not?"

"They have distinct sensitivities," she explained in a matter-of-fact tone.

"Then, let's take the left one, the one that belongs to the heart."

She stared at me; she was suffering visibly, and it seemed to me disproportionately. In any case, it didn't make me happy, as I had imagined it would (a fact which indirectly revealed the depth of her suffering). Though I had initiated this relationship as a game, I wasn't getting any pleasure from it. There seemed to be some sort of incomprehensible bitterness rather than embarrassment or moral outrage behind her suffering.

Finally she said stiffly:

"All right."

"All right, really?"

"Why, yes, can't you see by now that I'm not the type to go back on my word? And on the other hand, I have a stake in this thing, as a debtor. . . . So then, where?"

"And you really...?"

"Look, yes, really. Oh, you're all the same. When you finally get something that you yourself asked for, you lose your courage."

"Courage! It doesn't take much."

"You're sure of that?"

"I don't understand what you mean," I replied, more serious now, in spite of myself. "I mean if this is too high a price for you . . . It's a joke, after all."

"Oh, yes, you think so? Well, anyway, where?"

"You mean where should we ... go?"

"Right."

"Let's see, if you really want to..."

"Oh, now it's me who wants this! But you're not really wrong: I want to. I can't get out of it now, and my creditor is waiting."

"But I'm a kind creditor."

"And talkative!... Where?"

"My wife's at home."

"I figured as much. Come to my place, then."

"Your place... You live alone?"

"Yes, naturally: it's not dangerous for nice, respectable males. It's right around the corner."

"Oh, well: let's go."

"Let's go."

Without another word, she took a flight of stairs up to the old city, passed under three vaults and stopped before a house whose appearance was modest to say the least.

"This is it; come in."

Steep steps of gray porous stone; the usual odor of dishwater or meat left over for days and put up to stew; songs on the radio. Nevertheless, the inside of the little flat looked less depressing. The entrance hall had no windows, but through an open doorway you could see a dining room plunged in sunlight. Every object (sofa with tasseled fringes, and so on) gave the impression of age and emitted a peculiar odor; the entire house seemed frozen.

"It's as my mother left it before she died."

But not every object, not the whole house, to tell the truth. In the dining room, a large varnished table, one of those anonymous-looking assembly-line pieces, reflected the bright patch of sunlight. On the table, a diamond-patterned, cut-glass vase contained twigs (from the shrub called "miseria") bearing spotted leaves.

"Sit down there... no there. Would you like something to drink?"

"That's not necessary."

"Right, right, what's the point?... So, then, shall we proceed?"

"If you're ready."

She stood rigidly in the sun at the window, hesitating. Was she hesitating after all? Actually, she wasn't hesitating as I had hoped but for some other reason that eluded and annoyed me.

"Do you want to undress me or should I undress myself?"

"Look, I don't want to touch you, that's not what I wanted."

"But you wanted to kiss me, or kiss..."

"Only with my mouth."

"Oh, I understand, none of this will make sense unless I undress myself; nothing will be consummated, if I don't undress myself."

"'Consummated' is a heavy word. You're intelligent: don't you think that's a twisted or perverse way of looking at it?"

"Maybe, maybe; sure I am intelligent, intelligent enough to die a hundred times a day.... All right, I'll take off my clothes: watch carefully, and you'll be repaid in full. Afterward, I'll be free... and miserable."

"But what are you talking about?"

"Be patient for a second: you'll see."

She began to undress with a studied slowness. First she threw her coat aside, then stepped out of her (black) dress; and she stood like that, faintly alluring in her cheap lace underthings, her arms naked and the swell of her breast rising and falling. The shiny hairs that puffed out from her armpits were no less provocative than the hidden ones: since women have not one, but three, four, maybe five concealed, aching places, including their lips with that irresistible down.

"So, shall we go?"

"Yes, for God's sake." Now it was I who cried out anxiously.

Even more slowly, she pulled down the left shoulder of her slip (this, I knew, was the only screen between my real desire and her), still holding up this last garment with one hand. She looked at me again, darkly, almost questioningly, almost as if she were waiting for some impatient gesture from me; then she took her hand away, releasing the thin fabric; and finally, that left coral-colored breast was born, liberated anew.

"There," she added with desolate simplicity.

A breast: but was this vile and naked thing, this vilely naked, nakedly vile thing before me in the gold light a woman's breast? Hardly; obscene creases ran toward the tip of that pale flesh which was swollen, yes, but somehow dead; and the aureola, which in a truly feminine breast has the vividness of gums, looked colorless and sick, and was even surrounded by long black hairs; and the ultimate horror, the ultimate ignominy, was that in the place of the nipple (the source of supreme pride) was a sort of dark and flaccid flesh, like the mouth of an old, toothless man.

"This is the one which belongs to the heart.

"This is the one which belongs to the heart," she continued with forced gaiety, on the brink of tears. "But it's only fair that I show you the other one too: look."

Then she revealed the other, which was in fact the sister of the first one.

"So, then, you still want to kiss me, look, right here? Come on, be brave: I'm here, I'm not going back on my word. I told you I'm ready to pay my debt."

I had already decided. It's true, I had no idea how she'd been so reduced, and therefore did not know in what way or manner to comfort her; but I had no doubt about the necessity, the urgency, of doing so. Had it been a mere accident that had deformed one of the parts of her body that should have been the most glorious source of her feminine pride? Or was it the careless sentence passed by a gratuitously cruel fate? It didn't matter. In any case, I ended up following my feelings, which were rather different than I had anticipated.

"Of course I want to kiss you, and yes, right there. Come here."

"Oh, damn!" she exclaimed angrily, not moving. "After I reveal myself, or I might even say give myself to you as no other woman would have even known how, I deserve the insult of your pity? You can tell," she said weakly, "I'm a woman who pays, up to the last cent; be satisfied with that, don't throw your pity in my face! Nobody's forcing you to kiss my nipple . . . it's not there anyway; nobody's forcing me to suffer your nauseating kiss, and worse humiliation. Come on, aren't we already even and squared away?"

"But what pity are you referring to?" I countered a bit feebly. "You're kidding yourself: it's got nothing to do with pity."

"And what, then?"

"Look, first of all, can't you admit that when we pursue an urge, one image can take the place of another, or better still, that the first image can survive its own ruin? 'The shape of desire,' as someone rather inelegantly called it. I was attracted by your breasts down there in the street, by the way they bounced; and for me, this could be, I mean it doesn't have to be any different from the way I fantasized it. It could turn out to be no different, despite all actual appearances. . . . Am I being clear? Do you understand any of these confusing thoughts?"

"Yes, I understand; I understand that pity was never as well meant, as rational and charitable as yours. And I thank you; ah, yes, now I have to be grateful all over again."

"But no, that's not it!"

"Oh, but yes, assuming you're being sincere, it is if you think about it, unless, I mean, you're some sort of pervert."

Pervert? Well, maybe in a certain sense; for actually my initial disgust was slowly changing into eagerness, but whether this was wicked or legitimate, I don't know; but by then I longed with all my heart to sink my teeth into that pitiful breast. To sink my teeth into it savagely: who knows, perhaps I might draw out the hidden nipple by sucking it, and when it burst forth, restore peace, or some at least, to that humiliated woman. But of course something else altogether may have gotten into me.

"And if I were," I finally answered, "if I were some sort of pervert?"

She was standing in front of me with the top of her slip turned down, a blameless creature Someone had violated; so offended, so bitter and enraged that she had come to this—displaying her shame to a stranger. But, when I said that (certainly not because of it), suddenly...

I'll never forget the way her eyes lit up, a sudden, sweet, trusting light.

"You a..." she murmured, going pale. "No," she screamed. "That would be too perfect! I'm not used to things like this. Such a lucky coincidence: it's impossible!"

It was so simple, and yet I didn't catch on right away; realizing this, she went on:

"In that case, there's still hope for me! I could be a woman for at least one man! I wouldn't have to be mortified by that one man's pity, refuse it, swallow it; he would want me for what I am, and actually find pleasure in me; he wouldn't have to overcome his own nausea; he would actually desire me, my God, de-si-re!"

Now that I had finally understood, all I had to do was agree: "Well, then, I'm that one man." But, on the contrary, that same veiled impulse that had just driven me toward her marred flesh now pushed me toward a cruel, torturous inquiry, whose apparent motivation was either the impulse to satisfy my fixation or to plumb the depths of her bitterness (and allow her to unburden herself). I began, with outright foolishness:

"But everybody wants you."

"Yes, dressed!" she sighed in response.

"Why, you mean this has happened...?"

"Yes, it's happened before. They wanted to make love to me, had eyes for me, and when..."

"There were many, then?"

"No, of course not: one, only one, and that was enough for me."

"Who?"

"Who! You want his name and address?"

"No, I'm sorry: but what kind of man was he?"

"Handsome, young, a sweetheart. I was still in school; I still carried a schoolbag of useless books, but I already had these long

thighs, my waist was already supple, my chest swollen. My chest:
look, this. ... And I loved, loved him for his beauty, for his
stubborn will to dominate, but also for his misplaced desire, I
mean for me; I loved him before I even understood myself, before
I had any idea of the insurmountable conflicts that can arise
between ourselves and others—as if the fact that I was a certain
way should have been a sufficient guarantee of my right to live,
to be happy. It was raining that night. He was dragging his
schoolbooks too and left them on the counter of a closed newspaper kiosk where we had gone for shelter. He looked at me, and
I was naive, naive. ... There was a bandshell not far from there
under the plane trees in the public garden, and we went there;
it was getting dark; during our skirmishes it grew totally dark.
And he wanted to bare my breasts, these breasts."

"What did he say?"

"Nothing, nothing! What was there to say? In fact, he kissed
me everywhere I let him."

"And ... ?"

"Good God, your questions are nonsensical."

"Why? Tell me everything."

"How sweet of you; it's obvious you want to release me from
myself. ... His kisses were full of disgust, that's all, and that's
how they felt, all right. That's all, that's all," she laughed man-
ically. "And so, he vanished, or rather, I did, I vanished."

It was true, there wasn't anything left to say: I had reduced
her to the ultimate humiliation, which I had hoped would be to
her benefit. Now it was my turn to make a move, to touch bottom.

"So, come here."

She was still standing there bare to the waist like a huge statue
of the huntress Diana whose dissatisfied creator wanted to destroy,
to throw against the hammer; her slip was partly caught in her
belt, hiking up her skirt a little and revealing a bit of those thighs
she herself had praised. She was looking at me with the same
uncertain gaze, but without any sign of the insolence she'd had
before (this was already evidence of a positive outcome).

"You really mean it?"

"Come on."

She took another timorous step forward, the decisive one in any case. But now the problem was to somehow manage not to alarm her all over again with my kiss, thus plunging her back into hell. What was really behind my yearning desire to kiss that vile part of her? It was still disgust that I felt, however twisted, exalted or sublimated, but it was also a pledge of assistance; would I be able to hide the fundamentally shameful nature of my feelings once again? ... But on the other hand, this disgust, this very disgust, seemed to be a necessary, integral part of my perversion, which was, in turn, the only guarantee, if you will, for that woman, the only viable spiritual approach that precluded pity and might make a sincere relationship possible. But finally, I could make no sense of it at all, and I plunged ahead, trusting to chance.

She took another step forward and stood beside me, and I took her by the waist, actually by the bones of her hips.

"What long pale legs!"

"Yes, they're pretty, hm?" Though bitterness wasn't entirely gone from her voice, her tone was feminine now.

"And what a head of hair."

"Yes, yes, I know: it's shiny, soft, lustrous, isn't it?"

"And your mouth."

"Like coral, I suppose?" she joked weakly but indulgently, "a generous, promising mouth, right? Sure, everything is fine; everything else."

"Be quiet and come closer."

"Closer than this, how can I?"

"You'll see."

I grabbed her gently so that she turned that left and sinister bosom to me; it came right to my lips, not a hand's length away (I was sitting, she standing). ... Therefore, why was I still hesitating? The only thing to do was to plunge headfirst into the abyss, blocking everything else out, without giving her the time to be afraid. My imagination transformed the obscene withdrawn nipple—or maybe it had never been visible—into an obscene beast cowering in the fissure of a crumbling wall: as it peered out from its cave in a posture of challenge, I cast the image of a half-nude girl before my eyes, like a spell. Yet in spite of this, I mean all of this, I wanted to: then why did I feel some mysterious part of myself opposing a kiss that was growing more and more unopposable by the second? Wasn't I about to discover the bitter sense of violation for its own sake, and maybe even some unknown, extravagant pleasure—not to mention the inflated sense of a good deed done?

I kissed her, but it wasn't even her. I kissed—there, there. I don't really know what happened inside me then; too much, that's certain, something overwhelming, a headlong rush toward an uproar of images or feelings. I know that she murmured:

"Oh, so it's true, it's true, then?"

And I felt every fiber of her body respond to my kiss.

Come now, the rest, naturally, doesn't matter; if I refer to it, it is merely for the sake of conjecture or perhaps idle investigation, to see how what comes after can jeopardize what came before in the house of cards we call our feelings.

She was prey to hope once again, but let it be said immediately that my terrible success had already filled me with shame and remorse. In fact, let's be cautious: hope is false by its very nature. And it is not enough: she made the grave mistake of becoming attached to me, whereas it is clear that these minimal episodes of our lives do not have, cannot have, any history. In the long run, what could I have done with her, and more importantly, she with me? Everything ends badly, that goes without saying; and like the "fragile wall" of her breast, everything crumbles. . . .

It would seem that we must be contented by joys that are not only ambiguous and twisted, but even fleeting.

THE ETERNAL PROVINCE

1

I have a wooden leg (well, not really wooden, it's an American-made leg) but no one would ever know, and I barely limp; but it makes no difference. And that is why I hate women. The connection, I think, is fairly simple in itself; however, I might add, *ad abundantiam*, that women certainly have not missed any opportunity to make me hate them. And since I'm in this mood today, that is to rake up old stories, I might as well be more specific.

That first girl, for example, the very first one. She was very beautiful, with a great mane of jet-black hair, a well-sculpted face, vast, ponderous eyes; but—see how chance works—she had some trouble with her leg too (I never knew exactly what it was, a large, heavy leg that she actually dragged behind her). Why I fell in love with her, of all people, would be difficult, if it weren't too easy, to say: perhaps because she was impaired, and I was a tender and romantic adolescent back then; or perhaps because subconsciously I was hoping for greater understanding. Instead...

Her father was a gruff man, yet I managed to get an apartment right above hers, so it was easy for us to communicate with songs (she studied singing) and notes exchanged on the stairway. Ah, that first, fleeting meeting in a chapel outside the city, in the tradition of ancient poets and their beautiful ladies. I found her kneeling to pray in the attitude that best suited her beauty and at the same time best hid her deformity. She had assumed it spontaneously moreover, without any hint of calculation. And despite everything, other meetings followed; and she even risked having me at her house in her father's absence. . . . Life for us, for me, in those days was intoxicating and light like certain wines, like spring breezes! We were new, clean, with our baggage of hopes intact, and so on. . . . Us, or only me? Or perhaps not even me? I don't know. I happened to find one of my supremely poetic writings from those days. In it, I praised the nocturnal silence (in my little boarding room) and granted it the power to "weave" a misty, whirling dome of an apparently benign or protective nature which would crumble, to my gloomy disappointment, as the "voice" (hers surely, declaring her love in song from the floor below) rose. Was it a premonition that would pertain to the rest of my life? But I am digressing too much.

So this is it, briefly: she had that kind of leg, but nevertheless, she required her man to have two in good condition. And perhaps even with good reason: because she was determined to find the best man in me, while I (as I already said) was probably looking for a crippled girl in her. In any case, leaving the subtleties aside, as our intimacy developed, no sooner had she learned of my deformity, than she changed her tune. First in her notes, she accused me of lacking passion, and with a curious twist of sentiment, of being incapable of loving her "sick leg." And one fine day, she revealed brusquely that she was terribly sorry but she had been deceiving herself, she had to admit it now: but it was really so-and-so whom she had been feeling here—and I remember this well, she made a broad, shameless gesture from her crotch to her lips. So-and-so was another student of philosophy, with whom she had had an inconsequential relationship some time before.

Hence, my fall from the clouds, my desperation, my plans to get her back at any cost—that's how naive I was. Finally, as she was unyielding, the only thing I could do was to wake so-and-so on the telephone one night and persuade him to come down to the city from his house in the hills. I had to speak with him, I said, about some secret and highly intriguing matter. We hardly knew one another, but he didn't seem a genius; still, he wasn't terribly surprised when he learned the object of the solicited conversation, and he understood immediately what I so madly hoped for from him. The help, for God's sake, that one might ask of a rival who has fallen out of love (he proclaimed this right off) but still has the keys to the heart we desire. In his opinion, what should I appeal to to win over the woman again and generally speaking, what was his diagnosis and prognosis, and so forth. One of my ridiculous oddities, you see, as antiquated as "taking a seat at the enemy's hearth"; something between desperation, triumph, and my own personal style of chivalry.

What a good talker he was; perhaps he was just having fun, and I'm not denying that I was too. Needless to say, it was a lot of idle talk and nothing more: as if someone with a wooden leg could suddenly be rid of it! The girl held firm, and it was easy for her to avoid me. As for me... everything passes. She later found a well-grounded husband, and now she's a grandmother.

"In truth this has nothing to do with it," a poet once said—I mean, this whole little story. Except I must add that after this girl there were many others like her, I mean girls who acted in exactly the same way.

In conclusion, take it for what it's worth: I have a wooden leg and I hate women.

2

How many hotel rooms I've spent my life in! I have dragged my solitude, my boredom, my misery through them. Working or doing something is not for me. Fortunately, I am rich. Anyway, it was in one such room that the great idea came to me.

The hotel was in a small provincial city where you could have drowned in boredom. The heat was nearly unbearable, and to

make matters worse, my room was infested with fleas. The Lord
only knows why I lingered on there, if not for the usual reason
that I didn't know where else to go, and that I always found heat
or fleas or something of the kind wherever I went. In any case,
I used to spend nearly the whole day, especially the endless
afternoons, splayed out naked on the bed, managing with cunning
to save myself from the furious little pests. I flipped through
illustrated magazines, occasionally I forced myself to read a book,
but mostly I contemplated the whitewashed walls. And thus, I
soon discovered a spiderweb suspended there. I actually owe the
idea to that.

Not really a spiderweb, only a vestige of it; a simple scant
thread maybe two feet long, the kind you find everywhere, except
that I'm sure not many people have had the chance to observe
one's behavior. An otherwise imperceptible trifle of air would
make it oscillate, writhe, curl up; or I had only to blow lightly
in its direction or just barely whistle; or do nothing at all. Indeed,
I would say it was never still. By Jove, there are some summer
days when the air in a room positively doesn't move; and in any
case, I tried various experiments by stuffing the door and windows, closing off the cracks with blankets and clothes, and it
still went on trembling and twisting up there, though a little less
tumultuously. Whenever I turned on the light suddenly in the
middle of the night, it was shivering up and down. It was a
soul in agony, that's what it was, or more precisely, a soul upon
which someone was inflicting continual torment; and I liked to
imagine that I was that someone. It hardly mattered that it was
only a wretched strand of spiderweb. I finally felt like a master.
A kind of rapport existed between us. My breath was an atrocious inquiry and its contortions were its impotent answers, its
vain attempts to back away from the torture, its terror, its equally
vain entreaties. Yes, to put it one way, I held the right of life
and death over it. With one brutal breath I could nail it to the
ceiling, blow it out for good. And if it went on trembling even
when there wasn't a breath of wind, wasn't that in reaction to my

own breath, as if it sensed its executioner's presence?

Now, the step between these fantasies and the idea above was small, an elementary idea in any case: using my own humiliation as an instrument, I would unsettle, wound, humiliate any woman that I could in her most intimate and delicate feelings, thereby taking revenge on them all. I would open a wound in her soul, an incurable one if possible. In other words, I would make her fall madly in love with me, and when she was truly at a pitch, I would swiftly reveal, that is, suddenly force her to acknowledge my deformity; the violent shock she would experience and the inability of her love to overcome my physical defect (although I am now well aware it is not only that) would be my victory.

One might object that, surprises apart, things had been going that way all along, and that in fact I had already had my fill of such vendettas. But it would be easy for me to reply that in the first place, I was never at all sure of the sincerity or depth of the feelings I had inspired. Indeed I had had plenty of reason to doubt them. And whereas I was seriously involved in those previous affairs myself, now I would have a free heart and mind, guaranteeing me the right spirit, the resolute coldness I needed to enjoy someone else's pain. An indispensable premise (or so I thought) to the accomplishment of my plan! And lastly, let me say that it is all in the spirit in which it is done. There is, I mean, a great, a supreme difference between experiencing something and causing something, like the difference between the event itself and the power to bring it about. On the other hand, it might seem strange that I was basing my plan on something so uncertain: who can be so sure that he can make a woman fall madly in love with him? But truthfully, I am, or was, precisely one of those so-called ladies' men (hence, all the greater my rancor at their sensual betrayals: I hated them because I loved them, that's nothing new). I was handsome, well-built except for the invisible leg, intelligent to a certain degree, noble in feature and manner, capable of experiencing or feigning delicate, thoughtful, and melancholy feelings, and so on; and as fatuous as need be, too; one of those men whose friends would say, "Ah, if I were you, I'd make women fall at my feet and go into contortions for me." Therefore, I had no doubt that I could win the heart of some poor provincial girl and gradually exalt her emotions.

And thus, I became impassioned and infatuated entertaining this lovely idea. Now I had only to choose my victim.

3

When I was not lying in the hotel, intent upon blowing the strand, I used to sit at the main café in town, a place naturally located on the main street; and around nightfall all the young people from the town would parade in front of me. There were women of all kinds and for all tastes, beautiful and ugly, blond and brunette, modest and proud women; and I sat there observing them one by one with a kind of secret pleasure, like a cat on a stove might observe an unsuspecting mouse bounding across the kitchen.

Really, I had initially thought that I would not choose at all, but pick one at random, so that her sacrifice would be totally symbolic. Then I thought that by choosing the most superb—for a better example and my greater delight—I could humiliate the entire sex; but finally, I simply followed my more contemplative moods, or the natural tendency everyone has to put off his own pleasure, and made no decision at all, almost as if I were waiting for some special inspiration. I was perfectly aware that this unanticipated mood that had suddenly come over me represented a considerable danger; I ran the risk of developing some sort of interest in one of those women (whom I already knew in good part) and losing the required coldness; but so it went.

Soon after, anyway, one girl amid them all claimed my attention. Beautiful and shapely, a dusky blonde, she did not lack a certain natural elegance and was even well-dressed given her station (which must have been modest); and yet there was something uncertain about her that I couldn't pinpoint and which even interfered strangely with my faculties of observation. Perhaps it was the way she had of throwing back her shoulders one at a time and almost shivering, so that for a moment she looked as if she were being shaken by a sudden gust of wind; or an excessive length of leg; or the way she dragged her feet slightly when she was tired; or the barely noticeable prominence of her belly, almost suggesting an imminent pregnancy, which should have inspired tenderness, if anything, but for some reason, awakened cruel impulses instead; or the way that her shifting gaze, which occasionally faded or blanked out altogether, would suddenly darken; or all of that together—I couldn't say exactly what it was. But most likely, the feeling that she communicated was connected to her internal condition, to some unknown and blossoming pain. One thing, at any rate, seemed certain: she was a perfect victim. Thus, as much as the facility of the conquest (or so I deemed it) hurt my pride, she was my nominee.

But the point, frankly, was something else. The girl's supposed secret pain, in fact, only unleashed my most wicked and evil fantasies and promised me more refined pleasure: to open a suffering heart to hope, I told myself, and then to cast it back into desperation is a worse offense than wounding one which never knew hope because it never knew suffering; nor can you thoroughly measure the depths to which a person will fall if he has never experienced it before. And, who knows, maybe she was or had been suffering a lost love. . . . And other such nonsense.

All carts before a horse, obviously, that fit some conventional image of the provincial girl. Which only goes to show the futility of the ideas I was entertaining, despite all my apparent determination and my tremendous yet grotesque desire to cause injury.

4

During her strolls, the girl was almost always alone. I had seen her several times in the company of other women who simply seemed to be girlfriends and a gaunt young man who could have been her brother. One insignificant circumstance, among others, which clearly favored my design, but which I may as well say right off, quickly proved to be insufficient. Nor had the little complicities I had procured with my pennies (among the waiters at the café, I mean) improved the situation; and finally, the undertaking appeared much more arduous than I had, in my arrogance, allowed myself to imagine. In any case, the main stumbling block did not seem to lie in the customs or conventions of that narrow society. Somehow she herself kept slipping through my fingers. Although she now responded to and reciprocated my continual glances from the café table, she basically didn't seem prepared to offer much more. And while I had even learned her name, her circumstances and more from my accomplices, I still had not come up with any way to approach her, to break her will, which was openly yet blandly adverse. For example, once I tried to follow her, hoping that she would reach a deserted spot or street where I could speak to her without causing a scene or making her uneasy. She had turned back swiftly, and, I could see clearly from my lookout (which faced the main thoroughfare and major intersections), from that day on she took only busy streets.

It is true that in some cases café waiters are not enough to do the trick; and on the other hand, even if I had wanted to form solid relationships in town and snare the girl through the normal channels, I would have been prevented by the fact that I couldn't involve superfluous people in the affair, or even worse, fathers or mothers. Nevertheless, I could have easily acknowledged each obstacle as my own shortcoming or weakness; and that is not to say that I didn't, but my dominant feeling was one of rage and offended vanity, as though the girl's opposition weren't completely normal. Finally, perhaps I even expected her to run to me and literally throw herself at my feet, overwhelmed by God only knows what magnetic force or magical look which I then attributed to myself. Briefly, after a couple of days I was possessed by a sort of rage against myself, but really against her. Nevertheless, I rejoiced in this mood, since it was especially favorable to my purposes. If the undertaking was or appeared to be difficult, so much the better. Give it up? Never!

Now one day I watched the girl pass, and after exchanging the usual looks with me, she disappeared at the end of the avenue, in the direction of the country, or the adjacent public gardens, a rather wild and normally deserted place. Since I had stopped following her, her state of alarm must have ceased. Without losing a moment, I got up and ran after her.

I found her standing next to a tree, leaning her weight on one hip. She seemed lost in contemplation of the high mountain beyond the valley, gold in the late sun. There wasn't a soul in sight; the swallows were filling the air with a din. When she heard me approaching, she gave a start and quickly headed back toward town while I went on walking resolutely toward her. However, there was no way for her to circumvent me because she was now out on the edge of the ramparts that jutted out like a prow. I rejoiced in our inevitable confrontation and imagined having her in my clutches. . . . But when she reached me, rather than averting her face or looking down, she gazed at me intently and almost came straight for me without slowing her pace, or maybe she even stopped for a split second as if she were about to say something. But that isn't even the best part: the best part is that I let her go by without saying or doing a thing. And a moment later she was already far ahead of me, walking briskly and shuddering now and then in her way. But having reached her, now I stood there feeling like a brutal conqueror, and watched her walk away.

So why didn't I speak to her then? Perhaps because she had foreseen my intentions, even if partially, and had virtually taken the words out of my mouth. Or was it mere surprise? That evening, naturally, I went back over several explanations, overlooking (again, naturally) the most plausible ones. In any case, my curiosity had nothing to do with self-inquiry; and indeed, the incident had served purely and simply to aggravate my wrath. For one reason or another, and regardless of whether I had behaved like a fool, she had known how, had actually dared to muddle this city playboy, this master of the female spirit: so her punish-

ment would be even greater. I mean, I would have to hurt her as
an individual woman as well as a woman in general. Just how
detrimental such a personal complication would be to my plans,
I did not realize. Just as, in dreaming up the most suitable means
of bending the intractable creature, I didn't realize that I was
preparing to knock down a door that was open from the very
beginning. But the idleness of my life and my thoughts had
made me victim to a sort of supertraining (if that's the right word
for it).

As far as those means are concerned, it is useless to follow
the tortuous and somewhat contradictory courses that my reasoning took, thus let the conclusion suffice.

If her intention to speak to me, her inclination toward me, was
not merely one of my fantasies, the girl would have appeared
without fail at the same spot, at the very same time the next day.
I calmed myself momentarily with this thought. Then I went back
to consoling myself with the dangling thread, whose spasmodic
twitching raised me in my own esteem again.

5

She came. Walking hesitantly, head down, she never raised her
eyes until she was beside me. Dark blue eyes, whose depths I
just then began to discover. She looked at me shyly, without
uttering a word. Silently, I indicated a bench. She followed me
docilely and sat waiting: what the devil was she waiting for? For
me to speak, of course. But I didn't know what to say, or my
pride kept me from using one of the usual convenient little lines.
But why? What did pride have to do with a little fool like her?
But that's another story. Perhaps I got pleasure precisely from
that long absurd pause, from her anxious embarrassment, and
from my own feeling of ridiculousness? Yet, I sat there mutely
before her, while my twofold spite grew stronger.

At last it was she who spoke first. "It's pretty here," she said
doubtfully, looking around with a short sigh.

"Pretty! What do you see that's pretty?" I blurted, venting my anger. In reality, all we could see of the whole garden from where we were sitting were a few scanty trees and a bare incline which might have been a grassy hill before the daily infestation of dogs and children.

"But it's open, it's free," she protested, looking at me uneasily.

Ah, here finally was something for me to work on: she felt enslaved in her little city, her soul was gasping... et cetera; one could begin here.

"And so, poor soul," I declared, sharpening my instrument of seduction, "this is your freedom? Your little heart is so cruelly stifled that this narrow space really looks vast to you? Narrow it is, even if we can see a wide valley, a river, a distant mountain beyond. But we all have unbounded horizons in our senses, our minds, our spirits; and yet there's another freedom that isn't a mere escape from boredom and unhappiness, from the tyranny of other people and things, a freedom that will kill us, that will crush everything we care about or despise, before it rouses us again in another country, purified, under another sky, and takes the blood from our veins, before it abducts us...."

Damn, where on earth would it abduct us to? I had no idea why I had used that word a moment before.... Yes, I felt more ridiculous than ever. But then, I wasn't even sure that she was capable of understanding my lovely sentences. I recited and floundered. Maybe I wanted to stun her, or who knows, to arouse her admiration. I began again: "But there are places..."

"Where the soul can lose itself."

Her sudden, quiet reply, which though hardly original was ambiguous, only had the effect of heightening to the utmost my wicked anger and strange undirected agitation—either because she now seemed superior to the image I had created of her or better than my preconception, or because she truly seemed to be concealing an inevitable rejection. Good Lord, how else can I make it clear that despite all my airs, I really don't understand a thing about women?

"Because it's base, or if it is base!" I yelled, my voice strident

now. "A noble soul doesn't tremble, it confronts its own destruction if it must, to extricate itself from its own chains; it rejects
whatever deludes it and makes it cowardly, it doesn't make
concessions with its oppressor, with everyday vulgarity, with the
age-old prejudices, with moral sermons. And why destruction?
Yes, there's a deadly danger, but undoubtedly there's salvation
too. Those who want to live will live and triumph over all, and
those who perish so wish it; or those who must... those who lack
the strength of passion, do perish. ... But do you think this life
of yours, and mine if you will, is life? Is life giving up what
makes us smile, trembling before what isn't even frightening
except to those who tremble? Is it the soul's perennial contemplation of itself? Banging our heads against the bars of our own
prisons, tedium, torment? Is it other people's outrage, our shame
at our own reprehensible lethargy, our inner darkness? Ah, where,
what are the obstacles, the bars, the mountains that we imagine
shut us off from the horizon on every side and must be moved
with our own strength, and the rest of it, what are they if not the
figments and shadows of our own baseness, if not our very own
baseness?..."

Who knows how long I could have gone on: and all the while
I was thinking: there's a bit of sincerity, of truth in this vague
and ludicrous ranting, but the dimwit would never understand it.
Sitting beside me, she listened, watching my knees, her head
still bowed. But then she interrupted suddenly.

"What do you want from me?"

In my estimation, a stupid bourgeois question which nevertheless took me by surprise. "I... I? On the contrary, what do
you want from me: because you, your hair, your eyes, your sad-
ness, your mere presence in this town..."

"Forget it," she said, intuiting that my dim babbling concealed
some gallant impulse. "Anyway, I'm not really asking you, I'm
asking myself, just as maybe you weren't talking to only me
before. ... Look, you call it baseness. But is it base to tremble
at the very thing that gives the soul life, to try to save its secret

life, its illusions? I don't know. To ask yourself if you can break your chains without shackling an even heavier one to your foot, if breaking it might not itself be a new chain? To ask yourself if what you yearn for, if what will come after, is really better than what was before, really the best and the noblest and the most just thing? To mistrust giving up the most protective parts of ourselves for some unknown reward, or for nothing at all, giving it up in return for torment and mockery? It's not a question of confronting the destruction of one's own soul, unless that's just a way of putting it. And if the soul died! But it really never dies, it goes on dragging the weight of our crumbled dreams behind us, the inert ruins of our dreams and hopes, the wreck and rot of our outraged, derided feelings. Nothing can really kill it, nothing: exposing it to new disappointments and new shocks will only weigh it down, if they are on the mark, with some new, useless burden, sometimes an intolerable one, and debase it a little more; misfortune doesn't fortify the spirit, it only debases it. How can we blame the person who trembles? How can we blame him for wanting to see clearly his own destiny, which he is, or believes he is, master of, and for trying to secure an unglorified defeat for himself? This is not open ground, this is not an easy challenge where the just reward for defeat is death; it's not death that opposes life here—a life, in any case, that one merely hopes and dreams of deserving and redeeming after his victory: it's a long sordidness, an infinite ignominy. How can you blame those who don't want to battle with such inadequate weapons? Noble or base, they would always have good reason to hesitate: because though those things are less than death, they are worse. And that's also why . . . we can assume that whatever soothes us and keeps us distant from a struggle which doesn't even promise death must also possess some virtue that protects the best, yes, the most precious parts of us. . . . But you say victory is not uncertain, happiness is not uncertain. Ah, you can only believe that if you've never given up. . . ."

She stopped all at once, as though horrified that she had gone

on for so long and with such grandiloquence (if anyone had provided the example, it had been me myself). Among other things,
I had had the opportunity meanwhile to notice her strong local
accent.

Night had fallen, and like the air, her eyes had darkened though
at the same time they were burning in the pitch-darkness. She
was panting slightly, but more like a child who has been running
than somebody who was genuinely suffering.

6

But whatever was and is wicked in me still wanted to play its
part. Come now, what could have been afflicting that silly twit,
and in any case, why didn't she say it clearly? Precisely what
did her prolific subtleties hinge upon? Her speech was no less
vague or gratuitous than mine (it seemed to me). Maybe she
wanted to teach me a lesson: my reply, nevertheless (leaving aside
the fundamental absurdity, I mean the fact that I felt any need
to reply), could have only been as feeble and random as that of
an enraged woman who throws back in furious attack one, and
only the least relevant, of the words bandied about in an alter-
cation.

"Look," I said in a learned tone, "you speak of unknown or
nonexistent rewards: but couldn't it be that this is a soul's supreme
destiny, I mean abandoning itself without reward, or for the supreme reward of one's own abandonment: neither desire, nor the
hope of some other reward, belongs to the soul."

I considered myself a rather capable seducer. She shook her
head with a forced smile.

"But no, how could you say that!" she murmured weakly. "The
soul itself is nothing, I mean when it's alone and solitary: how
could one's own abandonment be sufficent reward? That's like
saying that having a clear conscience for a good deed is sufficent
reward for doing good. But such a reward is only a defense, it's
makeshift, even if our morals do sanction it. No, the soul needs
nourishment, and if it's abandoned, if nothing or no one embraces

it, it isn't nourished: it is devoured. By itself, the soul cannot even love, really love; it isn't love but the lack of love that causes it to languish and consume itself. Rather, you should say that abandonment is its wretched passion, the secret vice which despite everything it cannot give up."

Ah, this was too much: there was a moral too, and she even threw the verb "sanction" at me, the provincial fool! She wanted to outdo me, that was evident, though she didn't realize that we city intellectuals have the moral and all the rest of it right in our jacket pockets; so, now she would hear me out. But she continued, with a brief wave of her hand.

"You see, sometimes I try to reason things out, but I know myself how false reason is, even when it negates itself. But none of that matters; I really wanted to say... What are you doing here, in this city: why do I see you in the café every day, what are you trying to tell me with your looks? I understood very little of all your talk here this afternoon, except that somehow you're tormenting me, pursuing me. I know, in fact," she added decisively and almost coldly, "that you're getting ready to leave, that you're going soon, very soon: maybe tomorrow?"

Yes, this did outdo me, this sudden turn in the conversation which, in my conceited insipidness, I was utterly unprepared for. I couldn't even find a gallant line for my reply: and the truth is she wouldn't have listened anymore.

"I'm afraid," she went on, "of getting used to you... that I'm already used to you. So, why are you here? For business, studies, or what? And can one come, just like that, to a perfectly calm place without being invited and stay and do whatever he pleases? This town is surely not the same since you've been here. I don't know whether it's better or worse than before, and I don't care; but these old houses have become luminous, radiant, and the air is light and suspended... like in a dream. And I don't walk, I fly, floating; I breathe in the entire sky in one breath. And then I tremble too, tremble, whether it's noble or base; I fold myself up like a book and everything I see holds a threat: the facades

of the houses, though struck with sun, look colorless as though
a hurricane were imminent. I don't know if I should bless or
curse fate, so I'm blessing it. . . ."

That impassioned flow of words and what it had taken me so
long to understand dealt the final blow to my emotions, or at least
threw them out of balance momentarily. Suddenly tears came to
my eyes.

"My life," I babbled disconnectedly, "my life is a burden and
I . . ." Sobs clenched my throat.

She turned and brought her face up to mine, as if to scrutinize
me. There was no concern or compassion in her look, just a sort
of forgetful bliss. As for me, I remained there terrified, swallowing
back my tears. And then, she brought her lips to mine straight-
forwardly.

"Ah, you don't understand anything," she said afterward.

7

So that first ridiculous conversation ended in glory, full as it was
of abstractions and bombastic declamations, of evasion and floun-
dering. but mostly, of irrelevancies. Leaving myself (who should
have been the unmoving mover of everything) aside, what image
had she given me of herself? Undoubtedly, in the final analysis,
she must have gotten something out of that gobbledygook; but,
once again, who was the girl and what was she really looking for?
My God, it was useless to define who she was: she was no one,
she was all of them, and at the same time herself; she was a
woman. Of course, it was she herself who mattered. Who was
that self?

Or, to put it more clearly, why had I fallen in love with her?
Inherently, a question with no answer: on the other hand, it
certainly hadn't happened during our conversation. But regardless, this fact, which I could no longer fail to acknowledge, meant
absolutely nothing (I will come to that). I had fallen in love; but
as a result I hadn't stopped hating her, rather I hated her even
more: because she was woman, after all, because she was a

particular woman, because I had fallen in love with her and because I had fallen in love despite all my plans. But then again, no, something was still missing from the picture: I hated her especially and immediately because I'd been a victim of my own weakness in her presence. Oh, what had she taken my tears for, she who had been so delighted and who had deluded herself that not offering vulgar commiseration was sufficient recompense? No, my perverse will was not swayed from its design, if anything it exulted in it. Did I love her? But this was an unanticipated gift of fate, the utterly undreamed of and supreme crowning of my plan and of my whole life, in a certain sense! With one blow I would take my revenge on them, on her and on myself.

You can imagine the rest. I managed, I mean easily, to slowly bring our relationship to more intimate and carnal terms, but without going beyond a fixed point, which in any case coincided with the point at which she resisted. In fact, my plan required that the fatal revelation of my misfortune (which, as one will remember, was supposed to fatally shock the victim) come about solemnly in the course of a real tryst in a suitably private place: something like the first girl's unforgettable "confession." Certainly it was rather difficult to persuade her to agree to such a tryst.

I succeeded, however, with time. But, for obvious reasons, since I could not receive her in my hotel, I had to rent a house specially, furnish it like a love nest as best I could, and meanwhile justify my long stay in the town with some pretext. The civic library had the manuscripts of a celebrated, dead local poet, and while waiting, I actually began to examine them.

Finally everything was ready and the great day set. After having inflicted one last frenetic whirlwind on the suspended strand of spiderweb, I pinned it to the wall with a forceful burst of breath and left the hotel.

8

She was punctual. Although apprehensive and slightly sullen she had already made up her mind to everything, and all in all, she was happy (according to plan). She evidently felt required to act uneasy. I never found out whether she had any previous experiences of this kind.

It was raining and growing dark. Enthralled, we sat in silence watching the soaked countryside, then we drew the fake damask curtains and turned on the light, which I had wanted very bright. I was extremely careful not to lose my head in the usual preliminaries that followed; for as I said, the famous "confession" or revelation had to come about in a solemn manner, certainly not during an amorous scuffle, and to be well displayed. Thus, still in silence, we each began to undress ourselves on our own, a few feet apart. The bizarre and ill-defined feelings that assailed me were so intense and so conflicting that they were nearly painful, but they somehow merged into a single feeling of arrogance and desperation. Undoubtedly, that feverish exaltation one feels as he reaches a decisive moment, the event he has long awaited and from which he anticipates the greatest, the most dreadful satisfaction of his whole life, was a part of it. But it was also shame, first, a physical shame of my body itself, since I loved her; and besides that, a shame at what I was about to do because I did, but for other reasons too; and if that weren't enough, I also felt a sort of exhaustion or unexpected distress which made all my theatrics, my anxieties in general, my dramas and comedies, seem pointless and even pathetic with that rain, that twilight. . . . But my will wasn't broken—since I hated her too. And now as she pulled her dress over her head hesitantly, I observed her cruelly.

"Turn off the light," she said without looking at me.

Oh, no, not a chance: what would become of my effects, my real pleasure? I shook my head energetically, trying to assume a passionate expression, so that my refusal would seem the fruit of urgent desire. She didn't look straight at me, but she understood just the same. She made a little, sad gesture, or perhaps it was a lighthearted threat, and went on undressing without a word, turning away from me. Maybe she was enticed by my wanton ardor. A moment later, her long dazzling shoulders slipped out of her frothy underthings. She was naked now. I had also continued to undress, although more slowly. And finally I too stood naked, my leg shining.

The moment had come. But she still seemed to be poking around with something, and undoubtedly she was planning to slip between the bedclothes without turning around. No, I would have to make her turn around and face me. I called her name tenderly. She turned her head and neck, covering her breasts with her arms, and stared at me shyly with a soft, questioning gaze. But as I said nothing, she turned away again and bowed her head.

What! Just like that, and no more? I was perplexed, I was distraught. Even if she hadn't looked down, how could she not have noticed my leg, whose glint caught the eye in such a bright light? However, I couldn't be certain of anything, and in any case, she would not, she could not escape me, she could not cheat me out of . . . everything. I called her again.

"What is it?" she replied quietly, without turning at all.

"Come on, don't you understand," I said, not hiding my impatience, my excitement very well, "turn around, turn around will you? I want to see you, admire you, I want to . . ."

One of her shoulders gave a little nervous movement, a twitch, but she turned all the way around, looking me straight in the eye, seriously this time, without bothering to cover herself up. She was really quite beautiful, just a bit slight in the shoulders. She seemed to be waiting. She seemed to be everything but a woman offering herself to her lover's eyes.

"Damn fool!" I yelled, no longer taking the trouble to control my rage, "don't you see, don't you see? Ah, why are you acting like this?" I went on senselessly. "Why do you want to humiliate me, to take the little I have left, my last asset even if it is repulsive, even it it is horrendous?"

"What are you talking about?" she pronounced firmly, still

without lowering her eyes (they were actually glinting, as though full of repressed rage or challenge) or batting an eyelash, fueling my rage.

"What am I talking about! You don't see then, you don't see? Ah, this, this!" And I hit myself frantically on the leg, which made a hollow sound. How utterly ridiculous I was in my nudity, in my misfortune.

At last, she lowered her eyes fleetingly and went on looking me in the eye without saying a word and without betraying the slightest emotion. Panting, I looked at her. Several moments of nearly intolerable silence elapsed. What did this mean? I asked myself, my head spinning. Is she a perfect phony or what the hell is going on? And why on earth would she feign or conceal her feelings? Perhaps she had seen through my plan and wanted to undermine it, to be really wicked? But how could she have seen through it if she didn't know about me, or rather, about my leg? And if she didn't, then what to think? Anyway, her eyes were turning soft. Finally, she said:

"So what?"

"So what, you say, so what! You can say that? You can look at me, look at this without feeling stricken, broken up inside, my God, without feeling agony in your guts! You look like you've seen nothing. But is this nothing? How can this be nothing to you, or to anyone else for that matter? You must be numb—or are you hiding some diabolical plan beneath this indifference? You must hate me, or... or something, there's no other explanation. Or maybe you didn't get a good enough look yet, maybe you're not catching on, maybe you don't realize... Look, look! Do you see this? Look at it! Do you know what this, what this means for me, for you, for our love, if that's what it is, for everything? How can you not fall down struck—your heart, your soul, your hope, irrevocably struck? How can you ever recover after this? How can you not deny your own life now, deny providence, deny the heavens?..."

"Shut up! Why do you want to hurt yourself?" she interrupted quietly. She took me by the hand and led me over to the bed, just as we were, naked, and made me sit beside her. "No, no," I went on anyway, though suddenly almost calmed. "And I... you can't deny me this last right: to make you suffer, to suffer myself more than you, more than anyone in the world."

"So you've no intention of being quiet," she said. She pulled me toward her, made me rest my head against her shoulder and began smoothing my hair lightly, murmuring, "There's no other explanation, I heard you say just before? Yes, it's simple. I love you. Is that really news to you?"

I looked at her: she was smiling, tears in her eyes. And once again, I burst out crying in her presence, on her shoulder. But this time I didn't bother to swallow the tears or hold back the sobs, and I no longer felt the slightest shame. I even blurted: "But, no, it can't end like this, you have to at least tell me..."

"What do you want me to tell you? Let's hear it," she said cheerfully, between tears and laughter. "I can imagine what it is. Yes, then, I always knew."

"What... what did you know?"

"About this, what the hell else?"

"You... you..."

"We women, good sir, see everything. And then again, not even a guy like you can control everything or foresee every single eventuality. Sometimes, it only takes some trifle. If, say, you're sitting at the café enjoying the women parading by and you cross your legs, it's not so strange that your pants should finally hike up a little on one side. And you can't miss it, you know. It's so shiny and impressive. Besides, you can't delude yourself—you do have a very slight limp. So it was easy to put two and two together. Hey, why are you looking at me like that? It's not so terrible after all; no, no, it's fine; that I knew, I mean."

9

And thus the short affair would have ended. ... What, what do you mean ended, you protest? But the best part is missing here.

If not a moral, at least a resolution; or if not a resolution, some formal conclusion. Good Lord, you begin by stating that you hate women because you have a wooden leg (or whatever), and then it gradually comes out not only that you don't hate them at all, but that in fact you have no reason to hate them, indeed all the reason in the world to love them. What kind of game are you playing here? Or is it simply that you're making use of an easy narrative device or that you forgot to put the verbs in the past tense in the beginning? It seems too simple. Or maybe that's precisely what you wanted to show us by relating this little incident of yours, that this woman's love redeemed you from your shameful emotions, your malevolence toward yourself because of your misfortune, kept you from turning it into an accusation against others, and so on. But then say so outright, good man, and leave our hearts at peace. Although, to be honest, this also seems a little too easy. Or is there something else hidden in the convolutions of your not always limpid reasoning? Simply, you still owe us some explanation, that's obvious. And to begin with, you owe us some practical information, some sort of follow-up: you can't expect to leave us in the dark like this, right at the best moment of what seems to be a love scene....

Stop already. I married the girl, if that is what interests you. As for the rest, don't bother insisting, since I wouldn't know what to answer. In fact, I have often thought about it all. I mean the affair itself and not my story, and I've never come up with a clear sense of it. All of it is uncertain and contradictory, as they say of life itself (which I know so little about): precisely where does the accent fall or where is the most plausible shape of the matter to be found? I repeat, it really is a story which runs this way and that despite the particular direction it seems to take. Again like life, where nothing stands still and everything is random and seems to exist within its own margins or God knows what else, so that any interpretation must prove provisional and elusive, in other words, prove negative rather than positive, and even casual.

I don't mean by this that there is nothing to add. There is

always something to add, if it is done for the sake of discussion. At any rate, she was deluding herself. You pay not only for defeat but also for victory (according to her terms) with a long sordidness, not only for unhappiness but for happiness. Once I'd married her, for example, I began to wonder if the fact that she already knew about my leg could have in some way tainted the purity of her abandon and of our love in general; how beautiful and sublime it would have been, I thought, if she had been ignorant of everything at that point, and having no time to reflect, had reacted at the height of her feelings ... (yet, I admit the beauty of it lies precisely in the fact that she did have time to reflect). I thought about this, and the consequence of thoughts of that order is evident. I don't know what she herself thought, but I can well imagine. Anyway, this is just one example chosen from the least slanderous.

But perhaps I haven't been sufficiently clear. In any case, don't ask how it ended: everything ends badly. Even when the human creature rises above his sick nature and overcomes his instincts, his madness, his transience; even when he raises himself, establishing a reign of brotherly love, joy and freedom, and seemingly returns to his origins and accepts a contrary fate. And even when he joins the others who have been redeemed and ascends to the place he belongs, the home of the spirit—(rising to the occasion on a Pegasus or a nag burdened by eloquence) et cetera, et cetera—even then, everything ends badly, if only because wherever there's fuel there's fire.

BETWEEN
AUTOBIOGRAPHY
AND
INVENTION

PREFIGURATIONS:
PRATO

I (how many times have I written this damned pronoun?) was
a child who was brought before his dead mother at the age of one
and a half in the vain hope that her features would remain etched
in his mind, and who had said, "Leave her alone, she's sleeping."
This explains a lot of things (nearly everything) about my childhood, but certainly my situation in general. So, despite the efforts
of my father, who could never rest, and of other good people, one
in particular, the time came to put me in boarding school.

My father had various brochures, catalogs and pamphlets from
the most important schools in our country and all over Europe,
and he scrutinized this printed matter for quite a while; at last,
he decided in favor of the old, classical Cicognini, partly because
given the calamitous (and how many times have I had to write
this adjective?) times, foreign schools could not be seriously
considered.

We reached Prato early one evening in November, I think. It
was a biting autumn, and a foggy one, or so I remember it. As
we quickly crossed the city that first time, what struck me was
a statue of the carpenter Magnolfi (shown leaning on a long plane,
a corner of his apron caught on his belt), which I have never seen
or found again. We stayed in an old inn on the main piazza. The
next day began with a visit to the barber, under whose scissors

my hair fell to the floor, eliciting a certain emotion in my father, which I did not then understand: I still had my baby hair, I mean I wore it nearly to my ears. I don't remember how we spent the rest of the day. But then night came. . . .

I don't know how to describe the anxiety of that separation. Mine, because I was timid and pure as a virgin, a child whose characteristics were decidedly feminine, even physically speaking; and who harbored secret feelings, subtle and tormented sensibilities, though I had no anchor but him amid all that; his anxiety, which may have been even greater because he had to drive such a child out into a world he knew would be adverse. I remember, I will always remember, that last walk down the deserted school corridor leading to the front door, as he urged me to take heart and see the necessity of the separation (urging me and himself) and how I wept desperately, not wanting to listen to reason. Finally, in what might have been the most courageous act of his life, though he was probably aided by what he believed was his duty, he left, but only to run, I later learned, to speak to the principal about me—who I was and the care that had to be taken with me. This had the mere effect of eliciting astonishment and perplexed irritation in the latter, and understandably so. His only reply to all of that was that we had to have faith in the educators whom we ourselves have chosen, and that in any case, an overprotective attitude could be detrimental to the pupil. My father therefore started on his sad way home once again, while I, my arms still reaching out for his vanishing image, my heart torn, remained alone in the vast, or as the Russians say, the white world, the inhospitable and frozen region that is (or was before the changes in the regime) their world.

It was now a matter of getting to know and familiarizing oneself with the region as much as possible. But like a wanderer on the steppe, I was immediately frozen and paralyzed with horror. My companions were like all kids, neither good nor bad, neither warm nor overly adverse; they were only pathologically (or rather, physiologically) concerned with what was particular or exceptional in their companions, or deemed so by the majority. As is common, their social sense was quite developed in one way and quite deficient in another. This was enough to make me ill at ease among them, but I might have felt that it could be more or less overcome. However, what I found truly intolerable was their language. They talked continually of appalling and forbidden things which were unfamiliar to me. Or more precisely, they used terrible, unknown words to talk about them, words that nevertheless revealed some mysterious meaning; I mean they were loaded with a mysterious and abominable meaning; and they made me tremble. I said "more precisely" because I felt a sort of religious and superstitious love and terror of words back then (which stayed with me for a long time), and I fixed on them the whole weight of the meager reality which I was then discovering through various objects in the world; more simply put, words were practically my only reality. Therefore, I would have even been ready to close my eyes to the objects which my companions' words, I can't really say designated, but inferred or dragged behind them like mishaps, but not to the words themselves! And in the end, whatever reality added up to, couldn't those words evoke terrible things?

Indeed, they had a blissful orgy with them. They even started compiling a dictionary or glossary. I remember the voice of the editor. Five or six boys were gathered around a bench and one (I can remember his name) dictated: "Cucu: boyish language for: s——." And I will never forget the sly, bestial expression of pleasure which lit up his face as he pronounced this last word, which of course was among the most innocent and least disturbing. The strange thing too was that, aside from my horror of them, these words didn't hold the least attraction for me; at least that's how I see it now, though on this point, it's hard for me to put myself in that state of mind again. But to conclude: even that early on, I was formulating a plan to get myself out of there at whatever cost, as soon as the right moment came. Besides, I will leave it to you to imagine what kind of life I led among these companions of mine, in my ignorance of their concerns and my revulsion at their words. And to conclude in another way, I don't want to abandon this discussion without emphasizing that a man declines, grows vulgar, gross and obtuse, as or when his own religious sense of words declines. But nothing should be inferred from this, much less in favor of one aesthetic or another: I am only stating a fact which can be explained in various ways.

Meanwhile, other semblances, if not other realities, were taking shape around me. One evening, for example, as we were undressing in our room, I saw something turn red (I must put it this way to render the exact impression I had) between my neighbor's legs, a blond fellow. And yet, this companion of mine was remarkably different from me, certain withered parts of his body much different from mine! And undoubtedly, the way he used it must have been different too, or could I have put mine to the same unnameable, imprecise and certainly unimaginable uses too? I rejected that idea with dread and horror. In any case, even if words weren't losing their absolute meanings for me, they were beginning to lose their power in objects. I mean that those words were at least beginning to correspond with or to some definite objects.

But for me the main function, or perhaps I should say the parallel function of certain organs, aside from the obvious one, was, if not clear (in their nature), at least apparent (in their laws). Indeed, for the sake of explanation I will candidly confess something that might seem a monstrous anomaly and may actually be one—I noticed how thoughts of a given order provoked a given physiological movement in me. The fact is, anyway, that these thoughts weren't what one might think, weren't lewd but rather sad and sweet, and simply, deeply melancholy. More clearly: the movement came about especially if I thought of a dear dead person. Rather than add anything else, I will relinquish this, assuming there is any sense to it, to psychologists, psychoanalysts and those persons occupied in similar studies.

Since I never could get used to satisfying my natural needs in public or in the proximity of others, I waited until nighttime when everyone was asleep to slip out of my bed and withdraw to the most convenient or inconvenient place near the room. I should premise this by saying that one of the nicknames I had earned was "Buddhist" because I'd been excused from relgious functions in the school chapel. I should also add, by way of introduction, that our assistant housemaster, whose bed was sort of boxed in by a cloth curtain, came from Naples, or even farther down (in fact, at least back then, boys from Salerno or Avellino came to Prato for an education): a Tuscan, I mean, would have behaved differently in the following episode. So then, one night while I was waiting for the opportune moment to get up, this assistant poked his head out of his tent, made straight for the bathroom door and ostentatiously locked himself in, adding one of those little inarticulate grunts then in use among Southerners which meant: "Now get this and play along." Later, as this exemplary educator climbed back into his tent, a voice called from one of the beds, "Good Buddhist, aren't you going to go to the john anymore?" Why all this? Why were they doing me such an open injustice, making me feel as though I were on trial? And though I kept quiet, I felt only too certain that I was suspect, that everyone suspected me of something sinister and vile, though I could not begin to imagine exactly what.

That suspicion was verified, or nearly so, when I struck up a close friendship with a schoolmate (whose name I also remember), and naturally abandoned myself to it trustingly and openly. He was a rather sweet and understanding boy though vivacious and quite bold, and I liked him physically, in the sense that I have always liked, and still like, all my close friends and the people I love; and also in a sense which might be seen as somehow sexual, I don't deny that. But I don't know how this warm affection was interpreted then, or rather I know only too well now. And if the educators blew the whistle on me, here my father himself might have been fooled, for he gave me (or was it on another similar occasion?—during the most serious phase of the railroad strikes he practically lived in Florence, so as not to risk being separated from me for too long), he gave me a long and obscure lecture in which there was no straightforward reprimand though the final statement went like this: "When you grow up, you will know on your own what you can and cannot do." A lecture which, naturally, shook my innermost fibers. My God, him too! Aside from everything else, the general mistrust that surrounded my small being was so intense that it merely caused the radical sense of guilt that had accompanied me for most of my life to increase. Though I hadn't done anything wrong, I was guilty: but of what, after all, and what was I to conclude from this?

Meanwhile, the external life of boarding school went on, and good or bad, I had adapted to it; there was still something precarious and depressing about the school, which had been commandeered during the war, and the boarders had never entirely resumed their upper-class habits. The major events in such a life were occasional walks, soccer games in the park and the theater. But in this last regard, since the city didn't have great resources (as they say), it happened that we went to the same performances repeatedly. So, we went to hear *Aïda* two or three times, which is how *Aïda* must have infected me with that chronic illness which my male friends, not to mention my more patient girlfriends, know me for. One day they even took us to see a kind of huge seal, presented by an impresario with big hopes; the wretched animal (that I came to classify among the second order of deities) rolled about in a tank that was not terribly large, in the middle of an ordinary room. As far as my studies went, I cannot say that substantial readings nourished me (unlike my illustrious predecessor in the boarding school). On the other hand, following in his footsteps, I was writing something more or less on the order of an epic poem, something like a triumph of love, which regrettably I must have lost. At the conclusion, the triumph was physically and visually represented in the form of a kiss or embrace, exchanged, as the final caption informs, amid broken swords and myriad fragments. On the other hand, I encountered notable difficulty in the study of Latin (I won't even mention

mathematics), so much so that now and then my good cousin had
to send me her small, detailed translations of those simple texts;
on my own, I wouldn't have been able to ferret out any meaning.
I was utterly unable to acquire this language, and I was certainly
justified: Latin shouldn't be studied as a first language, at least
by people with any sense, but as a last one—leaving the parrots
free to do the opposite. Studying the violin was another problem
and annoyance. I can't imagine how I could have ever played
such an instrument, lacking as I do what they call a "good ear."
As far as natural gifts are concerned, alas, I can't say I had much
more than some general tendencies, and I was only able to ac-
complish anything through great labor and patience, slowly and
gradually adjusting my vision on distant sights, as it were, and
then painfully extricating some form from a nearly shapeless or
irrelevant tangle. That most supreme of gifts called facility was
practically unknown to me, and no road has ever been easy
for me.

But going back to the above-mentioned cousin, she once came
to see me, and by some exception was allowed to visit our room
and spend an hour with us, to take part in our lives. Naturally,
for me it was an hour, and then days and days afterward, of acute
suffering which was heightened by my companions' looks, for
although she wasn't beautiful, she was young.

I don't want to end this "homecoming" without remembering
the Bacchino, a little fountain by Tacca on a piazza in the city.
Aside from being a point of reference for our walks, it was always
the talk of the educators from Atripalda, who were inseparable
from their native soil; nor should I fail to recall the time some
hotheads caused an uproar, hurling stones under our windows
(the sons of gentlemen), while the Atripaldesi themselves yelled
up at us: "Get back, don't lean out."

Generally speaking, I made an exciting discovery toward the
end of my stay. Under the direction of the principal then in charge,
plaques with the names of all the boarding-school pupils since
its founding were hung along the vast corridors (they were to make

a special remembrance for the most illustrious among them, though what came of it I don't know); listed on one of them under the year seventeen hundred plus, I discovered the name of one Silvestro from my family, but I can't imagine which branch if his birthplace was Frattamaggiore. It wasn't much, I admit, but it was something.

And finally Christmas vacation came. Upon request, my father came to fetch me; that day too was damp and foggy. The first thing my father asked me was, "So, where would you like to go?" Naturally, I indicated our old house down in the village where my grandmother, whom I loved dearly, was living. He hesitated a moment: "Even if your grandmother isn't there anymore?" "That's impossible," I countered, my heart pounding. "But even if it were true," I answered, bursting into tears, "that's all the more reason to go." She had died over a month ago, but I had been spared the news until then.

The rest of the year passed somehow or other, and then I left Cicognini forever, as I had wished. Not that I went somewhere better. On the contrary, in the new school (I ran away, but that's another story) one might say that I fell from the frying pan into the fire, insofar as the things I've indicated here are concerned; and thus, of necessity, I too became a boor. Years later, when I saw and revisited parts of that first school, I had a vague feeling of desperate love, and the same pangs I had known in those days.

LITERARY PRIZE

Since his misanthropy and timidity were well-known, they blackmailed him. They said, or actually they wrote: "We have decided to award you the prize, only you must come to get it in person; otherwise..."

Well, it wasn't among the more significant prizes—around a million lire when all was said and done—but for him, given his situation, that was something; actually it was a good deal. So after all, what could he answer besides "Paris (or the farthest village in France anyway) is well worth the trip."

They made him an offer he couldn't refuse, which went contrary to the usual one: someone came to fetch him in a car and drove him to the place where the award would be presented. During the not-brief trip, he asked what was in store for him.

"Nothing special," his friend informed him: "they're all good, quiet people who simply want to get to know you and celebrate with you."

"Who are they?"

"Why they're officials, special guests, the reading public."

"Reading public... get to know me... celebrate: Oh, God, that's enough to make me run."

"No, no, calm down. You'll see, it'll be like a family gathering, yes, like a family, a reunion of us literati."

"That's even worse! And tell me: do I have to stand up and walk from the front rows to the judges' table to get the envelope with the check?"

"Uhm, I'm afraid that will be necessary."

"Then I'm not coming, and the hell with the million lire."

"Come on now: it will only take a second. Listen, calm down. We'll find a way to do it."

The award ceremony was supposed to take place the next day; but meanwhile, all those outstanding people were already there, assembled in the hotel reading room. A semicircle of people, half splayed out in spacious armchairs, waiting for me; their eyes were curious, intrinsically intelligent. Not surprisingly, it was like an exam.

"What do you think of ———'s last book?"

"I didn't read it."

"I understand, you don't want to jeopardize yourself."

And yet he really hadn't read the book in question: for a long time now, he couldn't have given a damn; in other words, he had given up on books and literature. Yet it must be said that he had sworn he would keep his mouth shut under the present circumstances, in any case; he had just come back refreshed from a long stay in the country where no one talked about anything, and where consequently he had lost his way with worthy, illluminating, literary, social words.

But they insisted covertly; they refuted some statement that appeared implicitly or explicitly in one of his works; they overlooked nothing in their attempts to call him into battle. And, in fact, it would have been strange for them to abandon their game now, this interrogation designed, yes, to embarrass him.

Then the young, supertrained historian leaped up: and he found himself in the midst of a heated debate (whose terminology was foreign to him). He heard himself replying, stammering, sometimes blurting things out, well aware the entire time of the inadequacy of his replies and prattle, the inadequacy of his damned, nearly vulgar manner of speaking, so halting and out of date. The other man was winning, he won, and when the torturous sitting came to an end, one of the judges with a chair at the university rated them thus: "Fine, good work: a ten in history for him [the questioner] and zero for ――― [himself]."

The literati's little games. Nevertheless he remained downcast, uncomfortable about what he had and had not said, and even more about the simple fact that he had said anything at all, quite contrary to his will and habit. A hot, enervating wind was blowing the pines in front of the hotel. . . . He realized he didn't even have a book with him; not that he wanted to read, heavens no, but to bring on sleep. He went off in search of his friend in one of the annexes (bungalows with stairs and ample balconies facing the sea) and tracked him down; his friend gave him a book, a depressing one—so much the better—adding, "Congratulations: you were brilliant tonight."

Brilliant? With a zero in history, hardly. That wasn't so serious after all, but . . . Zero in everything. Right.

The next day he found them at breakfast, amusing themselves by imagining (another game of the literati) who among them and their contemporaries, meaning writers, were good enough to be judged favorably by posterity.

"Two or three generations down the line, in fifty or a hundred years," one had said, "who will remain? Which of the works that please, excite or even outrage us today will still be considered valid, and which won't? Say we had to rescue ten books from time, from oblivion, let's see, who or how would we choose?"

"We all agree on the first four names," the man beside him at the table confided with an air of complicity and mystery, so that one could guess that among the four names were . . .

But he was thinking: Me, triumphant over time, me, surviving its fierce obliterations, among those who have contributed something to men? Me, who has never really had anything to say? Who far from triumphing over time has never even let it dominate me! And at the same time he was thinking, no less sincerely and disparagingly: Me, *among* the *first four*? Then there are three other writers who are my equals? Equal, at least in anxiety and desperation if not in their mastery of the art? So then, I'm not the only one, the only one who will be rescued from the weary, advancing mob? And he remembered that painter he'd offended by calling him "the greatest Italian painter" (he would have preferred to be called the greatest in Europe or in the world).

And then while the game continued, he thought: Ultimately what do they live for, what wonderful token? Perhaps desire, or a feeling of glory? Or perhaps some interest, some immediate pleasure, some sense of power? But what pleasure, assuming it were just one?... Literature: could there really be people who believed in literature, who invested it with a mission, with a message, with the power of consolation?

Yes, or so it seems. Let's take a closer look here: among these cordial, sensitive and basically kind people, there is the ambitious one, the strategist, the naive one, the suave one; one has the eyes of a woman (or a dog), another a pianist's hands, a third an athlete's biceps. And they all come together in this cult of a long-faded and long-impotent beauty?

He didn't know how to answer: he felt ensnared in an absurd plot; should he let himself go for a mere instant, he would fall prey to those same illusions and follies. But above all, he felt miserable and bored, felt an obscure malaise, an "age-old remorse."

And then came the award ceremony: to avoid putting his timid nature to too many arduous tests, they had him sit at the judges' table; all he had to do was extend his hand and the envelope with the million lire was his, his to hold against his heart. That was followed by the slight intoxication of mixed drinks, the accompanying effusive chatter and the (unsatisfied) urgent need for human communication, human assistance. At a certain point everyone retired; he was left alone with a woman named Aurora. She was a radiant woman but she had a dark gaze; in other words, she too had been violated by destiny, or so she thought. And she was the one who had to gather up his desperate longing for purity, simplicity, goodness: the longings of a drunkard. She, of all people, was the one who had to bear the assault of his ceaseless demands, his mad cries for help (yes, again) in the serious business of living. But let it be known, it was an assault against which she skillfully defended herself the only way she could: by pitting anxiety against anxiety, uncertainty against uncertainty, longing against longing.

Then, at last, the wind fell and sleep overtook the mists of drunkenness or rather saturated them; but in the quiet room, in the uncertain dawn, the time had come for a brief and futile examination of his conscience—whose conclusions it would be difficult to put down.

What did he think of those men, after all? Nothing that he allowed himself to think; only that they were incomprehensible, alien and remote to him. They took the essayist's ideas and theories seriously, took that novelist's amiable fantasies and that poet's severe rhythmical judgments to heart and just about fed on them. The more he became aware of his own abjection, his reprehensible despair, his inexplicable lack of faith, the more he envied them.

But despite his envy, he fell asleep; that is to say, he had reason to assume that the test of sleep and morning would prove his sentiments to be transient, occasional.

But, in the morning, he continued with the same sort of self-examination and anguish—who knows what twist or deformity of his internal springs was to blame? A raging, red sun lit the wild pines of the beach, the low-lying treetops, and as it sunk gently into the sea's depths, the water turned blue and changed hue. Meanwhile, those people left in their shiny cars, each to his own precise destination, a center of industrious life, some freely accepted activity—not a life willed to be void of reward or new stimuli. . . . And as for him?

Ah, yes, he would run there, put his whole literary prize in stacks of chips on number seventeen, and wait for that to bring some sort of solution (since there was no hope elsewhere)!

(Naturally, number seventeen didn't come up; the number alongside it, the stupid twenty-five came up, mischievous as a monkey. It's always the next number that comes up, it always almost seems . . . or seems. . . . And in the final analysis . . .)

THE GRACE OF GOD

I am writing from Venice, and anyone writing from Venice has things to say, especially now with the Biennale, the art shows, the conventions, the outdoor theaters and the rest of it. Not to mention the fact that Venice is, as they say, a dimension of the soul, so that one who habitually has a pen in hand must come to terms with it sooner or later.

And yet whether it is my mood or my shortcoming, this time I am inclined to leave the illumination of its official, spectacular, and general characteristics to others better qualified than I, and for my part, to seize upon a small experience that I witnessed in my aimless wanderings. This way, at least I will gain the praise of those who appreciate "candid shots of life." Thus, the reader is forewarned: don't look for anything but what I've promised in these pages. And to begin with, be prepared to hear about two somehow remarkable fellows whom I chanced to meet in these last few days.

At the top of the steps of the cathedral of San Marco, on the interior threshold, an imposing and rather ferocious character stands erect, taking a step now and then, dressed in eighteenth-century garb (that is, something like the doormen at the great houses of old or at some modern-day hotels), all in black, with a cane crowned by a brass ball and whatever else is required to instill people's respect. Fine, leaving him where he stands for a moment (we will come back to him soon), let's move on to any street of this regal city. Here the sweet speech of the place does not soothe our ears, but bristly Northern tongues rend them, and when we look around, all we see are hairy, knobby limbs, and arms and breasts that look like mortadella; or, considering the clothing rather than what it clothes, we see leather trousers poorly suspended by elastic waistbands, cotton dresses cut away broadly at the neck, and so on. And then the whole herd (which is actually made up of graceless foreigners, to whom the haughty Venetian people are obliged to pay their respects), the whole herd bawls, shouts, drags its big feet and huge shoes under a sun that cracks the pavement, pawing the guides, stopping in front of every knick-knack shop to expound on the displayed objects, and makes its way toward San Marco and the above-mentioned custodian, whose function must now be clarified.

Standing in the atrium of the church is one of these bare-armed women, at whom the man wearing black and a scowl points his index finger, as in many illustrious paintings we see the eternal father pointing at our ancient mother; and as if she were suddenly overcome with shame at her nudity, so her distant daughter is now ashamed of her exposed arms and stares in dismay at her accuser. The fact is that the Man of the house, that is, the eternal father, doesn't seem to appreciate female nudity, not even partial; or even, if we must guess, he seems to have become disgusted by his own creation after so long. Briefly, as the custodian of modesty orders, the female visitor understands that like Cincinnato, she must either cover her body or give up the visit with all the indulgences and charms it entails. And now two possibilities present themselves. Let us consider the first, that is, that the female visitor is accompanied by one of those men in leather trousers, yes, but who is fortunately equipped with a jacket. In that case, the Cerberus, giving in with a certain condescension, will advise the latter to surrender his jacket to the former, and satisfied, will finally let both of them proceed, the woman wrapped

in the masculine garment, the man almost naked as a worm, as
he is now left wearing nothing more than one of those so-called
tee shirts (aside from the infamous trousers) and either a Baedeker
or a camera, depending on his type: yet, nothing will be said
about this forced exhibition of calves, biceps, triceps and body
hair.

But what if the woman is alone, you ask, or if the companion
has no jacket to call his own? Ah, how you underestimate our
Beloved Italy's resources with such a question! Because, as Italian
as that person who measures centimeters of nude flesh is, the
humble creature I am now about to introduce, who sums up all
the industriousness (and likewise the moderation) of the race, is
equally Italian.

In the darkest corner of the atrium a sinister, little one-eyed
man stands with some rags, whose function is not immediately
clear, hanging off his arm. Looking again, one can see that they
are nothing more than that transparent material called "plastic,"
from which some raincoats are made, sewn together into sleeves:
these sleeves are tied into pairs with a ribbon that crosses the
shoulder so that they don't slip off the arms, and as you may have
already guessed, the little man rents them for a modest price to
the female visitors who have no other way to cover themselves.
Thus, finding a solution to the evil, everything would take its
course, as it always does among us, if the little man didn't suffer
a pathological timidity which prevented him from explaining himself openly to the foreigners in need of help, before whom, after
having taken a half step forward and babbled something incomprehensible, he can only wave his rags about. They go off, without
having understood a thing, and he withdraws into himself even
more.

But luckily, destiny has taken to heart this woman I have been
walking beside and observing, and with kind words, exhortations
and urgings, persuaded the little man to be more straightforward.
So that shortly after, we witness the following scene, described
here for the sake of exemplification.

An aged woman steps inside, and so to speak, stands facing the usual pointed finger. Far from being disconcerted or disgraced, however, she looks around with a vague air of triumph; the fact is, as my own companion notes with feminine acumen, it must please her to be judged provocative, or at least still womanly at her age (as true as it is that such foolish moralism always elicits an opposite effect). This is the little man's moment: in fact, nearly thrust forward by his good angel, he advances and blurts, "Fifty lire." The woman visitor doesn't understand, then understands, smiles and with the help of the little man puts on the sleeves, which are just long enough to satisfy the Cerberus's demands (and it matters little if they are transparent). He approves, and the woman visitor finally enters the church.

In that way, thanks to two rags, everyone is satisfied: the dark custodian is satisfied, the woman visitor twice satisfied, we who have been observing are satisfied, our Lord is satisfied, but above all, the little man is satisfied that now he will be able to bring a lovely nest egg to his wife, and his one eye is finally laughing.

When I took the train to come up here, there was only one other person in my compartment, but he counted for four, such was his presence, his seriousness and I am tempted to say his stateliness. Slightly bald, broad across the forehead and face, a little portly, a goiter bulging slightly (though he was somewhat pasty and oily-skinned), he looked out the window with a calm and knowing gaze, waiting for the train to move. When this moment came, he crossed himself, not in a furtive manner nor in an obvious one, but modestly, and yet consciously and confidently. Then he took down his one piece of luggage, a black leather bag which was rather stuffed, and pulled out three volumes which he placed before himself on the drop-leaf table. Meanwhile, moved by this ancient and pious gesture (our elderly always make the sign of the cross before undertaking a journey), I began imagining who this man might have been; and I had almost concluded that he must have been a professor at the University in

Perugia, I don't know why, and that therefore he would be getting
off at Terontola. But instead, he came all the way to Venice, et
ultra, as we will see.

Now he turns two of the volumes so that he can rest the third
against them; he opens the third and leafs through to the desired
place; from his pocket he pulls an eyeglass case, and from there
not only the glasses themselves but also a little yellow rag with
which he polishes calmly while watching the landscape; and at
last, he throws himself into his reading without further ado. I can
only wonder at the back of the book which he has unwittingly
turned toward me. There I read two titles of this kind: *The Heart
of Jesus in the Light of the Centuries* and *Mary, Virgin and Mother
in the Glory of the Heavens.*

My companion does not lift his eyes from this reading, more
or less until Florence. Here, while I supply myself anxiously with
an abundance of provisions and drinks, he makes a wide gesture
to call over a simple hawker and orders a single sandwich for
himself from that humble basket; he begins to chew this slowly
and solemnly, but not without giving me a slightly severe look,
as if to say that frugality becomes the wise. Having finished eating,
he immerses himself in his reading once again, while two sentiments war in my spirit. The first, natural, right and proper, and
I mean admiration; the second rather less clear and honorable.
I must truthfully confess that the sight of such types awakens
dormant fancies in me, and even a kind of glee; to put it plainly,
I have an impulse to take apart those heads to see what is inside.
But how to remove that mass, or simply strike up a conversation
with so much man? And then before I realized it, we had arrived
in Venice: he vanished down the Lista di Spagna, and I gave it
no more thought.

But once again destiny favored me. Tonight I found my man
again, at the casino. Towering over a roulette table, he was playing
a moderate and methodical game, with his usual decorous gestures. When I arrived, he was whispering something about the
"little orphans" (which, it must be said, are a series of numbers)

to the croupier, who was sitting beside him. He even looked at me without the slightest sign of recognition. Sitting at the same table, I was able to observe him the whole evening: every now and then, he jotted something in a notebook, and in general, his game continued with mixed luck. And we went on like this, up until two in the morning.

Suddenly when the employees had already announced the last three plays, that bulk of his seemed overcome by a sort of shudder, by a shiver, and his voice rose imperiously. He glanced at his notebook: "Wait a minute," he yelled at the croupier, who was on the verge of spinning the ball, "wait a minute: the thirty-two! I want to move to thirty-two." He was nearly babbling in his excitement, and all the while he kept on pulling an incredible number of ten-thousand-lire notes from his pants pockets, his vest, his jacket (and I suspect from the lining), which he pushed toward the employee for change. Then, he grabbed the handfuls of chips, and half standing, knocking down those beside him, sweating, muttering, he asked: "What is the maximum at this table? Can I put twenty thousand down on a single number?" He arranged huge stacks of chips on number thirty-two and around it, as well as on the simple corresponding combinations. With this spread completed, placed in various patterns, no less than a million was played. Then he sat down again, dried his perspiring brow and murmured to the bouleur: "I'm finished, go ahead now," and the bouleur spun the little ball.

Now he is not looking at anyone; I, however, am looking at him, and I feel, it's hard to explain, as if something is missing in all this. Or better still, as if I'm waiting for something, which, in fact, occurs not a moment later: as soon as the ball is released, the good man, who has now assumed all his seriousness once again, makes the holy sign of the cross.

A half-dozen wandering players stop at our table to witness the outcome of the play. The ball spins dizzyingly at first, then slows, collides, falls.

And yes, it lands precisely on thirty-two, and thus my friend pulls in a fair sum of millions (which he stuffs into his pockets with the usual calm)—all of which was to be expected. But then again: haven't you ever become fixated on a question that nobody can answer? That's what happened to me tonight. The thirty-two came up all right, but the question I keep on asking myself is why? In other words, to put the question in simpler terms: what did destiny (you can even call it providence if you wish) mean to reward, my friend's devotion or his mischief?

PRIZE
IN SPITE OF

Michele is a painter and a gambler besides. Two activities
without any connection, even if he were a good painter, for the
simple reason that the second connects with nothing, and makes
all else useless. To put it more plainly, Michele is a wretch who
barely hangs on. Now, one day as he was lamenting his condition
to a friend, the latter said:

"What do you need, cash? Nothing could be simpler. Just apply,
and in a couple of months, you'll be set."

Explanations followed. The application was to be presented to
some solemn assembly, perhaps to the chairman of a committee,
and considering it a lot of wasted effort, Michele wanted no part
of it. But his friend promised to guarantee everything, and Michele
had to consider the fact that he was the nephew of one of the
ministers in charge.

"They do have funds for this, for artists," his friend added,
"though some people—some fools!—don't know about it. Come
on, no excuses, I'll help you with the application, and I'll submit
it for you myself since I have to go to Rome. You'll see, within
a couple of months..."

Years passed and one fine day Michele got a letter from an
undersecretary, who informed him in a dry tone appropriate to
his station that a prize of two hundred thousand Italian lire was

to be awarded (or perhaps "conceded" to him), specifying that
such a sum would be signed over to him as soon as . . . and here
a sibylline sentence followed, whereupon it was revealed that his
case had yet to pass through various offices.

As impoverished as Michele was, his first impulse was to tell
the undersecretary to keep the money for his own personal use.
Nevertheless, he restrained himself, thinking that the money was
basically his anyway, as a taxpayer, and represented the resti-
tution of some minimal portion of what the government stole from
him daily, and above all, thinking that at the moment he could
damn well use it. His sole pleasure was in not responding to the
undersecretary at all. The payment voucher arrived anyway, oddly
enough, without delay. But other troubles began.

Naturally, the voucher was from an agency in Rome, while
Michele happily lived in a city very far from the capital. It was
inconvenient to go all the way down there. It was impossible to
collect it from any old bank because government agencies and
commissions were involved; and finally, taking the advice of people in the party, his only alternative was to send a registered
letter requesting a particular government agency to authorize another agency—likewise governmental—to transmit a certain document to a third office, upon which . . . and naturally, this registered
letter had to contain an obsequious salutation.

Understandably, in the course of the red tape and the waiting,
Michele's irritation only increased. Yet, between one letter and
the next, the Roman clerks somehow got around to his case, and
he was finally notified that the money was at his disposal at such
and such a city bank. But there, at any rate, only one hundred
ninety-four thousand of the two hundred thousand lire were signed
over for his benefit, the remainder representing who knows what
deduction, duty or other tax. An obviously fictitious operation (a
naive person might think it would have been easier to give him
an award of one hundred and ninety-four thousand lire, and call
it quits) but actually, if one looks hard at the dizzying succession
of taxes upon taxes, it was not an absolute loss for the state.

Michele took the small amount, but he was at the end of his rope; as soon as he left the bank, he headed for the casino with the idea of gambling all of it away, almost as an affront. But an affront to whom, after all, the greedy government bureaucracy? To himself, actually. So much the worse, then! Nevertheless, he thought it over on the way, remembering that his wife, who was shut up in the house, had been asking him for money (she even had debts, the poor woman) so he began considering the best way to divide the money. After calculating and hesitating, he finally adopted this as the best distribution: ninety thousand for his wife, one hundred thousand for him, that is to say, for the game; and four thousand for little expenses. He thus sent off his wife's portion and kept his own one hundred thousand net.

Except that now there were some technical considerations. Indeed, to gamble it all in a single sitting meant giving up any chance of a return match in the unpleasant but very probable event that luck turned against him: wouldn't it be better, and wasn't it a good ground rule anyway, to divide the capital into two nearly equal parts in order to give himself a greater margin and to appeal to luck itself, or at worst, to prolong his amusement or delay the final outcome of his match until the next day? Certainly, given the utter scarcity of the cash, but where could he hide away the rest for the return match? It would be useless to bring it home, since it would be too easy to rush there in a taxi to get it; he would really have to send it away somewhere neither too near nor too far. Michele singled out such a place in a town a couple of hours away by bus and wired the fifty thousand lire in his own name.

That was that. Now he could go to the casino calmly and lose the first fifty thousand in two rounds. Michele did this without further delay. But, when he consulted his watch upon leaving, he saw that it was still early. That is, it was still possible to reach the safekeeping (or saving) city via the post office, which was still open, retrieve the money he'd sent earlier and go into action

again. It's futile to point out that a single play could render all
his plans and considerations useless. And even as he was cursing
himself for not having chosen a farther city, Michele hurried to
the bus station and set out.

The small post office was indeed still open and had received
the wired money order, but unfortunately the cashier was already
closed; furthermore, he couldn't move those diligent clerks to
take pity on him. They could, however, send the money order
back to the office it had come from, where it could be retrieved
the following morning. And so, the money remained while Michele
started back home. The only consolation, he thought, was that
the affair was proceeding according to his original plan, if not
through his willfulness, then through the circumstances themselves, and this was a good omen. Tomorrow is another day, he
told himself, maybe tomorrow. . . .

The next morning, in fact, he found the money order at the
post office in his city. This clerk made it clear that he understood
precious little of all these transactions, but how could the wretched
little man have understood? Michele snatched up the money and
without wasting a second, holed up in the gambling den again.

Once inside, he lost first forty thousand of that second and last
fifty thousand. Left now with a widowed token of ten thousand,
he hoped at least to make it last as long as possible, and he began
to play cheaply, five hundred lire at a time. Thus the ten thousand
lire shrunk to five thousand. There weren't many choices left,
when suddenly Michele heard a little, frail voice saying, "Eleven!"

The little voice had spoken so distinctly, apparently from behind his back, that he turned around, astonished, and asked,
"What is it?" A young man standing behind him, blushing, blurted
out, "I'm sorry, it's not my fault, they're pushing." Perhaps he
was apologizing for shoving him. And then Michele realized that
the voice wasn't coming from outside him but from within; and
he placed fifteen hundred lire of the surviving five thousand,
three little white chips, on number eleven. It occurred to him
immediately afterward that there was no reason on earth that an

eleven should come up, but he left it there and waited. After a couple of seconds, the employee called out, "Onze."

A good take for someone down to the last of his small change. But how should he proceed now? Hold the position, for sure, but shouldn't he add to it? At this point, a voice called out again: "Eleven." Michele doubled his play, and eleven came up again.

To make it short, before nightfall he had won three million eight hundred thousand lire. He quit playing, went out into the open air, drank a lemon soda in a bar and sat down on a bench to reflect (he was reminded of "The Queen of Spades" and its hero).

He was not celebrating his triumph over fate this time, but rather the trick he had played on the government authorities. Yet trick isn't the word. It was pure and simple spite. (One can argue that the windfall had affected his mind a bit.) Ha, you give a man like me, a gambler to boot, two hundred thousand lire? Like it or not, honorable sirs, you awarded me this prize of four million, or "conceded" it to spite yourselves. How does that strike you, sirs, doesn't it make you angry? Ah, well, at this point all you can do is yell at each other.

But let's leave the government authorities and their damn stinginess aside. The fact remains that I can figure on having won a prize of four million lire. There's no point in thinking of the before and the after, or of how things might go later. This is how they stand right now, and one must start from here.

Thus, I have received a prize of four million lire; unpredictable, inconceivable and as foreign or, one might say, superfluous to my budget as it may be. And now, what should I do with it?

Obviously: I'll play it.

And once again, he climbed those stairs he loved and despised, although it's not my place to say how things ended. I won't entice the reader's curiosity like that.

LOVE
AND
NOTHINGNESS

RAIN

Usually, as soon as my wife wakes up, she goes to the bathroom to brush her teeth. It's only when she comes back, still glassy-eyed, that she utters her first judgments on the situation or on life in general, or else she digs something up. And that's what happened today. Except that, today, she came out with this extraordinary statement:

"Our carriage was drawn by a spider, wasn't it?"

Now, let's get things straight. I'm accustomed to my wife's occasional eccentricities, but the fact is that my beloved wife never went this far before. Therefore, it was best for me to play the fool like the husbands in farces of the good old days, and exclaim:

"Huh? What the devil are you saying?"

"I'm asking you," she replied without batting an eyelash, "I'm simply asking you if our carriage was drawn by a spider. What's wrong, can't you hear, or have you become a square?"

"A square? What does that have to do with it? But, who'd understand you? Your question just might seem strange, you know."

"Strange, why?"

"Why, why . . . where have you ever seen that, a carriage drawn by a spider?"

"In dreams, obviously."

"Ah, all right, in dreams; and how am I supposed to know or tell you the exact details of your personal dream?"

"You don't love me."

"What are you talking about! I adore you."

"You don't one bit, and that adjective is all the bitter evidence I need. 'Personal dream!' If you really loved me, we would share all our dreams; everything between us should be shared and mutual. Ah, it's easy for you. I dream of us going for a ride in a spider-drawn carriage, and you know nothing of it and wash your hands of the whole thing?"

"I see your point."

"Thank goodness."

"But what do I know if . . ."

"Perfect, excellent, I could have bet you would use that hateful expression! 'What do I know?' By the way, can't you try not to use such common expressions, and speak more correctly? But anyway, what language do I have to tell you in; if you really loved me, you would have the same dreams I do without any effort at all."

"Ah, hold on. It's reciprocal."

"Reciprocal, what kind of trick is this? Tell me, darling, do you really think you can enchant me with your difficult terminology?"

"No, listen. Do you love me?"

"Of course I do, unfortunately."

"Then why is it that you don't have my dreams, or if anything, have no dreams at all (which is exactly what happened to me last night)?"

"What rubbish! You're admitting yourself that you didn't have any dreams, and you actually believe that I should conform to your nothingness? That's enough talk! But, let me tell you something. We were actually fleeing in the spider-drawn carriage from a young man who was courting me. And let me tell you, he was gorgeous, and I must say, I wasn't entirely indifferent to his attention. When I saw him, with those sad, intense eyes and I felt his silent yet overwhelming plea for love, I felt a sort of longing in my heart. . . . So watch it!"

"Oh, really, a gorgeous young man? Was he fair or dark, wearing velvet or satin? And you felt . . . ?"

"You think it's a joke, my dear fellow? Don't you know that even dreams, or rather, only dreams are dangerous? . . . In fact, I want some proof from you."

"In other words?"

"Describe and explain this dream to me."

"Which I didn't have."

"Which you didn't have but which it is your basic duty to have, and in any case, you are obliged to know point by point. Otherwise, it will mean you don't love me."

"I get it."

"Finally; so go on, begin."

"Well, to begin with we had a tiff."

"Exactly, but about what? Let's see if you know."

"About my observations on the household expenses."

"Yes, yes, that's right. You expect me to perform miracles, but if everything keeps going up, if the prices rise from one day to the next, while your salary stays the same . . ."

"Quiet. And so, after we argued, we went out together, it was twilight. No, wait a minute: dawn."

"Yes, dawn. Everything had a strange glow, the sky was clear and empty; that's right, it *was* dawn, but what a joy to hear you say it."

"Let's keep going. We were still cross, and we were both looking away, and suddenly the young man appeared before us."

"The young man."

"Who began to stare and lurch at you eagerly."

"What do you mean lurch?"

"It seemed that at any moment he might hurl himself at you,

with those staring eyes of his, and he only seemed really substantial at those moments. And then he faded back in the distance."

"Oh, my God, perfect; yes, I like you better now."

"Eh, you know, I do understand some things. So, as I was
saying, he kept looking at you like that and I was very embarrassed
even though I realized that such an elusive guy had nothing to
do with me. When..."

"When what?..." My wife, on the edge of her seat, urged
me on.

But the truth was that I didn't know how to continue or what
else to invent before the spider-drawn carriage arrived; that it
would pull up without further mishap seemed too simple, too
elementary for my wife's character. Therefore I tried to stall.

"Let's take a quick break, for God's sake. We could stand to
clarify a few points. For example, you pompously call this thing
that's about to appear a carriage, just like that, and yet, on second
thought, it seems more like a common coach, a rented coach to
me, huh?"

I was really trying to penetrate the nature of her fantasies and
at the same time to go along with her. Except that she was
implacable.

"If you say so. Go on, don't get lost in trifles."

Now what? Now, unforgivably, I grabbed hold of an external
detail. It was raining out. I risked it.

"Well, in the meantime it had started to rain."

But now, damnation, she suddenly got angry, and pointing her
index finger, said coldly:

"No, really no! Save your other leaps of the imagination; no,
it wasn't raining, not at all. You're good at tricking a poor woman!
It's lucky that I've got a head on my shoulders. It wasn't raining,
my dear flatterer, my dear wicked seducer. And now I'll tell you
how you managed to be on target up to this point. You must have
some secret, diabolical ability to read minds since, when I thought

intensely about my dream, let's say, you intercepted something. But at the critical moment, when you really had to explain it and point out the significance of the various symbols, you gave yourself away. . . . Your mysterious and amateurish powers aren't good enough, your kind willingness to please the weaker sex isn't good enough: feeling, deep feeling is required, love! Do you take me for a little girl? Listen to this: it was raining! I would just like to know how you came up with rain. Raining in a dream! Have you ever heard of that? It rains in your damn world, it's raining now, but not in dreams. And I have to conclude from all this, I must conclude, as much as it hurts me, that you don't love me, like I said, that your chatter is meaningless. . . . Oh, wretched me, what a terrible mess I'm in, snared (isn't that how you literary types talk and write?).

"Come on, calm down. Maybe it wasn't raining, I might have been wrong."

"'Maybe, wrong.' But that's just the point! How could you have been wrong, if . . . ? You shouldn't have let yourself be wrong, or you should've not let yourself be wrong, if . . ."

"Don't you think it's complicated, don't you think it's ultimately irrational to demand . . . ?"

"I was waiting, I just knew you would come up with irrationality! All of you think you can resolve everything, not only with reason (that still wouldn't hold water), but with rational classifications: this thing is rational, that other thing isn't. . . . How dare you be so presumptuous!"

"Look, darling."

"Darling nothing, and there's nothing to look at! But I'm telling you again, watch out—I may end up going back to him tonight."

"Him who, you little fool?"

"To him, the young man. Don't say I didn't tell you."

And with that she burst into tears; she flung her arms around my neck, and sobbed and moaned. Staring out the window, she murmured over and over: "It's raining, raining mercilessly. The sky is all closed up, it's raining. . . . But only here, not there, for the love of God. You're mean, you shouldn't have done this to me."

A bit of hysteria, clearly, and with two teeny children! And yet nobody can convince me that when you get right down to it, she might be right. In fact, if you love someone, why on earth shouldn't you dream the same thing at the same time? Or, to put it less absurdly, why the perennial discord of our moods and feelings?

THE ECLIPSE

Complicated influences were at work in Giovanna, and although somewhat sophisticated, she was basically silly. But then again, no: it's hardly possible to explain away a human being so swiftly! Giovanna was subject to outbursts or phases (which were more unpredictable than periodic), or more precisely, to cloudings of her intelligence; though it remains to be seen whether they revealed her true nature, or were simply accidental, or even incidental. This question, one might add, was of no interest to her friends. Small, lean and pale, a dull blond, she was homely though not unpleasant-looking; but perhaps Enrico was the only one who glimpsed something more unusual in her.

The sun was flooding the Lungarni and a stinging wind chilled the air the day that Enrico met a certain friend of his—a German art critic, a stout, nearly bald bull of a man who seemed to understand nothing (starting with the Italian language) but who understood everything underneath it all, at least literally speaking. They walked, they discussed this and that, but then they ran out of things to do; the afternoon seemed empty and disquieting to Enrico, and perhaps to his companion too. And then the above-mentioned Giovanna popped up from somewhere or other: Enrico invited her to join them, inspired by the warmth she had shown him on other occasions. But nothing much hap-

pened. Finally someone mentioned that there would be a partial
eclipse of the sun that day, and one of the two men suggested
they go up to watch it from the critic's house in the hills. The
girl agreed and they started out.

His hillside studio was a spacious, comfortable room with picture windows that looked out on the large cupola; he served the
most delicate tea. But they soon found themselves in the same
situation as before. Nobody said a word in anticipation of the
eclipse. Enrico looked at Giovanna doubtfully. He liked her after
all, in his way, but was he intrigued by her? Yes and no; well,
a little. Mainly, he was looking at her head, for, in fact, the one
unusual thing about the girl was her hair, that is, the braids
wrapped in double circles around her head; and it was said when
loosened, her hair reached the floor.

"Hey, Giovanna, is it true that your hair... ?"

"Yes," she answered modestly. "All the way to the floor."

"No kidding? Would you show us?"

"Why not?"

"Go on, then."

Without another word, the girl began undoing her braids. But
Enrico, whose aesthetic sense was already titillated by the ancient, exotic image of a young girl with tresses to the floor, was
not content with this.

"Listen," he said, "I hope what I'm going to ask doesn't upset
you, but it would really be a spectacular sight if you..." He
didn't know quite how to express his thought, since he didn't
know if she was in an intelligent or obtuse phase. But she must
have caught on immediately, because she gave him a dismayed
look; nevertheless, she asked:

"If I what?"

"Umm..." Enrico floundered. "I mean, you would have to
take all your clothes off. It's hard to imagine a river, a waterfall
of golden hair over the kind of clothes we wear today."

It wasn't really gold, but that didn't matter. ... Yes, that would
complete the image: the girl completely naked, protectively

wrapped in hair (perhaps he had a mental image of flowing locks).

The girl fixed her eyes on him with a bizarre expression, which Enrico thought betrayed quite a bit more than an incidental warmth; meanwhile the big critic, delighted, excited by such a fantasy, came to his aid, uttering little phrases like:

"Why, yes, there's nothing, shall we say, wrong with it."

Giovanna looked away from Enrico and gazed at the other man with something like condescension and finally said quite simply: "All right."

She stood up. They pointed to a room, and she vanished. Enrico decided that she was in one of her brighter moments after all.

After several seconds she reappeared; her hair, baby fine, abundant beyond imagination, seemed to have proliferated in its freedom and waving down, it actually touched the floor. It clothed her completely, chastely, fiercely surpassing the lewd fantasies that the two men, as it happened, had entertained. Marvelous. But now that the first thrill was over, now that they had paid all the compliments, what could they say or do?

"Look," said the critic, "it's starting."

The eclipse was beginning. The sun, which could be watched through small pieces of glass blackened with a match, was already gnawed by shadow; and the vivid light in the room, though not obviously dimming, began to glitter and turn silver, losing stability, definition and confidence. Whereupon an utterly new spell was cast, not of the senses but of the imagination, a kind of diffuse uncertainty, as though another world were pushing up from beyond or from beneath the fragile fabric of diurnal gaiety that remained.

The three looked at one another, somewhat stunned. The shadow continued to gnaw at the solar disk, which now looked like a cookie that a child has nibbled at and thrown down on the ground, a fat crescent. The vague premonition had become an impending threat, the light now really weak. And though slight, an insinuating, subtle presence of gloom, which took the form of suspicion and anxiety, cast a shadow across their minds. But then a phase, or rather an instant of uncertainty or new equilibrium, took over, a chilling moment that marked the end of the celestial phenomenon; and throwing off the traitorous attack, the sun began to blaze again in all its golden splendor.

Nevertheless, under the pressure of those imprecise feelings or as a result of their natural evolution (if not involution), Giovanna began to cry. Silently, yes. The tears flowed down her cheeks effortlessly, as if from an inexhaustible source, while she gazed out of infinitely desolate eyes; and there she stood, all of her, pathetic and nearly ashen, despite her luxuriant mane, an asset which now seemed to mock her, a treasure with no power against loss.

Enrico's first impulse was irritation, and then bewilderment. Why the hell was the girl crying, what did she want? Perhaps being naked—hidden as she was—had upset her, and the waning sun had only intensified it, making her even more vulnerable? Or could it be rather that she had only now realized the violation? That is, some violation she thought she had suffered? Yes, without a doubt, she felt belittled by their unseemly pretexts and her own acquiescence: a base sentiment, after all. ... Or else, in accepting their pretexts, some deeper feeling, maybe her love for him (if he wasn't deceiving himself and if it was love) had been offended? But what did it matter now? What part had he, Enrico, played in all this? Or, what part should he play now? In what direction should he lead his uncertain feelings? But then, the very fact that he was asking himself was decisive; because if ... then his whole being would have gone out toward the girl, he would have surrounded her with protection, would have felt the need to offer himself as shelter, as a safe refuge, et cetera—a need that he didn't feel at all. And so, should he let her cry without interfering, much less explain himself or allow her to explain? Her crying was irksome, yes, but not irksome enough to clarify things, to purge an excessively muddled and turbid state of mind. It was only a bother, after all. But then, what was the source of Enrico's nearly unidentifiable guilt?

The big critic, on the other hand, seemed to understand the girl's dismay perfectly. Or perhaps he didn't question it at all, his tutelary nature satisfied by the mere fact that she was upset. Thus, he went out of his way to console her, wrapping his arm around her paternally, and even going so far as to cast a worried look at the other and calling her "little one." Finally, he pushed her toward the other room to get dressed. As usual, he was the least responsible who took the most upon his shoulders. Meanwhile the sun regained its roundness, its full powers restored, and when Giovanna emerged from the room dressed again, with her hair pulled back up, it had nearly triumphed over the forces of darkness.

Everything returned to order and now all at once their meeting, with all its tenuous complications, seemed pointless. The critic stayed up there, and the other two started down toward the city.

"Look, Giovanna, what I want to know isn't so much . . . what I already more or less know, but what does the eclipse have to do with it?"

"With what?"

"With what I know."

"You take me for a fool, don't you?" she asked instead of answering.

"No," Enrico answered, conciliatory. "I know you're not always one."

"Yeah, but I certainly was this time. I have no idea what the eclipse had to do with it. Seriously, I don't know. But look. As long as the sun is up there whole, you can even think of it as a huge gem set in the enamel of our sky, just a gem, not a real celestial body. But when it's threatened, like today . . ."

"It wasn't threatened. It was just the moon passing invisibly between . . ."

"Right, right the moon. . . . When, as I was saying, it's threatened, we suddenly get the feeling of a passage, a turning, a crossing of stars in which, it seems, our hopes and our feelings, have no place, or to be more exact, from which we can draw no solace. I mean those celestial events, for all the new perspectives they reveal, are utterly indifferent to everything in us, contemptuous even. They don't take our most secret desires, our most precious illusions, into consideration. It's horrendous."

"What illusions, specifically?"

"Ah, Enrico, your voice is so cold. So you want me to tell you mine, my illusions? Do I really have to?"

"No, don't bother."

She looked at him like a dog that's been whipped, her eyes reflecting an absurd, stupid yearning. Her eyes glinted, waiting for a gesture. He was afraid she was going to start crying again. Oh, no, for God's sake be quiet, not that again.

And as for him, he liked her after all, in his way, but was he intrigued by her? Yes and no; a little.

THE GNAT

It was pouring rain, a sudden rain after days of unseasonable heat. In the downpour, the usual garbage cans in the courtyard (objects with no apparent use) were sending forth a range of sounds, all of them gloomy. Perhaps the rain was keeping him awake. But when the darkness became too heavy, weighing intolerably on his chest, he decided to turn on the dresser lamp. A cone of light cast itself across a stretch of white wall.

Flush against the wall, a small winged and not easily identifiable animal, a sort of gnat, was struggling up and down. At least that was his first impression. Actually, upon closer examination, he realized that the animal was going up, and only coming down out of necessity or some adverse destiny. Briefly, the little animal was trying to latch on to the top part of the wall and succeeded. But since it was missing a foot or claw, once it got to a certain point, it ineluctably slid back down again.

Now, two inquiries are in order here, one technical, the other actually metaphysical. First: why wasn't it making use of its wings—or had they already proved useless in these circumstances? And: why did it want to latch on up there? In other words, where did it want to go and what point was it trying to reach? . . . But that's obvious, a pointless question; can a civilized and conscious man, a participant in the industrial revolution, enter a gnat's minuscule brain and identify with it? And yet!

They say there are deserts of salt in the world dazzling beneath the sun—arid, bitter, unfriendly. Well this unfortunate animal, in an environment of his own proportions, was lost in such a desert. In fact, the great smooth wall must have been something like that for it, leading (just like the above-mentioned deserts) nowhere. That was it. The little animal couldn't have wanted to go anywhere, for the simple reason that there was nowhere to go. And it was up to him to make that clear. The insomniac thus leaped up from bed, delicately grasped his waking companion and placed it a bit higher up on the wall, closer to the finish line it seemed to be heading for.

The gnat stayed in its new position for a moment with the help of its small wings; whereupon, it punctually began to slide down again nearly all the way to the floor, only to begin its arduous ascent once again. And then . . . ? In any case, such labor made one's heart pound. But since there was no way to help, he might as well turn out the light and let the creature get it over with on its own.

He had an appointment with his fiancée at noon. She was supposed to wait for him, and was there, at the bus stop.

How beautiful she was. A bit buxom perhaps, and perhaps she had a little too much apple blush in her cheeks, white and rose like a girl in a convent, or rather like a queen in a fable. She smelled, he could have sworn, of lavender (even though girls didn't use it nowadays) and she had vanilla on her breath. She was wearing blue, sky blue, a faint, and if it can be said, fainting blue. She wore a light rose-colored scarf, the exact color of delphinium around her neck. Every single fiber of her body seemed to be yielding to him, ready to give him pleasure.

"Where are we going?"

"I don't know. Wherever you say."

"But we're eating out, right?"

"If you want."

"But where? In what restaurant?"

"I don't know, anything's fine with me. Didn't you have something in mind?"

"Not really. Let's decide together."

"You decide. Anything's fine with me."

"Il Marinaio?"

"Why not?"

"Look, first of all, what do you want to eat, meat or fish?"

"I don't care. I have no problems with food."

"Oh, no? Then I suggest..."

"Fine."

"But I didn't say anything yet."

"Fine anyway."

But at this point, or maybe even before, he was gripped by a dull irritation. Was this girl a white wall too? One on which he, naturally, could inscribe his own hieroglyphs, arabesques or even frescoes? An enviable situation, in a certain sense, and yet extremely oppressive, because in order to do that, at least under the present circumstances, first there would really have to be a trattoria, some place in the wide world to go. . . .

"Listen now, you can't."

"What can't I? I can do everything if you're near me," the girl answered happily.

"You can't just yield to events or to me like this."

"Are you forbidding me?"

"But you must have a will of your own."

"I do. It's yours."

"Take it back, then," he spit, growing more and more nasty. "How many times have I told you? We must have a definite plan when we go out. For instance, we lunch pleasantly in a trattoria (granted) of my choice. We are pleasantly excited by the bottle of ——— by the bottle. Our stomachs are nice and warm. We feel reconciled to life. Fine, what then?"

"What then? We have each other. We'll go down to the port for a coffee in that café that's all glass. And from inside, we'll watch the blue water, the yachts, the fishermen coming and going, old retired men dozing on the seaside benches. . . . We're happy, what don't we have?"

"You're crazy: time. We don't have time, which means it keeps going forward. The first movie opens at three."

"But what do we need a movie for? We can do without it."

"And so how can we use our time, or our happiness, fool?"

"By talking."

"Talking about what? We've already said everything and every- thing's already been said."

"Our love always needs new words, or rather it can contain every possible word."

"Ah, but don't you realize, if you open your arms or wings wide enough, there won't even be any love there? What it always needs is justifications, that's all. Like faith."

"What are you talking about? Isn't its justification inherent in it, or to be more precise, can't all its justification be left aside?"

"Good riddance."

"What do you mean by that?"

"No, I'm saying good riddance to your academic arguments. . . . I mean, it's your place, sweetheart, to tell me what we're going to do and where we're going to go. Your place, yours, do you understand?"

"You're nervous today!"

"That's right, and I'll get worse as the years go by. . . . Just think, years, time flies, and then eternity. But luckily, you're here."

"A bit dismayed, I admit."

"You'll have to be brave. Otherwise you shouldn't have gotten involved with me."

"You're nervous. Maybe you need to be alone."

"On the contrary!"

"We could meet tomorrow at the same time."

"Tomorrow. If there is a tomorrow. . . . Give me a kiss."

"Right here, in the middle of the piazza, with all these people and policemen waiting in ambush?"

"They'll take us for foreigners and ignore it. Give me a kiss."

"A kiss kiss?"

"Sure, kiss me like a fiancée or a newlywed."

"I don't dare..."

"A kiss; a kiss, idiot. It's all we've got left. As bad as it may be, a kiss is a hook."

"A hook? You're taking the poetry out of it."

"I mean, to be perfectly honest, I can feel myself slipping, and if I don't hold on to something, I might end up on the ground."

"On the ground! Come on, big adorable boy, admit it: sometimes the things that go through your head don't make much sense."

LITTLE
TREATISES

AN ABSTRACT
CONCEPT

"Ah, dear boys, we've come to a slightly difficult part of the course. My scientific methods are more uncertain than ever here. The best thing would be for us to speak informally, and each of you can contribute whenever you see fit and ask all the questions you want. Only speak one at a time."

"Good, we like difficult things. Go on, Professor."

"Eh, take it easy, this is the most difficult part of all. But let's be brave and begin immediately. So, then, my dear boys. I must now speak to you about death."

"De-ath: What is that?"

"Slow down, slow down now: I don't know and it may not be possible to know."

"Oh, so?"

"But they have to know or had to, since they have or had a word designating it, and that's already saying something."

"They who?"

"What the devil, the beings we began discussing."

"The inhabitants of those remote worlds that . . . ?"

"Yes, that's right: the ones whose residence or galaxy you saw or barely saw."

"The last one, that very last one down there that looks like a little pale spot."

"Of course, but let's not lose time over idle repetitions. So then: death."

"But, Professor, if this... death, if they know what it is and you don't, we don't understand...."

"Hold on, I didn't state positively that they know or knew."

"Oh, that's even better! How can our investigation proceed without any context, then?"

"Context, noncontext! Listen, boys, we can't go forward this way. Cut out the preliminaries and the ceremonies. I mean, let's try to define or approximate the concept of death. I will help you in your, your hypotheses, or whatever you call them, and vice versa; and hopefully, we will arrive at some conclusion by working around this word. To begin with, you mustn't forget that if a person understands one thing, he can also understand something else, even if he lives millions of light-years away. Therefore, let's try, and in the end when we exhaust everything, you'll see how little I know."

"Let's try."

"That's how I like to see you. Now, it is best if we approach this from a broad perspective, otherwise we won't understand one another. Obviously, if I could refer to the concept of life, it would be easy for me to give you an idea of death, but the problem is that you don't even know what life might be, and I can't explain it without referring back to the concept of death. It's like saying that when we are through reasoning things out, life and death will become one and the same."

"Li-fe?"

"Yes, but forget that, for God's sake.... No, this angle isn't going to work: we need help from some concept which, shall we say, precedes that of life and death, if they're real after all. Let's see, let's see now: didn't the other professor tell you... I mean do you all know what time is?"

"Time? No."

"And space?"

"Space?"

"And if you don't know what time and space are individually, how can we reduce them to a single conceptual plane?"

"What are you talking about?"

"Nothing, nothing."

"Space, time: what funny words. What are they?"

"They aren't something: I asked if you knew what was meant on that last of nebulas by time and space or by time or space. But you don't even know that; just imagine if you actually understood the concept of duration, et cetera, et cetera. Ah, but you tell me then, how shall I do it?"

"Do what?"

"Oh, my God, give you an idea of death."

"Why, you mean you can't have an idea of death until you have one about this time and space?"

"I would say so; at least it seems that way."

"Explain time and space to us, then."

"Uhmm, but actually, thinking it over . . . Look, perhaps we're back where we started. Perhaps to talk about space or time, which are actually the same, I must necessarily talk about death, or else assume you have some notion of it. Do any of you know whether the concept of space or time generates the notion of death or whether it's the notion of death which generates that of space and time?"

"We don't."

"Neither do I. It may very well be that in reality they are two parallel concepts, or better said, the same concepts articulated differently."

"But what shall we make of that?"

"Make of that? Before we all lose our heads, let's start from the very beginning again, period. So, then, listen: what is being, do you know that?"

"Yes!"

"Yes!"

"Yes!"

"Ah, too many yesses. Go on, one person at a time. What is being?"

"Being is our consciousness."

"Uhmm, yes. Indeed, this is the definition in our manuals. So being is some kind of feeling or at least a subjective relationship. But to what, let me ask you that."

"What do you mean to what? Oh, great, to the activity of our own thoughts and feelings, that is to everything that makes us what we are."

"Namely, it would be the consciousness we have of our consciousness. I say, do you understand this or does it seem like a little game to you?"

"But, if you put it like that, certainly..."

"I said exactly what you said. But listen, I think we must see it as a meditation instead, in other words, our consciousness must have a connection to something besides itself.... In any case, we are probably digressing here, and overstepping your background knowledge as well. I mean, didn't it ever occur to you that this relationship we've called subjective could almost tend toward an objective entity, in other words, that being might represent our state of being, rather than an image we've made?"

"A state!"

"The concept of state we more or less understand, but..."

"Ah, yes, I knew that you would lose your tempers. I know you were going to say that since our state is constant and eternal, it is not a state."

"Of course! The concept of state presupposes the possibility of change."

"That remains to be seen: the very fact that we can say 'immutable state...'"

"Uh-oh, now what?"

"What kind of discussion is this! Are you playing games with us?"

"And what's supposed to come of all this anyway?"

"Calm down, calm down. Okay, you might even be right. So let's try to work around the difficulty. Tell me something, do you all know what nonbeing, nothingness is?"

"No."

"Ah, that's understandable because all our speculation is based on positive concepts. But there are negative concepts too, blessed be God, or we must assume so from the news, I mean the ideas that have reached us from that distant nebula."

"Negative concepts, what are they?"

"Concepts which refer to things unrelated to things that are."

"Professor, be patient, this is not making a bit of sense."

"I'm not surprised. Let's say they refer to things that exist in a different mode than the things in question."

"In a different mode? What does that mean?"

"Oh, God! They refer to another possible condition of any given thing."

"You mean to an impossible condition?"

"If you like. But I mean, for example, nothingness would be that which is not being."

"But that which is not being doesn't take shape."

"Agreed, but you can think about it."

"Not really, because that which isn't being could represent an infinity of (other) things."

"No, no, you're wrong here: being represents an infinity of things too, but to the extent that it can be taken as a single concept, it is well defined and self-contained. Likewise, there's only one mode of nothingness; that is, the concept of nothingness is a self-contained concept, a precise idea."

"Forgive us, we still don't understand. You say likewise. But in order for the analogy to be acceptable, not to mention complete, this nonbeing would have to represent an infinity of things, within its own limitations, just as being does, and not merely be something that can be represented in different ways. . . . I'm not making myself clear, and I don't know if you understand me, but our objection isn't what you apparently think it is. And one thing is clear, if you'll forgive me, you're pulling a fast one on us. On one hand, you're giving us a single all-encompassing concept, and on the other hand, you're giving us an equally single theory which unfortunately encompasses nothing and relates to nothing."

"Damnation! You're too smart and not smart enough. Not enough, because without realizing it, you're contaminating abstraction with reality. In other words, let's say that being is not a real concept whereas nonbeing is. Yes, the concept of nonbeing is pure, since it corresponds to nothing."

"But you'll have to depict it for us somehow."

"No, actually I will do that through the process of elimination: I'll depict it as a mere intellectual construct."

"And we'll have to swallow this whole and be satisfied?"

"More or less, I dare say."

"Well, guys, let's swallow it, even if we can't digest it. Let's do this, Professor: you continue, and maybe what is to come will clarify what came before. But come on, Professor, is this any way to speculate?"

"We are not speculating. I, I repeat, am trying first to reason something out for myself. And in any case, it wouldn't be the first time that what came later clarified what came before."

"Fine, yes, go ahead. But to begin with, how do you get from your nothingness to your time and space?"

"Who the devil knows! Not directly, I suppose."

"Forge ahead, Professor."

"Ah, well, then: does the idea of nothingness imply an idea of limitation or does it not?"

"Uhm."

"Uhm."

"Eh, no, there's really nothing to whine about: it does imply it, I think."

"How?"

"But if there's a nothingness it means that being isn't, how can I put it, total; rather than embracing everything, it leaves a certain margin instead."

"Eeeeh!"

"Pfui."

"Come on, really, we've come to whistling too? Try to be more serious."

"And yet, Professor, now you're the one who is contaminating abstraction with reality. But nothingness isn't: didn't you just call it a mere intellectual construct?"

"Here now, you others, instead of making noise, open your mouths and speak. What! Of course we're discussing intellectual constructs, and I didn't say nothingness was anything but an abstraction: seeing that our ultimate point of destination, or rather, our first stop, space or time, is nothing more than an abstraction."

"Yes, yes, this time you're actually right. Forgive us. But just tell us: what is a mouth?"

"Mouth, I said mouth?... It's something they have down there but never mind. Maybe we'll get to that too."

"Let's go on, then."

"Yes, let's go on." (But how?) "Now, if being is not everything, in other words, if one can conceive of it as bounded by nothing-ness..."

"Yes?"

"Yes, nothing, my boys. I don't know how to go on, and perhaps you are sneakier than I. Nevertheless, I have a hunch that if we start from such a premise, we might be able to come to a dis-tinction of elements, conceptual elements, of course."

"What distinction and what elements?"

"Yes. .... Here's being and here's nothingness: meaning that at a certain point being becomes nothingness, and vice versa, that at a certain point nothingness ends and becomes being, right?"

"Well, in a way, yes, since this idea of ending is not terribly clear. What do you mean by ends?"

"It means merely, for now, that being is quite distinct from nothingness, doesn't it?"

"There's no doubt about that, insofar as it relates to your rather nebulous definition. But look, dear Professor, there is a lot of hocus-pocus here: words within words, words explained by the words that should explain them, et cetera."

"All right. But what can I do about it? Anyway, it only seems that we're playing hide-and-seek: in reality, like it or not, something or other remains. Words in themselves are already something, and hopefully they will come clear all at once."

"Well, go on a bit."

"So, being and nothingness are different. Now, are you able to conceive of or imagine two separate things, to put it one way, within being?"

"Do you mean even if we separated being from nothingness before? Not very well."

"But first of all, wasn't it one of you who just spoke about thoughts and feelings, which are two things, and didn't all of you agree that being is an infinity of things?"

"But, first of all if everything were so straightforward, why would you feel the need to interrogate us, and besides, it was just a manner of speaking: an infinity of things is the same as a single thing. And thoughts and feelings aren't two things either, they are two words."

"That's enough now. So let me ask you: can you imagine something distinct, or even something corresponding to a particular word, within the context of being?"

"What kind of question is that? Certainly, we've just finished saying you can find as many words as you want in being."

"No, I didn't make myself clear, or maybe I actually made a mistake, but it doesn't matter. I mean (but what do I mean?), I mean... Look, for example, can't you actually conceive that something that is in front of you at this moment is distinct from the rest, can't you isolate it by dint of abstraction?"

"Your question, Professor, is terribly obscure, not to mention beside the point and badly put. You mean, for example, presume that a star is qualitatively different from the sky which surrounds it?"

"No, not qualitatively! Can you assume—I don't know how the hell to say it—but I'll have to go back here—assume that it's distinct from the rest, an entity, a thing in itself?"

"How in itself?"

"Ah! Another example: can you imagine that two stars could be two ends?"

"Ends of what?"

"Of the sky."

"Oh, you mean actually imagine the sky is contained between those two stars?"

"Not at all, but rather that in the sky there is another sky contained between the two stars, that there's a little one up there in the big one, a part in the whole, or that the sky is made up of many little skies."

"Eh, come on. . . . But, basically, we're beginning to understand what you mean."

"Oh, praised be God! Then we're approaching the concept of space or time."

"But what's the use of such a fantasy?"

"Forget its usefulness for now, though its use is precisely that you will finally come to understand space and time. For you, for them down there, ehm, it's a whole other matter, and I don't know if it was even a fantasy for them."

"But after all, what would space or time be, what would represent it in this hypothesis or image or fantasy?"

"Take it easy. Let's sum up instead. Therefore, there are all these little skies within the sky, which is the same, I think, as saying all these little beings within being: they're actually infinite because your possible points of reference are infinite. Are you following me, this far?"

"More or less. And these minor skies that are finite for us, or these little beings as you call them, each of them is space or time?"

"No, no! What a dickens of a mess you're making: those minor ones, though they are limited arbitrarily and only abstractly, are still something, while space and time are nothing, are only concepts, or at most methods."

"What do you mean methods?"

"Methods to do what, for what?"

"Come on, come on, don't get caught up in words; perhaps what I said will be clear to you later, and perhaps not. Period!"

"But will you tell us: what are space and time? For goodness sake, it's all becoming vague and it's time you spilled the beans."

"Well, here it is briefly: space and time are no more and no less than the very possibility of clearly and effortlessly conceiving of those little skies and little beings."

"What, what?"

"That's a vicious cycle of a definition!"

"What a disappointment!"

"But wait! Let's try to explain it: the idea of space or time is really a conclusive one for them."

"Conclusive?"

"Yes, in the sense that it moves toward an end, no, even contains the end in itself. It's an idea that limits more than it distinguishes; they call it an idea of . . . duration."

"They: but now we're in the dark again."

"But why, if we just now said . . . Look, if I posit, postulate, one sky here and another sky here . . ."

"You mean where one ends the other begins, or anyway that one must necessarily end so that the other can begin?"

"Ah, right."

"Right, you say: but ideally speaking, how are they represented in the hypothesis, leaving aside the fact that the two supposed skies are of one identical nature; do this end and this beginning occur as a change in state or modality?"

"No, no!"

"So how, then?"

"Only as an end and a beginning; and in the case in point, you can do away with either of those terms, whichever you wish."

"Eh, no, that's too easy, or—we don't want to offend you—too difficult: this image has no substance. We refuse to go on."

"Therefore, you can't separate the idea of beginning from the idea of ending?" (What an intelligent question! If they could, they would already know what death is.)

"No, no, these are ideas of relationship, nothing else; and we beg you not to confuse us anymore."

"Nevertheless . . . !" (But, damn it, as far as I can see, they're right: do I know what death is myself?)

"And then there's another problem: if your little skies or beings are infinite by your own definition, we really can't endow them with any sort of ending or beginning."

"What, now you're taking back what you just conceded?"

"We're not taking back anything, or yes we are, but it seems that ultimately there're no two ways about it: you either see them as infinite or as a single thing."

(They're right about this too, even if they're not terribly consistent.) "Come now, let's see: they are infinite, but you can always think of a limited number of them."

"No, thinking it over again: we can think of them as a limited number, provided that we keep in mind that they are infinite, that is to say, that our fiction dissolves at the same time that it takes shape or should take shape."

(It doesn't make sense, for God's sake! . . . or does it?) "Listen, let's forget these punctilious fine points. We could try to approach it from a different angle instead, and hopefully, we will get there slowly. But I don't think that will be necessary. You know what I really think? That in talking like this you've already demonstrated a grasp of the concept of space or time."

"If you say so. . . ."

"Yes, and somehow I anticipated this: concepts get clearer as you go along, as you talk about them, even if you don't understand what they're about. You certainly can't explicate them directly or take them by the horns."

"Uhm."

"But in any case, we're going to pretend this is so: and if you still don't get it, I mean this blessed concept, there's no alternative but to forge ahead anyway and hope for the future, which is a dead end for now."

"Uhm, let's pretend and forge ahead. But, did you mention 'death' or something like that in the beginning, or are we mistaken?"

"Eh, sooner or later we'll get to that."

"Go on."

"Now, can you actually manage... Good heavens, it's even hard to say it.... Can you actually manage to imagine yourselves contained in one of those things, those hypothesized entities that we called little skies or beings—I mean each of you in one of them?"

"What?"

"What?"

"How could that be?"

"No, really."

"Professor, you've lost your marbles; being contained in a part of itself, more within less, the biggest within the smallest?"

"Ah, ah."

"Pfui."

"Good, now be quiet! And first of all, what do you mean being? I said each of you."

"Being, being itself; each of us is all of being."

"Good, what diligent college and prep-school students you are! And though I feel desolate, actually desperate, I must ask you once again to make this imaginative effort, this speculative leap, or whatever; otherwise we can't proceed and we might as well give up."

"But it's impossible to conceive of oneself contained in anything whatsoever."

"I understand myself that it's impossible: besides, it would be even more impossible, if that were possible, to actually be contained or enclosed, so from greater to lesser impossibility..."

"Damn, he's throwing everything together at random."

"But, there might be a way to conceive of such a thing: for instance, once I threw myself into it, I succeeded, even if poorly. And in any case, this is how they seem to understand it down there, with or without good reason; and if one wishes to grasp this matter, if I want to myself... But I know very well... I know very well I have no right to ask you to accept such a hypothesis."

"So, let's make him happy, guys; what's it to us? If we don't he might start crying."

"Don't be insolent; instead..."

"Sure, sure, fine: the biggest within the smallest. Are you happy now? Each of us contained in a little piece of sky."

"Not only that but..."

"Oh, that isn't good enough for you?"

"Stop it, I said, and try to pay attention."

"Ah, Professor, Professor, you've reduced us to the point that we'd even admit that the universe is infinite, or finite, or whatever other absurdity you want. We're beaten down."

"Me too. But when this struggle is over, you'll see that it certainly isn't my fault if they are contained within a little piece of sky, as you put it, or of, of time."

"What, what... they? How can it be, how can they be? Let's hear the next thing, perhaps we'll catch on a bit, if you're right about what comes later helping one understand what came before."

"Oh, that's good, have a little faith."

"In whom?"

"In yourselves above all. And now, you were right to pay such close attention because now the most difficult and unbelievable part is really coming. What we were dealing with up until now was a piece of cake: just a minute ago we were playing around with the idea of lesser and greater impossibilities, and now we're approaching the latter head-on: therefore, they..."

"Go on, be brave: nothing can amaze us anymore."

"Well, everything still amazes me."

"Eh, well, as long as we are dealing with impossible fantasies, the most impossible is also the most amusing."

"And anyway, I don't know how to explain it; if I did, I'd already know quite a lot, but the opposite is the case. So we must now proceed by guessing. Bah, all I can really do is repeat what I've already given you a taste of: where they live, the greater is something that takes shape in the lesser, or I should say in as many lessers as they are. Is that clear?"

"No, no, not at all: it doesn't make any sense . . . ,it's utterly incomprehensible, even as a sentence."

"I know, nevertheless, it is so: I'm saying it like this because I don't dare say 'it's true.' In other words, we are facing a factual situation regardless of whether or not it's comprehensible."

"Factual?"

"Well, yes, insofar as we can accept or conceive of factual situations."

"Can't you at least explain yourself better: what is this supposed factual situation all about? Because from what you've told us so far, we don't get its meaning."

"Oh, God, I've already told you, how else can I say it? Infinity completes itself or materializes, or let's say defines itself in the lesser, though it remains greater or maybe it doesn't, how should I know? In other words, their being is somehow broken up into small pieces. Ah, I don't really know if it's broken up or merely exemplified . . . in many lesser beings."

"But then it's not so much a matter of more in less, as of so many lesser beings forming a greater one."

"No, at least this is the obscure point; I said 'somehow' broken up, and only to try to help you understand."

"But we don't understand anyway: so can we say that a division of being is active in each of them?"

"No, no (although . . . oh, forget it). Rather, each one of them is one of those little beings, those minor beings and nothing more, even if they do perhaps contain the totality of being or participate in it. I mean, each of them is, in fact, a limited thing in the sky or in being which takes up a limited area of sky or being."

"What, how, didn't you just say that they themselves contain, participate, et cetera?"

"From one point of view or consideration, they are a portion of being, but from the other they are all of being; from one point, they begin and end, and from the other, they may never begin or end."

"Mystery upon mystery! Look, Professor, we're giving up."

"But, no." (I just realized that maybe I can dispense with this whole complicated method simply by reminding them of their sense of individuality: if they have any or if it's distinct enough. They're always willing to listen, but the trouble is I already know how they'll answer.) "Pay attention, boys: I don't see what you find so strange in this arrangement: when you get right down to it, aren't we in the same situation? We are also contained in something, that is in our own distinct personalities or individualities, aren't we?"

"Ooooo."

"Fff."

"But I mean, are you actually many or are you one in this room here?"

"You know very well, neither many nor one, and we can't understand why you enjoy asking these questions. It's simple: we are ones, singularities in the plural, or better still, plurality singularized."

(Just as I anticipated: let's hurry back to our initial points before the situation becomes even more complicated.) "So be it: let's go back to our previous point. Or better still, let's leave aside whether or not they participate in the whole of being, since in the final analysis it's beside the point or premature, and go back again for a moment or change our viewpoint just a bit. . . ."

"But kindly tell us, what viewpoint do you want to change if there's nothing to see! Listen, what does it ultimately mean if they're limited in the sky, or in being, or wherever else you said? It can only mean that they see themselves as limited, right?"

(One would have expected that they wouldn't understand anything—with my explanations. ...) "No, but then again, this is
the heart of the matter. ... Or, in the final analysis, yes, but ...
Or at least it doesn't only mean that." (God knows how to put it!)

"Ah, okay, Professor, if you're not feeling well let's put off the
rest for another day."

(They're right: what a sham my explanations are when I'm the
first to get bungled and beat around the bush.)

"Why this dignified silence?"

"Keep silent yourselves and listen. Look, I don't know if the
monstrosity which I will try to explain to you (and myself) is an
effect or a cause, but the fact is that they are not restricted to
seeing themselves as limited, but they are, regardless of what
they think they are." (Look at this: I can't even find the right
words and have to repeat this nonsense!)

"Come again! What do you mean?"

"I simply mean that being what they can be and what they
know, and God knows what else, they are still really enclosed in
something smaller which you can abstract or hypothesize, or
ideally, isolate, as you did before with the sky; each of them,
then, is hopelessly enclosed in this lesser thing, or to stretch the
metaphor if you like, in time and space."

"Hopelessly enclosed? You mean, self-contained by a rigid
concept?"

"My God, no. I mean enclosed enclosed: each of them is a
hard thing, an object, with a particular consistency, presenting
a resistance to external agents, and so on; each of them has, as
they themselves call it, a body!" (Oh, what's going to come of
this?)

"A body?"

(Nothing's happening, they're still too flabbergasted. Maybe
I've quelled the hurricane.)

"Body! We only know one meaning of that word: heavenly
body."

"Yes, imagine something like that, proportions aside, or actually no. Bodies of varying proportions."

"And each of them has... what do you mean has? Is, you mean?"

"Yes... I said has because... I really meant is."

"Each of them is a heavenly body?"

(They're not getting it.) "No, not a heavenly body, simply a body. In fact, they are attached to various heavenly bodies upon which they depend and can only separate from with great difficulty."

"You mean they are satellites?"

"Ah, no, but then again, why not? You could even imagine them as satellites, it's just that if they were satellites, they would certainly be sui generis: but they have no orbit of their own. They actually cling to the heavenly bodies, rather like fleas, parasites."

"Fine, but so what?"

(I wasn't ready for this calm: they still must not really understand.) "What do you mean, so what?"

"But... what does this have to do with... No, Professor, look, we'd better be frank: this presentation of yours, assuming it's valid, this tale of yours, assuming one should believe it, doesn't make any sense whatsoever to us. To be perfectly frank, we don't get it at all."

(I suspected as much.)

"What use is this body of theirs, how does it behave, and ideally speaking how could one justify this mode of being?"

"Too many questions too fast! Let's be content to say that these inhabitants are or are also bodies, let's even use the word substance."

"Actually substance?"

"But, yes, what's so unusual about that? Even though we are not bodies, we are substance, everything is, in other words, combinations of energies. In their case, it's a matter of a greater degree of compression of the material or energy."

"Yes, yes, but we don't get, we don't really understand how this thing works. Listen, let's try to discuss it again, perhaps from

the beginning; why don't you try to familiarize us with this absurdity. I don't know, for example, you just said you didn't know
if this body or 'body being' was an effect or a cause: well, what
exactly did you mean? Explain that point."

"What I meant is obvious: the body or its presence might be
a result of their way of conceiving things."

"Conceiving what?"

"Their way of thinking in general; of conceiving, being, everything."

"Uhm; well, and if it weren't?"

"If, if it weren't, the opposite case could be: that is to say, it
may have been the presence of the body which created and in
some way necessitated their way of conceiving things."

"Well, then, you see? That's already a bit clearer: we're beginning to get the question at hand."

"Good boys."

"Yes, but what now?"

"What now?"

"What are we to make of this body? In the first place, what is
it like?"

"You mean what does it look like, what form and characteristics
does it have?"

"No, no: *how is it*, in what mode does it exist, what is its
purpose within being, what is its relationship to being, et cetera."

"Oh, listen here, don't attribute more science to me than I
actually know; at most we can guess, debate and discuss for the
sake of discussing."

"Oh, no, first you dazzle us with preposterous revelations and
then you begin to waffle."

"I . . . I'm telling you what I know, and it's useless. . . ."

"Listen, have you made up your mind to tell us about death,
or did you forget about it?"

(They're getting insolent again: a good sign actually.) "Yes, I
think at this point we can start to talk about it; indeed, this is
the perfect moment to get to the heart of the matter."

"Go on."

"Hence, those so-and-sos are limited in space..."

"Or in time if you prefer. We've already clarified that."

"No, wait a minute. Space and time become the same thing, yes, they are certainly one concept, but only as a concept or concepts go, and not as..."

"As what?"

"I don't know!... Look, they distinguish the two, or they have for quite a while, or at least they've considered them as a sort of double or twin concept, I suppose... I don't know exactly what to tell you. I suppose too that one can't arrive at a unified concept of space or time, I mean that they couldn't have arrived at it, if not by first separating them as two parallel concepts, or rather by abstracting them, like a concept within a concept."

"Ay, ay, what a muddle."

"No, wait. Even though I am limited like everyone else by my imagination and suppositions, I've formed my own personal idea of this, and to get to the point, I believe definitively that if one wants to have an idea or to have an awareness of death, he must consider their ancient distinction valid."

"Okay, let's skin this other cat, then. So work backward if you prefer it that way, but do it in an orderly fashion: space, then..."

"Space is space, and I know you already know enough about it."

"Ah, yes, fine. And time?"

"Time: look, for one reason or another, they have postulated a succession of events..."

"What do you mean?"

"Yes, a succession of events within being."

"But what does succession really mean? System?"

"Yes and no; something more than a system; let's call it a dynamic system, with each event following upon another spatially...." (I don't know what the devil I'm cooking up here.)

"Incomprehensible, but let's go on. And if so, why, what's it all for?"

"Do you think I know? Perhaps above all only because they are bodies."

"In any case, so far the concept of time is still no different than that of space."

"You're right. But look ... Oh, God, what saint should I turn to? Look here, that star is limited in space. Are you following me thus far?"

"Uhm, yes."

"That is, at a certain point it comes to an end."

"Or rather, it doesn't really come to an end, since it is of the same nature as the rest, but let's have fun imagining it does."

"Okay, and let's have fun imagining this: suddenly the star disappears."

"Disappears, how?"

"Yes, you remember, I don't know exactly when, but that star exploded right before our eyes? Well, what was left in its place?"

"Nothing apparently, but only apparently."

"Hold on, now. And let me ask you this: don't you see a difference between the two endings, the ending of whatever it is in space, and the ending, the explosion, the disappearance of the star in question? What do you think they are, two distinct occurrences or two things that are one and the same?"

"Yes, of course. But still, on second thought, perhaps we're getting your drift. And this second ending is time?"

"Not time: that which brought about or might have brought about the concept of time for those people, like the first ending gave rise to the concept of space. At least this is the fact upon which they must have initially based their distinction, which, I must say, is entirely off target to my way of thinking."

"So time would be a system of endings?"

"You might say that for the moment."

"But as you presented it to us, space is also a system of endings."

"Yes, but ..."

"Ah, ah, we get it: the first kind of endings that we imagined apply to space, and the second kind to time."

"Precisely."

"So be it: thus, as they see it, these endings bring about two distinct systems or concepts. So what next?"

"Hold on with the distinctions: I differentiated the two concepts, but only to reunite them immediately. In fact, these seem to come together again in the other concept, of death; indeed, it happens that death reveals their nature better than anything else."

"Oh, then why did you have to wear out our brains with such an irksome distinction? What kind of wild-goose chase is this anyway?"

"I distinguished them for two reasons: because as I said, you cannot take them as a unified concept until you have split them into separate ones, and because death actually seems to follow from the second one, the second aspect of that idea rather than from the first, as incomprehensible as that seems to me."

"What kind of hunches and contradictions are you handing us? You mean death represents more of an ending in time than in space?"

"More or less."

"But then they are two concepts."

"No."

"Oh, fine, you just want to joke around?"

"Not really. My flimsy doctrine undoubtedly ends here, and I really don't know what to tell you or how to justify my . . . my impressions. Nevertheless, perhaps we should try to change our terminology? For example, we could assume that the concept of space or time, relatively speaking or in relation to the idea of death, and in this one case, wouldn't really be a concept at all, but a function. Think of it like this if you can: space and time are two functions of one another."

"Which wouldn't be a function at all! And even so, what would we resolve?"

"Oh, God, nothing, but it might be easier to accept the preponderance of one over the other."

"Not at all: on the contrary!"

"And what if we resort to the concept of variable function?"

"But don't you realize how carelessly you're throwing these terms around? A function, variable or not, cannot be relative to itself. And then you throw these concepts back in our face; and now, to top it off, you lose your head. And finally, we're getting lost in these useless details that refer, as you yourself said, to mere impressions."

"It's true, it's true, I am losing my head."

"Hold on, hold on, Professor: just tell us what to make of this blessed death? Is it an ending in time or space, or both, or in something which both of them unify and assimilate? And is it really an ending in the first place, have we interpreted your vague explanations correctly?"

"It is really an ending, or that's how they conceive of it, and to be more precise, an ending in time and space: in both, or to be more precise, in time or space. Yes, let's stick to that for now."

"Oh, good, at least that part is clear, as obscure as the rest of it still is. So it is an ending. That is, fundamentally the idea of an ending. Anyway, let's say a tautological idea: if they're bodies, it is understood they come to an end."

"They're finite, limited in space, right, but..."

"Yes, but..." (Oh, good heavens.) "Look, first of all, saying they're finite or limited doesn't mean that they come to an end."

"Yes, but this distinction lies only in our consciousness."

"Good! And then, here's where whatever I just said, here's where the concept, or false concept, or half-concept of time could be useful to us: they don't only come to an end in space but in time too, in other words they come to an end in space as long as we see space as space or time, time being the more preponderant of the two. Did I explain myself?"

"No."

"You must go back to the example of the exploding star and

for two different reasons. Or else, to proceed as best we can, it's not a matter of their understanding of themselves in abstract terms, as much as something that happens. Even if, as I said before, their way of conceiving things made them who they are."

"Your connections are a little loose: the thing that happens is death?"

"Yes."

"So in this new configuration it isn't a concept or idea anymore."

"What the devil: it is the abstract idea of the thing, and in a word, the same thing."

"Eh, what a glib, smooth talker! The bad part is, as you yourself admitted, that you can also see a thing abstracted from an idea."

(Damn them!) "But my dear little wise ones, what would that change?"

"Let's sweep it under the rug. So now, you're going to tell us that they explode like heavenly bodies?"

"I don't know if they actually explode, but they end; but go ahead and say they explode if you want."

"You mean they are subject to such a strange eventuality?"

"Eh, no, here's another diabolical point: it would seem that it's not a matter of possibility, but of necessity."

"Necessity! You mean that they must, necessarily, explode?"

"That's what they think anyway. Clearly this could be a mere postulation of theirs, but nevertheless it seems to be confirmed by reality. In other words, up until now it has always gone as they thought it must: they are, and are, until at a certain point, they are no longer, I mean, they die."

"But that's absurd: what is, in other words, everything that is, cannot cease to be."

"But it can alter its state: otherwise how could you explain the explosion of a star? It ceases being in respect to what it was before."

"Uhm, this all sounds like a sophism to us."

"What do you mean a sophism? Can't a star explode or go out anyway, or cease being what it was, perhaps to become something else?"

"Sure; but the point is it can, it doesn't have to, which makes a huge, a real qualitative difference."

"It's not that they must. Ah, what do we know? Couldn't this be some sort of natural and universal law?"

"You mean the one concerning the ending or altering of states? Come on!"

"I'm just saying: that's what they think, anyway."

"And where did they come up with such a law?"

"But . . . from experience. I am continuing, of course, to reason things out in their way, or rather according to their facts."

"From experience! But experience is the most treacherous research method or point of departure. You can always come up with anything and its opposite from experience; you can make experience tell you anything you want. Anything: from the fact that a star explodes should we conclude that all stars must explode sooner or later, or that, hypothetically, if one of us ceases to exist, all of us must necessarily cease to exist? What kind of faulty reasoning are you getting caught up in here?"

"That doesn't negate the fact that if we saw a star exploding or going out every second, and if these cases generally were to multiply, they, I mean all future events leading back to that might appear to our way of thinking as an increasing probability and would ultimately seem as almost necessary."

"What are you telling us! Forgive us, but didn't you teach us yourself not to trust facts, to keep our calm, or as you said, our virginity, in their presence? Besides that, anyway, you say future events leading back to that. But no random event is connected to another, a preceding one to boot. And nevertheless, increasing probability or near necessity is still not necessity, they are, in fact, the opposite. And finally, let's say we accept the first case: okay, what is the ideal relationship of the second to the first, is it free? Are we free in relationship to it? I mean our minds could already be made up or conditioned by that first random event as a necessary result of our concept of it. Therefore the necessity or the lack of necessity of the second event would always be subjective, and we'd never be able to prove it. And we're talking about the second event: just imagine the third, and subsequent ones."

"Yes, yes, but meanwhile they die."

"But maybe because they're convinced they must die. Perhaps if we shared such a conviction it would begin to happen to us too; you can see what I'm getting at."

"And didn't I tell you that?"

"But no, they should find the courage to say 'it's just too bad for the facts' for once and for all. That's what they should do. In any case, let's go on; bah, anyway, do they die or just think they do?"

"Isn't it the same thing, at least insofar as our reasoning and the concept we're trying to specify are concerned? Indeed, indeed, if they only believed it but didn't really die, it would be even worse, or rather, we could take this as an *a fortiori*. But perhaps it's not as simple as it seems. Let me ask you, for example: would you be inclined to admit to the existence of other natural laws elsewhere, or of particular places where other laws are in effect, whose people are subject to different laws than those which govern us?"

"The question, excuse us, is rather badly put since no law governs us, but we are the ones who invent the laws and then govern them; the laws are our interpretation of . . . But assuming your question were better formulated, if we try to intuit your meaning, we would definitely say: no."

"Huh, no?"

"How or why should there be other laws? What the devil, if thought abdicates unity, everything will go to ruin. Our interpretation of . . . must be unambiguous and uniform."

"Good, good, you've learned the lesson from . . . the other professors well. But may I humbly point out the fact that you've left a certain sentence dangling at least twice: 'our interpretation of...' Of what?"

"Oh, of the universe, of everything."

"You mean of something outside us?"

"But... now you're trying to trip us up too."

"Of something outside us evidently, otherwise there would be no reason for the term Interpretation or anything comparable to it, and the very word Thought would lose all meaning. A person, to put it plainly, cannot interpret himself, since in order to do so, he would have to use a part of himself, that is, assume that what he is interpreting has already been interpreted or, at the very least, interpret himself only partially."

"Perfect, now you are the one repeating the little lesson, only you do it a bit more swiftly!"

"No, this has to do with what I'm about to ask you and to introduce my next question: won't you even admit the existence of other, or apparently, distinct laws?"

"Ehm, ehm, that, yes; provided they're traceable...."

"Yes, yes. Well, then, consider death one of the many possible appearances."

"Eh, you and your tricks. But how? Then there's no need to fuss so much over... over what, anyway? Is it an appearance or a concept?"

"It could always be a specious concept."

"Another charming deception!"

"Then, let's say an apparent concept or a conceptual appearance; in other words: a concept insofar as appearances go and an appearance insofar as concepts go."

"Long live clarity and above all long live decisiveness! And what do you want us to understand and retain from this?"

"Whatever you have understood and retained."

"You mean nothing."

"No, no, you've been talking about death for half an hour now, and that means I've succeeded in giving you an idea of it, or actually, to tell the truth, you have succeeded in forming an idea of it."

"Don't delude yourself: until we come to some definition..."

"Forget definitions, at this point they're impossible for us. I don't want you to forget, in fact, that I am not nor was I talking about death in any real sense, but merely trying to represent their idea of death, and their nonidea. In other words, for you, for us, death remains a concept, even if it isn't or wasn't in and of itself."

"The umpteenth little game you're playing! And such a crystal-clear context!"

"No, the little game we're playing is logic."

"But how are you going to represent death if you don't know what it is yourself? And anyway, a concept can and must also be defined."

"How *did* I represent it, you mean to say. Come on, come on, you must more or less know what this death means by now: everyone knows what death is. And we've arrived at the point we wanted to get to."

"We know without knowing."

"Better still: this is real science. You see how much, and at the same time, how little, words matter."

"So death is a word."

"If you say so."

"A word that means nothing!"

"Good."

"For now death is only something that disturbs our vision of the universe...."

"Excellent."

"Without giving us anything back in return."

"Exactly."

"Will you cut out your riddles."

"But the fact that they are riddles is taken for granted. Death is a riddle for them: think for a moment, for me and for your-selves."

"What can I say, guys, maybe the old man is right, and you can understand his position, or what he's asking us to do. . . ."

"Right, fiddlesticks."

"Ah, some old man and some fiddlesticks: may I remind you to be more dignified and composed, even if you are kind enough to say I'm right. . . . It's a riddle that one can not only reason out but even presume to solve."

"Let's reason it out."

"Eh, listen, fellows, at this rate we run the risk of taking a tour of the universe, or of trying anyway. I should actually remind you that this lesson has gone on too long. We've gotten to a certain point. . . . Good, the next time . . ."

"What, have you lost your mind? You want to leave us like this?"

"There won't be another time, go on and don't complain."

"Spit it all out."

"Pfui, pfui."

"You should be ashamed. If there weren't other reasons for interrupting this lesson, you're giving me a perfect one now: this isn't a lesson anymore, it's a rally."

"A rally, what's that?"

"Bah, it's something from those parts down there: something very important for them, it would seem."

"But at least tell us a little more about it. Come on, we apologize: just a little something."

"About the rally or death?"

"Don't play the fool: some little trifle so we can think it over and be in better shape the next time."

"Ehm, what do you want to know?"

"Well, for example you said that at a certain point they die or something like that; at what point?"

"I think there's a fixed expiration, more or less."

"A fixed expiration?"

"Yes, well, you must know that they have elaborated a second concept which you should be able to understand immediately by

now: the concept of life. Elaborated in a manner of speaking—
not that they made much of an effort—since it's really the same
concept reversed. In short, whatever isn't death, they call life.
So then, after a certain period of life that is nearly the same for
everybody, they die."

"Oh, great! This is even more absurd: and how do you explain
it?"

"Ah, even if there were an explanation, that would take us too
far."

"And what does a certain period of life mean? A period that
is still infinite: if not on one side (forgive the expression), then
on the other, if not after death, then before it. You mean equally
infinite, that is, not a period."

"Eh, no, I don't know what you mean, but you're forgetting
that they're limited in time and space, or so they suppose themselves, thus isolating the lesser. Thus, actually, they not only end
but also begin. And they call this beginning a birth."

"Which presupposes an ending, a death?"

"Undoubtedly, just as an ending presupposes a beginning,
death presupposes birth. But where are you dragging me? Let's
not make a question of the before and after, or we'll be back
where we started."

"Before and after: what are they?"

"Come, come now, for goodness sake."

"But is there finally any sort of apparent rhythm or cycle in
their being?"

"Yes, you big geniuses, that's it exactly, even though we can't
really say in their being. In their terminology life isn't and can't
always be identified with being. So to put it another way, they
don't know what they were before death nor what they will be
afterward."

"They don't know!"

"No, that's the point."

"So, how do they come to be ... to live: is that the way to
say it?"

"Another time for this too. But if the stories are true, I can tell you that this rhythm you brought up is exemplified by their very lives."

"How is it exemplified?"

"Well, during their lives they have some sort of little or minor births and deaths; apparent ones, of course, or doubly apparent. How should I know: almost like attempts at the final death and repetitions of the initial birth. And to come to the point, the funniest thing is, they are born and die like this the exact same number of times, seeing that the first birth, meaning the real one, is not preceded by any evident death and that the final death is not followed by any evident birth. Which is why only half, and exactly half, of their life is actually such."

"That isn't clear: their life is thus made up of births and deaths?"

"Not made up of, marked by."

"That is, a period of time follows the first birth, which is soon interrupted by a death—a period of death—which is in turn interrupted by birth and a relative period of life, and so on until the final death."

"That's less clear than ever."

"Wait. Not only are these periods equal quantitatively but also qualitatively as incredible as it may seem: that is, these minor births and deaths also take place at nearly fixed periods."

"What you're saying is finally clear, but only what you're saying. . . . Oh, how can it be? And another thing: what does period of death mean?"

"The period of time, we can put it like this now, between one of these minor deaths and births."

"What a sneaky professor: that was more or less clear. But we're asking something else, and that is—if death is some sort of ending, how can it be a period?"

"Because we're talking about appearances here, about apparent death."

"Ah, that period of time is a lacuna?"

"On the contrary, their existence does not cease during those periods, rather it becomes more intense in one way and nearly fades out in another. Do you see?"

"Oh, sir, so many incongruities in so few words! First of all, evidently their existence doesn't cease even after the major death. Rather, as you said, what ceases is life, which to complicate matters is still existence, even though or insofar as it is part of it. And one could go on. But truthfully, you must have deliberately chosen an ambiguous or inconclusive term like existence to save yourself from embarrassment. Just say so."

"I will not say so, not even hypothetically."

"Hypothetically?"

"I won't say anything of the kind. Look, you see why I don't want to add anything when a lesson is over? There's no rest with types like you; everything, the least word, requires explanations, and endless specifications. That's enough."

"Let's be quiet, otherwise he'll leave."

"Oh, all right, calm down; we'll pretend to understand and you can make your point again. So during those periods their existence becomes more intense in one way and nearly fades out in another; fine, in what other way?"

"Uhm, what characterizes existence, existence or being, as you all see it?" (This will end it.)

"Sensations, images, thoughts."

"Uhm, in that case, there's no doubt that they exist or are to a greater degree during those periods of apparent death than during actual life."

"Therefore, aside from some obvious observations you made about the way existence expresses itself, your analogy was false and it would be better if you reversed the order you just set up. It begins with a death and ceases with a birth, it seems."

(These devils are embarrassing me.) "Reverse it, if you like, in the end it makes no difference. However, you are not putting enough of an emphasis upon the fact that they have a body or are . . . In reality, who knows what we're fishing up here;

their alternate periods or states of apparent death and
life...."

"... Apparent?"

"Don't interrupt! Those states of theirs, which incidentally are
generically and respectively called sleep and waking, are the
reverse of one another, and one can no longer tell which is true
and which is false."

"True and false, what do they have to do with this?"

(These guys are no fools!) "Anyway, one no longer knows
which to focus on and sometimes one comes to the conclusion,
as some of them have even thought, that these people are made
of two halves, one of which would be the body, and the other..."

"The other, the other?"

"What do I know! Evidently, something that isn't a body, that
actually opposes the body in some way."

"No, Professor, this won't do: we cannot, we simply cannot
actually go so far as to conceive of two distinct coexisting natures.
You must tell us whether or not they are bodies."

"Listen for a moment, my darlings, my young, oh, so petulant
friends, we're not going to perplex one another any longer. I'm
not taking my notions any further, and offhand I don't know
how to put the matter to you. .... Uhm, but listen, couldn't there
be something inside their bodies like those celestial bodies with
a hard crust that have a fire inside?"

"And why then doesn't whatever is inside break the actual
crust or render the body useless?"

"Good gracious, a good question: and why, may I ask you
in turn, doesn't the internal fire of heavenly bodies erupt? But
then again, I really don't see how you got it into your heads
that freedom tends toward greater freedom, that, for instance,
a free element like fire must necessarily tend toward some sort
of liberty or epiphany. Actually, it slowly closes in upon itself,
and on closer look, freedom tends rather toward a state of
slavery. It is not a value, not even an aspiration, it's simply
one of those false presumptions that our myopia has created.

It is in our nature to make analogies, and thus inspired by the partial processes of the liberation of energies or forces in nature that we witness every day, we ended up with the conviction that freedom is the supreme end and good, even the best means! But we cannot see the ultimate end of all this, its ultimate and perhaps its positive end. That's for certain! If there is anything we don't begin to understand it's freedom; but actually it isn't even anything, it's a breath, a nothing, awaiting its definition and its destination, which as I said, is slavery. Freedom cannot be an objective; or anyway pity upon those people and those epochs that considered it as such. Or in more pertinent terms, one could also say that the regulating principle of the universe is not a dilating, excuse the ugly word, but a constricting one; not, excuse me again, an expanding but a contracting one.... Oh, but diligent boys, why are you making me give these night-school seminars? We are clearly digressing (it isn't really all in vain!) and this blessed lesson really should have ended long ago. Let's go back to our guns. But no, let's not go back to anything. Good-bye until the next time."

"And so?"

"So what?"

"So their lives are made up of both, of sleep, and what did you call it, waking?"

"Right."

"And then they really die?"

"Really: how do you mean really?"

"What, what?"

"No, this time you're not going to get me; leave the rest for the next time."

"But at least tell us how this death is manifested?"

"Damn it, they cease to be what they were. For example, they cease moving."

"Why, did they move when they were alive?"

"And how! Movement is one of the fundamental principles of life for them: and from their own point of view, they're not all wrong. Are the heavenly bodies ever still for a moment?"

"They move! This is too much!"

"Yah, and they always, for example, and it's just an example, lose their bodies."

"Huh, what do you mean 'for example, just an example,' and how do they lose their bodies?"

"Oh, no you don't, my dears." (It will never end at this rate.)

"Oh, what a shame. Let's jump ahead, then. So they die, and then what?"

"Then what? Nothing?"

"Oh, no way! Where one thing ends another must necessarily begin."

"Come back tomorrow."

"Come on, Professor, be nice, just a moment: tell us another bit of nonsense."

"Nonsense? Hah."

"No, no, in the sense of some trifle: Professor, the fun has only just begun; up until now, you've only been demanding unpleasant leaps of our imagination, but now it's time you started telling us properly about everything...."

"Come to the next lesson on time."

"Oh, this is infuriating!"

"But what studious and thoughtful youngsters you are! Nevertheless, I better not exaggerate this either. Good-bye."

"Just a moment. I have a question: you said that waking and sleep are the reverse of one another."

"Yes, they are each the simulation of the other."

"But..."

"I understand what you don't get, and I don't know what to say. You'd like to know if... or which would prevail in an ideal order?"

"Yes, yes."

"Look: since I don't know, I can only imagine that waking simulates sleep much more weakly than sleep does waking. Or anyway, sleep is automatic while waking is not."

"And what are we supposed to make of that?"

"I don't know."

"But do you realize that if such a fact is true, it can be interpreted in two different ways?"

"I realize it."

"One can choose either waking or sleep randomly as the more important."

"Choose."

"We choose the second interpretation."

"Fine, congratulations."

"So real life is sleep?"

"You may think so if it suits you."

"And the body plays almost no part in sleep?"

"It seems so, or it surely plays a minor part." (If I'm not careful, they're going to drag me back, and I'll be answering, and discussing, naturally.)

"Therefore what or who or the thing that ultimately dies is the latter?"

"What the devil are you saying? What kind of deduction is that?"

"Why don't you tell us: if they didn't have bodies, if they weren't bodies, could they die?"

"I don't think so."

"You see, so the body *is* death."

"I didn't say that."

"You mean you don't want to help us anymore."

"Not now. Good day."

"No, no, wait! Just one more explanation for the road: just a little nothing of an explanation; we'll wrap things up in two words."

"It better not be three."

"Why did you begin by using the present tense and past simultaneously and then stick only to the present in talking about all of this?"

"Look what you're cooking up now! I limited myself to the present for the sake of simplicity... but actually... You know what happened, don't you?"

"No."

"Well, the ones who went down there never came back; and at the outset they sent us communiqués, though not terribly clear ones, then those stopped too. ... Finally, we don't even know if those people, the natives of those distant worlds, are still there or not."

"You mean if they're dead or became something else now?"

"Um, right, we could put it that way."

"And when did we go?"

"Who knows! Certainly the great western star has cut the celestial equator more than one hundred thousand times since."

"Oh, Professor, tell us this story!"

"Nothing doing!"

"What did you say?"

"It seems to be or to have been an elegant expression they had for 'no.'"

"Oh, ah! You're really unyielding?"

"Unyielding."

"You mean this lesson is really over?"

"Over, may God be praised."

"And this is the famous death after all?"

"This is it. But what? I have tried my best to encourage you, but now I have my doubts: God only knows what you've all gotten from it. Anyway, summarizing what we've said up to this point..."

"No, let us summarize, so you'll see what we've understood."

"Hurry up, then."

"So, we understood that we didn't understand anything."

"Marvelous, that's more than I expected. One of their essays read: 'All I know is that I know nothing.'"

"Not so stupid for someone subject to death."

"I forbid any more delays: are you finished?"

"Look here: in final conclusion, it isn't known what death is, and consequently it may not occur at all, and the fantastic concept of death is the most absurd and inconceivable thing that..."

But just then something happened suddenly that truly put an end not only to the lesson but to the entire course, and to all good. The sky, the whole sky, was lit as if by a frightening aurora borealis, and in no time those drapes, trails, fringes, curtains and swords of light turned a violent and wicked scarlet color; the entire visible universe burned and bled. In several seconds, the temperature rose millions of degrees. And one brief second later, the stellar earth that had sheltered those relentless speakers exploded.... One can't even say thundered apart because there was nobody left to hear that great thunder.

I must confess how providentially this cosmic catastrophe coincided with the then intolerable boredom I, the teleteletelestenographer, was suffering. So I must now ask myself: what did eternity want to show? That death not only occurs on those remote galaxies but actually reigns supreme? Or did it simply want to punish those good people for their peculiar quibbling?

How petulant they really were, and what fools, too; how can anyone get so excited over things everybody knows? And full of pretenses and an obsession for speculation; alas, in this regard, they didn't let up. They would grab any little word and start to paw it as if it were a woman's breast, if you will. But, truthfully, was that speculation? Instead of rowing on a great river, they threw themselves into little rivulets and splashed about blissfully, like little beavers; without any thought to the connections, the relationships and everything else that make our real speculation glorious and supreme. Yes, yes, fine... but what about the poor fellow (like me) who had to sit there and listen?

Yet it's undoubtedly preferable to adopt their point of view, and I'll tell you the wherefore. There was one thing those people were undoubtedly right about: no matter what eternity may do, death does not occur, it simply doesn't. Thus, some part of them must still be, even if they are out there rambling. And since they are indeed out there rambling, their spirit, or some part of it, may well have entered one of our bodies. And everyone, save the creators of speculative science fiction and galaxoids or nebuloids, has some self-respect.

WORDS
AND
WRITING

PERSONAPHILOLOGICAL-
DRAMATIC CONFERENCE
WITH IMPLICATIONS

"Gentlemen! I am the author of a short story entitled 'The Walk,' which heralds an equally short collection, *Impossible Stories*, published by the fellows over at Vallecchi Publishers."

"So who cares!"

"A rude yet, we must admit, frank opinion. But hold on, gentlemen: either I am deceiving myself, or the matter in which I propose to engage you is, as the saying goes today, of general interest."

"We hope you're not deceiving yourself."

"Judge for yourselves. So then, a number of obsolete or difficult words appear in this story."

"Good for you, but why?"

"It will soon become clear."

"Go on, then."

"'At times funereal, the voice...' Oh, well, so wrote a know-it-all of hack-magazine literary criticism...."

"What a great description, but this sounds more like a hatchet job than a hack job."

"A know-it-all who is well-known for his scanty familiarity with the Italian vocabulary defined mine as 'invented.' And then, another top critic of the same ilk states, and I quote, 'Innovations of this kind abound in the recent *Impossible Stories*, beginning with the sort of imaginative exercise on the first pages of the little story, 'The Walk,' in which dialect (probably from the Pico region) is displayed in narration and dialogue, the result of which is an utterly indecipherable and mysterious language with the usual polemics and playfulness.'"

"And so?"

"And so, I got fed up."

"So what?"

"So I decided to break my usual silence and state the facts as they are."

"We're listening, though we're hardly interested in your facts."

"Oh, for heaven's sake! Am I holding this conference or are you?"

"You, you are unfortunately."

"In that case, let me say my piece. And if you do anything, make yourselves comfortable as one does at all conferences in this world: snooze."

"Very well, but don't yell any louder than necessary and wake us when you're finished."

"No, no, don't take me literally! Just pay attention. Now, then, we will divide my counterdemonstration into two parts; in other words, first we will respond to the first critic. So, my words are 'invented'?"

"But if a know-it-all of et cetera... asserts..."

"Oh, really, really? Then, let's get down to things.... First of all, is each of you equipped with a common Zingarelli dictionary?"

"Common?! Why common?"

"I mean a dictionary that everybody uses, even those little professor types."

"Hmm. Anyway, yes, we are all equipped with our Zingarellis."

"Very well. So, the—let's call them the incriminated words— are, if I am not mistaken, the following.... I'll write them down on the blackboard." (...)

"But there are so many: nearly one hundred."

"Ah, yes, my intentions required that."

"And you have yet to explain them to us."

"Silence. We must proceed in an orderly fashion. Come, then, take the first: Look it up in your Zingarellis."

"Sst, this isn't a classroom, you know! Nevertheless, tst, tst, is it possible?"

"And this second word? Unheard of?"

"And what about this one with a complete definition!..."

"Look at that, your words seem to have precise meanings."

"No kidding. Come on, get busy.... Anyway, no encouragement is necessary. I'm glad to see the entire assembly is avidly and noisily consulting their Zingarellis and finding the proper definitions for *all* the words in question."

"Your writing, therefore, has a common meaning!"

"Extremely common and obvious."

"And you have the last word over whoever he is."

"No, no, wait a minute. So far all we have done is refute the first critic's opinion and the second one's judgment insofar as he claims the language I used (or 'displayed' as he more elegantly writes, to give him credit) is 'utterly indecipherable and mysterious'; thus, it remains for us to refute the rest of this judgment."

"You mean that it is neither dialect nor that of the 'Pico region' (as the second critic, this time, so inelegantly states)?"

"Exactly. So... did you bring your Tommaseo-Bellinis?"

"What! Should we have brought our wagons too?"

"Calm down, if you don't have it, I do, I have one. See? Is this a Tommaseo-Bellini or a chicken goiter?"

"Wait, take a look.... No, a chicken goiter it certainly is not. ... Yes, indeed, it is a Tommaseo-Bellini."

"A Tommaseo-Bellini: a dictionary specifically for the literati, which even half-baked writers keep in their libraries."

"Fine, fine, go on."

"Let's consider the incriminated words one by one to see if they are if not from the Pican dialect, from any dialect at all, or if they are not actually of good Tuscan usage."

"That will take quite awhile."

"Let's choose some randomly, and you'll have to take my word for the rest."

"Don't worry, we're beginning to give you some credit."

"It's about time. Well?" (. . .)

"Ah, agreed, we don't need more. You win."

"No, I want to take this opportunity to point out that this other presumptuous critic is, if not by birth, still from a good Tuscan family."

"Please, have pity! Didn't you promise us something of general interest?"

"Well, you should have gotten some idea from all this, I hope."

"That literary critics don't know the Italian language?"

"Too well, honestly. And too little."

"Explain that."

"Gladly. What we do not demand from the critic, although we hope for it, is a knowledge of many strange words. But what we do demand, and have the right to demand, is a certain philological flair. . . . Stop me if I am mistaken."

"You are not mistaken. But spare us your chatter."

"Is it possible that among the hundred words in circulation here right now, among all of them, not one of our meritorious men recognized a familiar sound?"

"It really does seem impossible because, by definition, a critic cannot be thick as a log. Nevertheless, forgive us, but the meat of your argument escapes us: it is quite possible that the above-mentioned critics did recognize some words. . . . But anyway, what's your point?"

"Very simply that the impossible is always really possible. If indeed any of them, these critics, had the slightest doubt about even one of the harassed words, and if as a result they had realized that this one word was normally listed in any old scholarly dictionary, then they would have looked them all up and would have discovered unequivocal meanings for all of them, and they wouldn't

have brought shame upon themselves with feeble-minded statements."

"By God, you're right."

"Thank you. But there is more, and it's worse. Let us assume
that we didn't demand a certain philological flair from the critic.
Friends, let's be honest: at the very least, a literary flair . . . this
character who proclaims himself the interpreter of others' works—
shouldn't he have a literary flair?"

"What do you mean by literary flair?"

"If he is, or presumes to be, a critic, this person must know
that D'Annunzio and I don't invent words: the ones in our beautiful
language suffice us and it is easier to use them (a fact which is
even more mortifying for these critics in question)."

"Oh, ya ya ya ya ya. You can pride yourself on having convinced
us."

"Well, I confess, to your credit, I didn't expect anything less
than comprehension from you; and yet I flatter myself in thinking
that you will likewise hear me out, for I am about to articulate
my general conclusion, in anticipation of your questions."

"Articulate it."

"As you wish. Now, then, should we concede to these critics
the right to judge our works when they don't understand (as we
have just seen) the alphabet?"

"Noooo!"

"Thank you for that general consensus. But once again, there's
something else, or actually more of the same, which we can
illuminate with a clear example."

"Something else, the same? To tell the truth, we were hoping
. . . we were afraid the conference was over."

"Have no fear! . . . But I ask: why did I go to so much trouble
to reveal the critics' ignorance and stupidity, which after all have
been well-documented for so long?"

"You answer that."

"The answer is: because their incorrect interpretations render
all my labors futile."

"Speak more openly."

"I mean, rather than 'playfulness,' my 'Walk' was meant to be a bitter indictment, or if not an indictment, then a bitter demonstration. As if to say: 'Look, we can't even speak the same language.' But apparently, those critics and I truly do not speak the same language; so it is not that we cannot understand one another *even though* et cetera, but simply *because* et cetera. Which makes quite a difference, as far as my conclusive conclusions go."

"Why don't you stop jumping to these conclusions of yours, and tell us instead: isn't it possible that the critics had their own good reasons, or at least justifications?"

"For what?"

"For not penetrating your intentions; since for one reason or another you enveloped your bitter indictment or demonstration in obscurity."

"And (once again), gentlemen, what about that flair?"

"What do you mean?"

"The tone and atmosphere of the subsequent stories or little stories should have certainly illuminated, for the knowing reader, the first one, which could have ideally been considered the *key* story of the whole collection."

"Ehm. It could be! Actually, we understood precious little of your answer. But allow us to call your victory anyway."

"Hold on, hold on. Just like that, without any further comments?"

"Why, do you have anything else to add? Some little point?"

"My files are as extensive as Versailles or Escorial."

"Out with it, then."

"Something recent, you mean?"

"Whatever you want."

"I don't know. A certain highly qualified critic, a regular contributor and perhaps a column editor for that exclusively literary paper... But it's not worthwhile discussing: there is nothing new or unusual in this."

"Why, yes, go on, just to give us an idea. This critic...?"

"He doesn't know how to copy an Italian sonnet. A normal administrative task, as you well know."

"Oh, my God, no! Evidently the printer was at fault."

"This age-old and merciful lie could be exploited once again if the very title of the article were not taken from one of those copying errors; and if, more importantly, other factors didn't arouse our bewilderment."

"That is?"

"In conceding to me, this gentleman was good enough to attribute to me and to extol with words both learned and enthusiastic my (I'm sorry if it isn't much) my *Winter Story....* * But no more of that."

"No, no, just one more critical anecdote to instruct and amuse us."

"Eh, but we might get into hot water; and anyway, what could I tell you? Perhaps something concerning 'Mozart's sublime "Scherzo for Elisa"'?"

"Slow down! 'Scherzo for Elisa,' Mozart? You're pulling our legs!"

"I'm not and neither is Mozart: it's the other way around. That attribution was firmly stated in the remarks of a leading critic, (the same one, by chance, who deemed the words from the above-studied little story 'invented')."

"Ah, but therefore, ah, but then...!"

"No, that's enough now, really. Actually, give me your attention again because, going back to our main discussion, I have a trick up my sleeve, or rather a bomb under my hat."

"Oh, marvelous!... Go on, go on."

"Coming here for this instructive and delightful conference, I was handed a sheet of paper which I see bears snippets of rumors heard recently when I was judged deserving of a piece of that

---

*Landolfi's highly regarded novella is titled *Racconto d'autunno* (Autumn story), not "Racconto d'inverno" (Winter story), as it is mistakenly referred to by the critic here.

literary award (I don't know for what special merit)."

"Please, don't bore us like this: first you promise us seas and mountains, and then you make us fall asleep in our seats."

"Ah, well, I would like for us to read this paper together."

"A great idea: we're all ears."

"And particularly this passage where... Yes, here, here: '*Impossible Stories* contains some of the most revelatory pages of the author's present condition, and above all of his narrative and stylistic "epoché." It opens with the brief caprice or pastiche, 'The Walk,' in which the myth of incommunicability is playfully exorcised and ridiculed by the introduction of an "impossible" lexicon, which is glossematic (and yet belongs to the dead periphery of the Italian language) in the highly traditional nineteenth-century syntax; and ends with...' So, how does that strike you?"

"That, considering your intentions, one couldn't say anything better."

"Right, not better, but maybe slightly better."

"And so, just because it happens to all of you so often, you have led us around by our noses? Thus, not all critics are gross, as you would have us believe?... And for heaven's sake, what about your bomb, or your trick?"

"That's simple: it's that we can celebrate the archeminence of this last and archeminent critic, but we can't reveal his name."

"Why, is he involved in anonymity?"

"Yes."

"Why so?"

"That's simpler still: to avoid his colleagues' insults."

"Fantastic!"

"What?"

"The man, but also your argument. Which is good reason to proceed to your long-overdue victory."

"What, what, did you really take this seriously? Don't get excited, calm down, good!... Or do you want the authorities to intervene?"

"No, anything but the authorities!"

"Good, then. May our farewell be both sensational and subdued."

"So be it. How about something like 'May God always be with you, great Italian.'"

"No, no, something a little less idiotic, and contrary in feeling. For example, 'Adieu, faithful followers, and my insults to your families, if you're stupid or wretched enough to have any.'"

DIALOGUE
OF THE GREATER
SYSTEMS

In the morning when we get out of bed, though we may be astonished to find that we are still alive, we are no less shocked that everything is just as we left it the night before. Thus, as I was staring in stupid absorption out the window, my friend Y announced himself with a precipitous series of knocks at the door of my room.

I knew him as a timid and cantankerous man, dedicated to strange studies that he carried out like rites in solitude and mystery; therefore, I was not surprised when I observed that he seemed to be in the grips of great agitation that day. While I dressed and we spoke of this and that, he swung with extraordinary rapidity between profound dejection and a happiness that struck me as feigned, and I soon realized that something curious or terrible must have happened to him. When I was finally ready to listen, he recounted a strange story which, for the sake of simplicity, I will relate in the first person. He premised it by asking me not to interrupt him regardless of how strange or pointless what he was about to tell me might seem, and that he would make it as brief as possible. Taken aback and curious, I complied.

"I must tell you," Y then began, "that many years ago I dedicated myself to a minute and patient distillation of the elements that come together in a work of art. And as a result, I came to the precise and incontrovertible conclusion that having rich and varied means of expression at one's disposal is hardly a favorable situation for an artist. For example, in my view, it is greatly preferable for one to write in a language he only partially knows than in one with which he is wholly familiar. But I needn't retrace the involuted and tortuous path that brought me to this simple discovery because I think the same clear arguments still prove valid today: when one doesn't know the precise words to indicate objects or feelings, it seems he is forced to paraphrase, that is, to substitute with images—and you can imagine the artistic advantages. And when technical words and clichés are eliminated, what else could prevent a work of art from coming into being?"

At this point, Y stopped short, probably momentarily satisfied with his argument, and gazed at me through half-shut eyes, his woes forgotten. But noticing the stunned and questioning expression on my face, he drew a breath and began again hurriedly.

"Having reached the conclusion I just mentioned, I happened to stumble upon an English captain, a monster of a man (you'll soon see why I'm calling him a monster). Oh, God, why didn't you spare me this misfortune? Now my peace of mind is lost forever! He had a weak countenance—but what's the point of telling you this? He used to eat in the trattoria I frequented, and he always bragged of his numerous adventures to the vast circle of subordinates who flocked around him. He had been in the Orient for many years, though I don't know how long, and knew a great many Oriental languages (or so he said). But he boasted particularly of his knowledge of Persian and often bandied three or four strange words at the waiters, who merely stood blinking in astonishment; it would turn out that he wanted to order a glass of wine or a grilled steak. As you can see I hated this man, even though he managed to strike up conversations with me; and one awful day he offered to teach me Persian. I was anxious to test my theory on myself, so I finally accepted. As you might have already guessed, my plan was precisely to learn the language imperfectly: well enough to express myself but not well enough to call things by their names.

"Our lessons proceeded in a normal fashion—but why can't I resist the temptation to tell all the pathetic details of this story? . . . I made swift progress in the new language. In the captain's view, languages must be learned through practice: therefore, during that entire period I never saw a Persian text (anyway, it would have been difficult to get hold of one). Instead when we took walks, my teacher and I conversed solely in Persian and when we sat down in some café to rest, we quickly filled the blank pages before us with strange, minute signs. More than a year went by in this manner: toward the end, the captain praised me ceaselessly for the facility with which I had profited from his instruction. Then one day he announced that he would soon be leaving, for Scotland, I believe, where indeed, he fled and where, I hope, he will find just reward for his trespasses. I haven't seen him since . . ." My friend Y fell silent again, as if to rein in his emotions: the discomforting memory curdled on his face in a pained grimace. Finally, he composed himself and went on:

"Meanwhile, I already knew enough to carry on with my experiment, and I did so with great zeal. I forced myself to write only in Persian; or actually, I expressed the outpourings of my soul, my poetry, solely in that language. From then up until one month ago, I didn't write one poem that wasn't in Persian. Fortunately, I'm not a terribly prolific poet, and all the work I produced during this period only amounts to three brief compositions—in Persian!—which I will show you."

I could see that the memory of having written in Persian was unbearable to Y, but I still didn't understand why.

"In Persian!" Y repeated. "But now I must explain, my poor friend, what the language which the reprehensible captain had named Persian really was. A month ago, I was suddenly overwhelmed by a desire to read a certain Persian poet you don't know in the original (one never runs the risk of learning a language too well when reading a poet). I prepared myself for this demanding task by diligently reviewing the notes I'd taken with the captain until I deemed myself capable of understanding. After great difficulty, I finally succeeded in obtaining the text I wanted. I remember that it was handed to me carefully wrapped in tissue paper. Eager for this first encounter, I went straight home, lit my small stove and a cigarette, adjusted the lamp so that all of its light was shed on the precious book. I arranged myself in the armchair and unwrapped the package. I could only guess that there had been a mistake; the signs before my eyes had nothing in common with those I had learned from the captain and which I knew so well! I will make my story brief. There was no mistake. This was a real Persian book. My only hope then was that even if the captain had forgotten the characters, he had nevertheless taught me the language, and what did it matter if he used imaginary symbols? But that was a false hope too. I turned the whole world upside down, I rifled through Persian grammars and chrestomathies, I sought and found two authentic Persians, and at last, at last . . ."—and here poor Y's monologue gave way to a moan— "at last I discovered the terrible truth, as horrid as it was: *the captain had not taught me Persian!* Need I tell you that I searched desperately to find out whether that language was at least *Jakuto* or a *Hainanese* language or Hottentot: I contacted the most famous linguists in all of Europe. Nothing, nothing! Such a language doesn't exist and never existed! In my desperation, I even wrote to the ignoble captain (who had left me his address 'for whatever you might need from me'), and here's the reply I received last night." And bending his weary head, he held out a rumpled piece of paper on which I read: "Honorable Sir, I have received your letter of . . . etc. I have never heard any reference to the language you refer to, despite my remarkable linguistic experience." ("Shameless!" Y exclaimed.) "The expressions you quoted are completely unknown to me and believe me they must be a figment of your fertile imagination. As for the bizarre signs you wrote in the note, on the one hand they resemble Amharic characters and on the other hand Tibetan ones; but you can be sure they are neither. As to your reference to the pleasant period we shared ... I can only respond sincerely: it is possible that in teaching you Persian, I might have forgotten some rule or word after so long, but I see no reason for alarm, and you should be able to rectify any inexactitude I might possibly have imparted to you [*sic*]. Please keep me abreast of your good news ... etc."

"Now I understand it all," said Y, rousing himself. "I wouldn't want to assume that the miserable fellow simply wanted to play a joke on me. I rather think that whatever he taught me was what he remembered of authentic Persian, his own personal Persian, if you will; an idiom, I mean, so deformed, so altered that it bore no relation to the language which inspired it. I must therefore assume that this mutilated knowledge in the wretch's haughty mind did not represent any sort of fixed values whatsoever. In the face of his fading knowledge and perhaps in the hopes of slowly reconstructing the lost language, the miserable fellow began inventing this horrible idiom as he taught it to me; and, as often happens to such improvisers, he later completely forgot his creation and even marveled at it in all sincerity."

He announced this diagnosis with perfect coldness. But added immediately: "He completely forgot it, you must keep that in mind! You wanted the truth, that's the truth!" Y yelled in conclusion, momentarily turning his anguish against me.

"The saddest thing," he continued in a broken voice, "is that this damn language I cannot name is beautiful, beautiful ... and I love it very much."

I waited until he calmed down before I spoke.

"Look, Y," I began, "what happened to you is certainly unpleasant but in reality, aside from your wasted labors, what is so serious about it?"

"That's how you all think," Y came back bitterly, "but don't you understand the serious part, the horrible part of the affair? Don't you understand the whole point? What about my three poems? Three poems," he repeated, choking up, "into which I poured the best of myself! What kind of poetry can those three poems of mine be, then? They may as well have never been written than to have been written in a nonexistent language, those three poems! Isn't that so?"

I suddenly understood the matter at hand and the gravity of the situation struck me. Now I too bent my head.

"It's an extraordinarily unique aesthetic problem," I admitted.

"Aesthetic problem, you say? An aesthetic problem... All right, then..." and Y leaped up violently.

What great times those were. We gathered in the evening with our contemporaries to read the great poets, and a poem was inestimably more important to us than our bill at the trattoria, which increased daily and was never paid up.

The next day Y and I stood knocking at the door of the city newspaper office where we were to confer with a great critic, one of those men for whom aesthetics holds no secrets and on whose shoulders the spiritual life of an entire nation rests at peace, since these men know its foundations and problems better than anyone else. It had taken miracles to obtain an appointment with such a man, but Y's spiritual health depended upon it.

The great critic greeted us with a smile. He was still young, and permanent ironic creases surrounded his lively eyes. He fidgeted as he spoke, first toying with a steel paper-knife and then pushing a hand-bound book on its spine around the desktop. He sniffed a tarnished container of almond glue now and then, and continually traced broad shapes in the air with long, glinting scissors and then combed his mustache with them. He often appeared to be smiling to himself, especially when he imagined that his interviewer thought he might have embarrassed him. However, when he addressed us directly, his smile turned affected; and generally, he affected an exaggerated courtesy. He spoke softly with sober gestures and lofty words duly intermingled with foreign expressions.

After he had heard the matter at hand, he seemed perplexed for a moment, then he smiled to himself, and as if distracted by some point above our heads, he said:

"But, gentlemen, writing in one language rather than another is unimportant" (and he lowered his eyes and produced a worldly smile on "portant"). "A language needn't be very widespread for one to write, let us say, masterpieces in it. In this case, Mr. Y, it's a language that is spoken by only two people: there you have it. *N'empêche* that your poems can be of, uhm, the first order."*

"Wait a moment," said Y, "perhaps I failed to mention that the English captain completely forgot his improvisation of two years ago? Moreover, seeing this turn of events, I myself burned the old notes which alone could have served as the grammar and key to the language. Therefore, we must consider the language non-existent even for the two people who once spoke it for several months."

"I wouldn't want you to think," replied the great critic, "that the elements that establish the reality of a given language are not identifiable outside the context of its grammar, syntax and even its lexicon. If you simply consider your language dead, and only reconstructible through a few documents which have survived (in this case your three poems), the supposed problem will be resolved. As you know," he added, conceding, "we only possess a few inscriptions from some languages and hence a scarce number of words, and yet those languages are very real to us. And let me say too: even those languages which are only certified by the existence of indecipherable, I said in-de-ci-pher-ab-le, inscriptions, even those languages have a right to our aesthetic respect." And pleased with this phrase, he fell silent.

"But, sir," I then broke in, "let's overlook these other languages you just spoke of because I don't think I grasped your concept, and go back to those you spoke of before; those languages, I mean, are still real insofar as they are presupposed by the inscriptions, scarce as they may be—but beware, presupposed in

---

*I must point out that it was the great critic who chose to address us in the rather antiquated second person "you" plural; we followed suit obediently. As the reader will note, this lent our discussion an amusing aspect of the fantastic.

the complex of their lexicon, grammar and syntax. The inscriptions, that is, bear the trace of a structure, of an organization, which places them in time and space and without which they wouldn't be the least bit distinguishable from any other sign on any other rock, just like those indecipherable ones. Those inscriptions throw light on an unknown past, but they also draw their meaning from it. And that past is merely a complex of norms and conventions which attribute a fixed meaning to a fixed expression. Now, what kind of past could the three poems in question have and from what would they draw their meaning? Nothing stands behind them but momentary whim without any codification whatsoever, a whim which vanished as hopelessly as it emerged."

The great critic looked at me askance, still pondering that "beware" which had annoyed him. Not in the least intimidated, I continued:

"A language reconstructed upon scarce inscriptions only acquires validity if that language, and that language only, proves to be reconstructible through those inscriptions. But in our case the sum of data is so small that one could construct or reconstruct not one, but one hundred, languages. One would thus witness the lovely little example of a poem that could claim to have been written in one language just as easily as in one hundred others which, moreover, are profoundly different from one another and from the first. . . ."

And here, satisfied with my sophism, I stopped. But the great critic said:

"This seems little more than a sophism. In the first place, philology operates upon precisely such suppositions in cases like this: suppositions which have the characteristics of relative certainties, it is true, but are suppositions nonetheless; besides, theoretically speaking, more than one language can be reconstructed on the basis of certain inscriptions. And secondly, what do you care if a poem could have been written in more than one language? The essential thing is that it was written in one, and it hardly matters if this has something in common with another or one hundred other languages so as to permit the kind of interchanges that you are speaking of. Finally, sir, I'd like to point out that from a more, ehm, elevated point of view, a work of art can arise not only from linguistic conventions but from all conventions, and it is its own only judge."

"Oh, no," I yelled, seeing the best part of my argument slipping through my fingers, "you're not going to get out of it like that. Now you're verging on a sophism. And, then, you're taking it for granted that this is a work of art. But that is really the matter in question: where and what are the criteria by which you judge? Let me go back to my previous thought for a moment. When I said that a complex of norms that can be apprehended stands behind inscription, I also meant that some of its purely linguistic data are verified and buttressed by a knowledge that is not merely linguistic: I mean by an ethnic knowledge. On the basis of what we know about a certain people we can take it for granted that a given expression is valid not only in a certain position, but also in all analogous positions. For example, the mere knowledge that a given language has served a people in their internal and external relationships is sufficient guarantee of the fixed significance of a word. An entire people, sir, stands behind an inscription! Behind one of these poems there is only a whim, that is evident. And thus, who will guarantee us that the meaning of the same expression won't be radically altered from one occasion to the next? Please note that you will not find one word repeated twice in these three poems. Theoretically, sir, one could imagine that each of the three poems unfolds a certain image (or concept, if you prefer), and at the same time, seeing that none of the words have a well-defined meaning, one hundred, one thousand, one million other images (or concepts)."

"Excuse me, excuse me," shouted the great critic, beside himself now. "Thus the question can be swiftly resolved: the inscriptions, that is the poems, can be considered bilingual. Mr. Y, who is now present, can communicate what he wanted to say by translating them. As you can see, your objection doesn't hold." And he looked at me triumphantly. But I wasn't moved:

"You're forgetting, sir, that a poem is not only an image (or concept), but is made up of an image (or a concept) in addition to something else. If you judge my friend's poems on the basis of his translation, you will find yourself in the position of the person judging a foreign poet through a translated version of his work. Admit it, it is neither honest nor honorable. Besides, my friend himself, in point of fact, can't know what he wanted to say"—Y glared at me—"since he conceived his compositions in the language initially. The result is that this would be no more than a version, comparable to a translation which you or I might do if we had to, and therefore by its nature incomplete and fallacious. It might also be completely arbitrary and have nothing in common with the text; it might be a false interpretation, after all. Finally, I needn't remind you, sir, that, more generally speaking, a work of art is, by necessity, an accomplishment relative to particular conventions and can only be judged by their standards. An accomplishment, by its very nature, can only be appraised on the basis of the means employed. No absolute results exist, outside of God, and the very concept of a creation is a relative one. Creations fall into place along an infinite, ideal scale, even if within the limits of a single moral standard. But let's not digress. Very well, sir, what criteria will you employ to make your evaluation?"

The silence of a tomb fell over the great critic's office. The man, his eyes lost in thin air, pretended not to hear my question. He pretended to rouse himself, and then to kill time he said to Y with his most beautiful smile:

"But meanwhile, sir, why don't you let us hear some of these famous poems that are stirring up such a 'pleasant war of wits'?"

"I only have one with me," hesitated Y. The great critic nodded, and encouraged, Y pulled from his pocket some papers covered with bizarre and minute characters that were all points and commas, and he read in a trembling voice:

"Aga magéra difúra natun gua mescíun
Sánit guggérnis soe-wáli trussán garigúr
Gùnga bandúra kuttávol jeriś-ni gillára.
Lávi girréscen suttérer lunabinitúr
Guesc ittanóben katiŕ ma ernáuba gadún
Vára jesckílla sittáranar gund misagúr,
Táher chibill garanóbeven líxta mahára
Gaj musasciár guen divrés kôes jenabinitúr
Soè guadrapútmijen lòeb sierrakár masasciúsc
Sámm-jab dovár-jab miguélcia gassúta
    mihúsc
Sciú munu lússut junáscru gurúlka varúsc."

(according to the transcription that Y handed to me).

In the long silence that followed, the great critic waited, smoothing his mustache with the point of the scissors, while Y looked at him questioningly. He finally blurted out: "But do you hear how the *u* is repeated in the last lines and the rhymes of the *usc*! So what do you think?" The poor fellow had forgotten that he had yet to give us some explanation.

"Indeed, indeed, pas mal, really pas mal," the great critic said. "And would you be so kind as to translate now?"

Improvising from the text, Y translated:

"And her weary faced wept with joy
as the woman told me of her life
and promised her fraternal affection.
And the pines and larches of the avenue bent
    gracefully
against a warm-pink sunset in the background
and a small villa flying the nation's flag,
seemed the wrinkled face of a woman who didn't realize
her nose was shiny. And for a long time after
I felt that bright flash,
mocking and bitter,
leap and twist like a little playful fish
deep in the shadows of my soul."

"Why that's good, really quite good," the great critic exploded in compliments. "Now I understand why the *u* is repeated in the last lines! Bravo, bravo: it's an appropriate thing, fortunately, not one bit formulaic."

With this formality expressed, he turned to me.

"As you can see, your suspicions were unfounded and hasty," and he smiled. "Did you see how quickly he translated?"

"But no," moaned Y, "that free translation doesn't render the original even remotely. The poem is unrecognizable in translation, it has lost everything; it is devoid of all meaning."

"As you can see," I said in my turn, "that only brings us back to the same old question. A little while ago, sir, I took the liberty of asking you what criteria you, yourself, would adopt. Allow me to repeat the question."

The great critic could no longer slip out of it and was forced to comply and reopen the discussion, which he did once again by skirting the difficulty.

"Truthfully," he began, "I'm not, as you've rightly made clear, competent to judge one of these poems; thus, I'm not thinking of the criteria I should adopt. The only one who is competent to judge is the author himself, since he is the only one who knows the language regardless of how well or poorly."

"If I'm not wrong," I interrupted, "I've already implicity excluded this way out. As I've already told you before not even the author..."

But Y, who had been silent up until then (though I'd noticed more than once that he looked like he was up to something), preferred to take a different tack.

"You mean something can qualify as a work of art, even if there's only one person in the world competent to judge it, and that is, precisely the author?"

"Exactly."

"That means that from now on when one writes poems, he can base it upon sound rather than idea," Y then went on and one must take pity on him. "He can put beautiful and musical, or suggestive and obscure, words together and then attribute a meaning to them, or merely see what the outcome is...."

"Excuse me, I don't really see the connection between..."

"But, yes; nothing prevents one from arranging the first sounds that come to one's ears according to a certain rhythm, and then attributing a lovely meaning to them. In doing this, he will create a new language: and what does it matter if it is inadequate and limited to a few sentences (those in the composition), since there will always be one person who knows it: its very creator, and always someone competent to judge the composition: its very author."

"But look, you shouldn't take things to extreme conclusions. I'm in full agreement, at least with the first part of your reasoning, though, forgive me for saying so, it doesn't seem much to the point; but as far as the second point is concerned, come on, you shouldn't *emballer* in a dangerous *Weltanschauung*, or raise such problematical *topics*. Personally, I prefer the *commonplace or places*." The great critic had outdone himself.

But Y answered:

"I'm sorry, I don't care if my reasoning seems to the point or not, now I have another more pressing concern. But you say, you agree with the first point?"

"Certainly," declared the great critic, "we cannot lay our profane eyes on what unfolds in the innermost penetralia of an artist's soul. Certainly, an artist is free to put words together before attributing a meaning to them, free even to expect those words or one single word, to confer meaning and sense to his composition. As long as this is ... art. That's the point. I wouldn't want you to forget, moreover, that this meaning and sense are certainly not indispensable. A poem, gentlemen, can also make no sense. It must merely, I repeat, be a work of art."

"Therefore," Y continued, "a work of art can also lack a common meaning; it can be made of mere musical suggestion and suggest one hundred thousand different things to one hundred thousand readers. It can, in other words, have absolutely no meaning?"

"This is a thousand times true, sir."

"But then why the devil won't you admit that even if those sounds are taken from a nonexistent language, the resulting product could just as rightly be called a work of art?"

The great critic glanced furtively at the clock and perhaps deeming that the interview had already lasted long enough, announced:

"Fine, if you really insist, I'll admit it."

"Good Lord, now you're talking," smiled Y. But his smile seemed slightly diabolical. In fact, he added with a sudden theatricality:

"Well, then, I'll relinquish the meaning of these poems, and I'll bring them to you written in beautiful calligraphy with the transcription on the facing page, since you prefer to judge them without their meaning."

"Absolutely, absolutely!" blurted the great critic, caught off guard, "but . . . why, after all, do you want to give up their meaning? Just think how much easier your road to glory would be if you are the only person capable of judging, appraising and glorifying and you have only your own opinion to take into account. Trust me, it's better to have to deal with only one person rather than too many. Trust me. . . . Don't be afraid if you ultimately come to believe yourself a great poet, as I predict you will; your glory will be just as great, just as whole, and not one bit inferior to Shakespeare's. Thus you will be glorified by everyone who understands your poetic language, which happens to be only one person; but it doesn't matter. Glory is not a matter of quantity but of quality. . . ."

The great critic made biting jokes, but he was obviously in a cold sweat.

"Well, then, I yield to your point of view," Y finally said, and I saw him sneer to himself once again. "But can you assure me that we're in total agreement on that first point?"

"But yes, yes, totally, by God!"

The great critic looked at his watch openly this time, stood up and said:

"Unfortunately, my professional duties call me elsewhere. Hence, to reach some conclusion on the problem that brought you here, I would say in the course of this interview we have ascertained that the only competent judge of these three poems is their very author Y, whom I heartily hope will relish undisputed glory which shall not be sapped by envy or malevolence."

Now that he was out of danger, all his confidence had been restored. Accompanying us to the door, he slapped us familiarly on the back.

"May I still come to see you once in a while?" Y asked him.

"Why yes, whenever you like."

I was not in the least bit satisfied, and before leaving I tried once more:

"But art..."

"Art," interrupted the great critic with an impatient smile, "everyone knows what art is...."

The rest of the story is too sad for me to relate in its entirety. The reader need only know that after that visit my friend Y seemed to have gone slightly mad. A good deal of time passed, but he persisted in bringing the strangest poems without beginning or end to the newspaper office, demanding publication and pay: everyone there knows him by now and escorts him unceremoniously out the door.

He has never gone to see the great critic since that day when the great personage himself was compelled, in order to free himself from the nuisance, to push him down the stairs: or just about.

WORDS
IN COMMOTION

In the morning when I get up, naturally I brush my teeth. Thus, today I thrust the brush with half a squiggle of toothpaste into my mouth and brushed vigorously; and then with my mouth still full of foam, I sucked a gulp of water from the faucet. I'm saying this to point out that I did everything as usual.

I rinsed my mouth and spit. But now, instead of the usual disgusting mixture, out came words. I don't know how to explain this: not only were they words, but they were alive and darted this way and that in the sink which, luckily, was empty. One slid, nearly disappearing down the drain, but it caught on and saved itself. They seemed sprightly and happy, though a bit silly; turning around as rabbits sometimes do in cages, or otters caught in rapids, they then decided to climb up to the mirror. Not really the mirror: they wanted to cling onto the brackets, and I don't know how but they managed quite well. And then I realized that they were also conversing, or actually shouting in terribly high-pitched voices, which were nevertheless faint to my ears. They danced, played games and curtsied on the brackets as if they were on a stage, and then they began to gesture, so that I understood they wanted to talk to me. I strained my ears and leaned my face close so that I could hear without struggling; and when I focused my eyes, I began to recognize some of them. I really should say, single them out or read them because I knew some words that were somewhat similar; in any case, I saw the words Locupletale, and Massicotto and Erario and Martello, among others.

"We're words," began Locupletale, who seemed to be in command.

"I can see that," I answered.

"We're words and you're one of them."

"Them who?"

"One of those people who deal with us and misdeal us. That's why it's fair that it's you we're turning to for justice. In these times of revenge, of redefinitions and other such re's, it seems strange that we, alone, are left out. But now that we're all showing up together, you're in trouble: in short, we demand a redistribution."

"What redistribution? Of what, you fools?"

"Of meaning, to begin with. Does each of us mean something or not?"

"I would say so, even if some novelists or journalists may not think so."

"All right, listen. Take me, for example: I'm Locupletale, and what do I mean?"

"More or less, you mean pertaining to wealth."

"Sure, because you know; but what if you didn't know?"

"What a question!"

"No, look, I do mean what you said, but do you think it's fair? I should really mean pertaining to a brook or generally to flowing water."

"But why?"

"By God, Lo-cu-ple-ta-le: do you have a tin ear?"

"Uhm. But to begin with, you may not even exist. I know locupletare, locupletazione, locupletatissimo, but you...? And if you do exist, you're so rarely used, so what are you complaining about?"

"I do exist, I exist! And the fact that I'm rarely used doesn't mean anything."

"Tell us," another leaped up, "I'm Magiostra: so what do I mean, then?"

"How should I know?"

"Good, I mean if you're one of them; but so much the better, actually. I mean, take a rough guess. What do you think I sound like?"

"I don't know... something like a straw hat?"

"No, no! You're thinking of Maggiostrina; forget words that sound similar or things will get even more complicated. You have to try to look at me without any particular idea in mind. So just guess the first thing that comes into your head: what do I mean?"

"Then I'd say some kind of tent or lodge."

"You see?"

"What?"

"Actually, I represent a very large strawberry. You think that's fair?"

"And me," a third interrupted, "how would you size me up? Because you can do this in reverse too. Look, then: I'm Martello, isn't that an utter outrage?"

"What you're saying is Greek to me!"

"What's a Martello: maybe you know that? Well, never mind— a hammer should be called something other than Martello."

"Oh, and what should it be called?"

"It's obvious: Totano."

"I see what you mean, but I don't see how this concerns you, you in particular. You're Martello, and if you're saying that a hammer should be called Totano instead, you're sorely mistaken, because in that case, you would be a squid and not a hammer; you're only a word, you wretch!"

"You don't understand anything at all," interrupted Totano herself. "It's so simple: we two want to switch meanings, so that at least this matter would be settled, isn't that right, Martello?"

"Not at all, sweetheart!" screamed Martello. "What would happen? You'd be fine, that's for sure, but I would end up designating some kind of cuttlefish... uugh! You're kidding yourself, honey: Martello can only mean some sort of... of tree, that's it. Something vegetal."

"Calm down," I said. "One thing's for sure, two females and a goose make a market in Naples!"

"What do you mean two females? The proverb says three females."

"And you two are making enough confusion for three. Wait a second: you, Martello, didn't you say you'd rather be called or rather be, Totano?"

"Not at all, what are you, a real nitwit? I only said that the object, a hammer, should be called a squid, which makes a hell of a difference."

"Oh, for Pete's sake, you're making my head spin. And so?"

"So what?"

"So nothing. I certainly can't exchange my meaning for Totano's, even though Totano should take mine. Do you understand?"

"No."

"In other words, I give up and should rightly give my meaning to Totano, but I don't want hers in exchange, hell, no! I want someone else's."

"Whose, for example?"

"For example, hers; see over there, Betulla."

"And what about her?"

"Who, Betulla? She'll take someone else's since hers—birch—doesn't suit her anyway; let's say she'll take Trave's and mean beam."

"What, what," squealed Trave hearing herself named. "What are you, nuts? You mind your own business, and I'll mind mine."

And they were off and arguing.

"I Iridio," began another with an air of importance, "can only mean a file, it's obvious."

"And do you expect me to take your name and saddle myself with a meaning like iridium?" Lina rebutted. "Going by your rule, I can only mean something very soft, hardly a metal, let alone such a hard one. At best I could switch meanings with Guanciale or Cuscino and mean pillow or cushion. . . ."

Anyway, by now they were all screaming and squeaking at once; I felt as if I had a handful of pins in my ears. I lost my patience.

"But will you tell me what's gotten into your heads, you scamps?" I yelled. "Now watch what a neat little thing I'm going to do now so we'll all be equals."

"What are you doing, what are you doing?" they jeered.

"Wait a minute."

Blind with rage, I ran into the kitchen, got an empty bottle, then went to the studio for a sheet of paper and pencil, and came back.

"Now I'm going to list all your meanings very neatly here, then I'll throw you all into this bottle, and finally I'll let you out one by one. That way, whoever gets it gets it: the first to come out will take the first meaning, the second, the second, and so on. You will take them and be content, like it or not. Come on, let's begin."

They didn't want to cooperate and put up a struggle, trying to befuddle me, but I forced them to explain themselves point by point. But they didn't want to be caught, to say the least, and fled every which way, so I caught and squeezed them in my cupped palm; and then holding them between the thumb and index finger of my other hand, I finally managed to bottle them all. They seemed like trapped mice, they were screeching so. When they were all inside the bottle, I let them out one at a time, as planned; and each one, as I said, had to be content with the meaning she got. As soon as they got out, they fled, God knows where, and I lost sight of them. And that's the end of the story.

Right, but now there's one big problem. Because each of them took a meaning and kept it, and that's fine: but precisely who took what meaning? That's the problem. I don't know if I'm explaining myself; do you understand the question? It was all done on friendly terms, in good faith; but in the confusion of the moment, I didn't think of noting down how the various meanings were exchanged and assigned; and I was left with nothing to show for it, no documentary evidence. So now, to sum up, they know what they mean, but I don't. It's awful.

Besides, I'm a little worried. Yes, I said God knows where they went when they got out of the bottle: but surely they are somewhere in the house, and you'll see, sooner or later, they'll jump all over me again.

There's just one thing I'm happy about: now, I finally understand the meaning of the expression "to rinse your mouth out with words."

TRANSLATOR'S
AFTERWORD

Tommaso Landolfi's life is shrouded in mystery, a mystery that he himself created and sustained. Both his life and work reveal a penchant for the bizarre and extravagant. A recluse who cultivated the image of dandy and gambler, he shunned colleagues, critics and neighbors. In fact, he forbade his Italian publishers to print any biographical information in his books, and the inside jacket was always left blank at his explicit request. However, on the flap of *Gogol's Wife*, an American edition of nine of his stories (New Directions, 1963), there appears the now infamous photo of the writer thrusting a splayed hand toward the camera.

Likewise, the work he produced over a forty-year span abounds with enigma, with outlandish and horrifying premises, disturbed and disturbing characters, preposterous situations. As Italo Calvino notes in his Introduction, Landolfi's work is a feast for psychoanalytical speculation and interpretation.

Italo Calvino's instructive essay orients the unfamiliar reader in Landolfi's complex universe; having known him personally, Calvino brings his opus and his life into a broader perspective as few can. Therefore, I will comment here only on those aspects of Landolfi's work significant in the selection and translation of the stories. I am referring principally to the element of obscurity, be it of vocabulary, as in his usage of obsolete, dialectic or invented words, or in the abundance of arcane references, allusions and literary echoes.

For instance, in "Personaphilologicaldramatic Conference with Implications," a colloquy between Landolfi and an imaginary audience at a literary conference (or "fake conference," to borrow Calvino's definition), the writer defends his story "La passeggiata" (The Walk) while railing against the attacks of two outraged critics who found its "invented lexicon" incomprehensible. He misses no opportunity to mock and insult the critics who, he claims, have misapprehended the story because they "don't even understand language." Landolfi then prompts the audience to look up the words in question in two august and authoritative dictionaries, a classical one and an updated literary one, ultimately proving to the dazed spectators (his reading public) that these words are indeed legitimate, even if they have fallen out of current Italian usage. "If indeed any of them, these critics, had the slightest doubt about even one of the harassed words, and if as a result they had realized that this one word was normally listed in any old scholarly dictionary, then they would have looked them all up and would have discovered unequivocal meanings for all of them, and they wouldn't have brought shame upon themselves with feeble-minded statements," he declaims with a convoluted pomposity that borders on the comic. Still, he tells us that he wrote the story as "a bitter indictment . . . or bitter demonstration, as if to say 'Look, we can't even speak the same language.'" Thus, the unsuspecting reading public, and more so the critics, who should have known better, have been doubly duped and humiliated, while the writer, having won the game, is redeemed.

Landolfi's story is often a game, and the act of duping or manipulating the reader's intellectual and emotional reaction is the writer's characteristic stance. Like the compulsive gambler he was in life, Landolfi constantly ups the ante in his writing; he seems to intentionally arouse the reader's sense of bewilderment and frustration, to test his patience and suspend his disbelief to the breaking point. Then, the moment of unexpected denouement or fatal twist, or occasionally flat anticlimax, announces the reader's defeat, simply for having fallen for the trick. However, in Landolfi's game, there is not a single trick or twist but a series, which the reader stumbles upon one after another even as he anticipates them.

In his discussion of the stances and attitudes of Landolfi's personae, Calvino seems to suggest that the intelligence that animates them is at once instructive and good-natured. For instance, he says of that infamous story "La passeggiata" (The Walk): "the author simply set up a rule to use as many obsolete words as possible. (He himself couldn't resist the temptation to reveal this secret in a later volume, thus poking fun at those who had not caught on.) So Landolfi the 'mystifier' becomes the 'demystifier' par excellence."

In fact, "this secret" is revealed in the story discussed above, "Personaphilologicaldramatic Conference with Implications." In translating the story, I read Landolfi's intention quite differently from Calvino; rather than whimsy, I sensed behind it the bitterness which Landolfi himself admitted to; rather than "poking fun," he is flinging mud at the literary establishment that he saw himself at odds with—an entity which included his readers—and enjoying it.

In fact, since a translator's involvement in a book is generally more focused than an average reader's, I was often keenly aware of Landolfi's ironic and explosive presence lingering just behind the page. Early on, in moments of bewilderment, I regretted the fact that Landolfi was not alive to consult, for the illumination that a collaboration might bring. But as the work proceeded and I came to know the writer better, it occurred to me that as translator, I embodied both the archetypical reader and the critic; and that as such, I too would somehow be perceived as the nemesis, were Landolfi alive. Thus, working through my list of apparently nonexistent words and hermetic references, I often imagined Landolfi delighting in the sight of his translator planted before stacks of dictionaries and encyclopedias and often coming away without a glimmer of clarification. Well aware that Landolfi himself was a translator, and a superior one, I still couldn't shake the sense that I had fallen prey to a flawless literary strategy—"a perfect victim," as he says of the young woman he singles out to "revenge all women" in the "The Eternal Province."

The enigmatic and occasionally unresolvable element was both the greatest challenge and stumbling block of this translation, for writing as rich with sophisticated literary tricks as Landolfi's forces the translator to constantly confront the specter of the "untranslatability" of the text. There are, for instance, a number of words and expressions that have no obviously discernible meaning and indeed do not appear among the most authoritative or specialized Italian dictionaries because they are invented or dialectical. The "labrena," the creature whose name may trigger delightful suggestions to the Italian ear, merely falls on a deaf English ear. In fact, "labrena" is not, as the opening of that story suggests, a Venezuelan word, and we will probably never know what reasoning or association gave rise to its invention. Then there are words and whole passages that may be rich with reverberations, with irony, pun or double entendre for the Italian reader who has a linguistic and literary precedent in mind; but for the English reader who lacks the privilege of that patrimony, the text will suffer, falling flat or making no sense whatsoever. Certainly, all good translations arise from recreation rather than slavish reiteration, and this is true to an even greater degree with authors whose use of language is uncommon or idiosyncratic. The translator, therefore, must recast the pun, wordplay, or allusion by drawing upon whatever resources his own language and landscape offer—needless to say, with varying degrees of success.

As for the plethora of obscure literary, cultural and historical references scattered throughout the stories, they almost beg for footnotes. However, for a number of reasons, I decided against notes except in those cases where their absence would have forbidden understanding. Firstly, although Landolfi is a difficult writer, he is also supremely entertaining, and I did not want to weigh the collection with a burden of esoteric footnotes. Secondly, a poll revealed that the literate Italian reader was, in most cases, left in the dark just as often as the English reader would be. Landolfi's obscure references are not in the domain of his average Italian reader (and thanks to his demanding style, those who read him are already a select few), but often require the specialist's frame of reference; indeed, the breadth of Landolfi's erudition, in fields as remote as ancient history, linguistics and Russian literature, is remarkable. Nevertheless, my own research indicated that a curious and ambitious reader could, with the help of an encyclopedia, a host of dictionaries and a generous share of patience, solve most of Landolfi's little puzzles. And wasn't this an essential part of his intention, the reader's "turn," as it were, in the game which a Landolfi story proposes?

A word about the selection of the stories here: all but four were taken from *Le più belle pagine di Tommaso Landolfi*, edited and introduced by the late Italo Calvino. I also borrowed Calvino's categories in arranging the stories. Of the four chosen from other sources, two are dialogues, a form which Calvino admits he did not favor. They nevertheless represent a form which Landolfi often used—occasionally to quite humorous effect—and they lend the collection a diversity that his straight narratives would not have.

Finally, I would like to mention Italo Calvino's initiative in introducing and promoting the work of other Italian writers; certainly *Le più belle pagine di Tommaso Landolfi* helped to make this new translation possible. His intention in "reintroducing" Tommaso Landolfi's stories to the Italian reading public was to reveal the startling range of his voices, those both rough and polished. In editing the English edition, I have attempted to preserve Calvino's vision.

KATHRINE JASON
August 1986

LIST OF SOURCES

"Maria Giuseppa" and "Dialogue of the Greater Systems" from *Dialogo dei massimi sistemi*, 1937

"The Werewolf" from *Il mar delle Blatte*, 1939

"The Provincial Night" from *La spada*, 1942

"Gogol's Wife" and "Prefigurations: Prato" from *Ombre*, 1954

"The Grace of God" from *Se non la realtà*, 1960

"Two Wakes" and "The Eternal Province" from *In società*, 1962

"An Abstract Concept" and "Chicken Fate" from *Racconti impossibili*, 1966

"The Kiss," "Prize in Spite Of," "Words in Commotion" and "The Eclipse" from *Un paniere di chiocciole*, 1968

"The Labrenas," "Personaphilologicaldramatic Conference with Implications" and "Uxoricide" from *Le labrene*, 1974

"A Woman's Breast" and "The Test" from *A caso*, 1975

"Literary Prize," "The Gnat," "Rain" and "The Ampulla" from *Del meno*, 1978

Two previous volumes of Landolfi's work have appeared in English:

Gogol's Wife and Other Stories (New Directions, 1963)

Cancerqueen and Other Stories (The Dial Press, 1971)